A DO-SI-DO WITH DEATH

by Grant Michaels

Foreword by Leigh Ann Wallace

ReQueered Tales
Los Angeles • Toronto
2022

A Do-Si-Do With Death

A Stan Kraychik Mystery, Book 7

by Grant Michaels

Praise for Grant Michaels

"A delightful debut with a gay hairdresser-investigator who gets his fingers into a lot more things than hair. It's a promising start to what looks to be a successful series."
— George Baxt,
The Dorothy Parker Murder Case

"This is a first-rate mystery with an Agatha Christie lineup of very possible suspects and Stan Kraychik playing a terrific Poirot."
— *San Francisco Chronicle*

"*Love You to Death* is an engaging murder mystery that epitomizes the best in the genre. The one-liners fly as fast as bullets and there is a surprise in nearly every chapter."
— *The Advocate*

"In *Dead on Your Feet*, Michaels hands another case to out-of-the-closet, loud and proud Boston hairdresser Stan Kraychik in this witty, fast-moving romp."
— *The Advocate*

"In *Mask for a Diva* Grant Michaels invades the world of opera with often hilarious results ... The people and plot are engaging and the ending leaves us with an intriguing hint of what we may expect in Stan's next adventure in mayhem."
— *Pittsburgh Post-Gazette*

"*Time to Check Out* is another entertaining haywire adventure for the sleuthing Boston hairdresser."
— *Library Journal*

By GRANT MICHAELS

THE STAN KRAYCHIK NOVELS

A Body to Dye For (1990)

Love You to Death (1992)

Dead on Your Feet (1993)

Mask for a Diva (1994)

Time to Check Out (1996)

Dead as a Doornail (1998)

A Do-Si-Do With Death (2022)

A DO-SI-DO WITH DEATH

by Grant Michaels

Table of Contents

Foreword

I love ReQueered Tales' mission. There are so many orphaned books out there, so many lost authors, having ReQueered putting these largely forgotten books out there for new readers is, to me, everything. So, when they asked me to do the foreword for Grant Michaels' last book, I went through a lot of different emotions. Shock, astonishment, happiness. Disbelief. Fear. All in pretty much equal measures. Even with all that, it never occurred to me to say no, but I was totally freaked out. I didn't know Michaels, wasn't a family member or a friend. I'm not even a published author. Who am I to write the foreword for the very last book of this wonderful series?

After a bit of thought, it came to me.

I'm a fan. A *big* one.

I love Stanley Kraychik, have from the very first book. His snark. His guts, and his heart. His inability to do anything but follow a trail to the very end *no matter what.*

Not that he's perfect. In Stan's personal life, he's all over the place. Self-absorbed, insecure, illogical, combative, and stubborn. He's lonely and looking for love, but when he finds it, he can't bring himself to trust it. He's also honest, generous, curious, creative, and quick witted. A Gemini, which pretty much says it all.

I like character-driven books. Michaels' writing is smart and funny, and the plots are a blast, but from the very beginning, it was the characters that kept me engaged. Nicole and her pastel cigarettes. Roger the Ranger. Ramon. Calvin the Creep. Sugar Baby. Tragic Rafik. Cozy Dinette. Russ. Sweet, sad Russ.

And last, but not least, Mr. Tall, Dark and (probably) Unattainable, Lieutenant Vito Branco. Or, as Michaels put it, "A big, contented tiger about to engage in a playful bout of get-the-gazelle." Love that.

Michaels' characters aren't cookie cutter. Even with the "minor" ones, you get not just what's on the surface, what they show to the world, but also their vulnerabilities and weaknesses. Their humanity, warts and all. You may not like them all, but you know them.

Roger, in *A Body to Dye For*? His death killed me. Even though he was only there for the first chapter or so of the book, he was a real person, a good man. I mourned him and understood completely Stan's motivation when he went after the killer. It wasn't only because Roger deserved justice. Not just that Stan suspects Calvin and the creep is an entitled ass. Stan was grieving the loss of what might have been. What he and Roger could have had together, given time. Stani's all about the what-ifs.

That kind of loss is a recurring theme throughout the series, the worst when he lost Rafik, not through murder, but stupid failing brakes. That kind of reality is what makes these books, and the characters, stick with you.

Which is the reason why, when I found out through a casual online comment by Greg Herren that he had a copy of the seventh, unpublished Stan Kraychik novel, I went a teeny bit nuts. A little fangirl.

Okay, a *lotta* fangirl.

I had to know what happened next! How is Stan? What is he doing? Is he still in Boston? Do he and Branco get together? Does he have a new sweetie?

Damn it, does Stani get his happy ending?

I was obsessed. My brain was in overdrive, trying to figure out how we could get that next, last, book published. Was there some reason it hadn't been published? Was it just because Michaels passed before he had a chance to finish it? Or was it still in the first draft phase? If it were that last one, maybe a ghostwriter could take it over, polish it, get it out to us. Get it out to me.

I had to let it go, though, after a few weeks. I was getting stalkerish and I didn't want to be "that" person. That whole "Misery" gig. Hand me my ax, will you?

I moved on to other passions.

Then ReQueered came along with the announcement that they were going to release the final book in the series and BOOM! Cue the joyful shrieks and the resurgence of my absolute *need* to find out what happens next. It's embarrassing how fast I fell back into it.

So. In *A Do Si Do With Death* our favorite hairdresser is building a new life. Not back at Snips with Nicole (and believe me she's got tons to say about that) but as a private eye, after a short stint at the police academy. It's quite a switch from hairdresser to gumshoe, but it makes sense. Stanley *does* like unraveling mysteries and he might as well get paid for what he's going to do anyway!

His first case as a budding P.I. is an innocuous case of petty theft which inevitably leads to murder. What else? We've got a cowboy convention, Chester and Paladin, Miss Kitty, platinum collar tips and Russian Revolvers. These "Mucho Macho Honcho" characters are Michaels' usual well-rounded fabulous mixture of good guys, lost guys, and people you really hope are going to be the next victim.

Oh, and an old friend of Stan's pops up. Benji. He's had a thing for Stan for a long time, but he doesn't fit Stan's "type", so he's determined to keep Benji in the "friend" slot. Which probably means he's absolutely perfect for Stan.

As to our Italian stallion, Stan's a bit at odds with Branco in this outing. What's new, right? Well, hold on to your hats. Our "paragon of virility" has done something so unexpected, so what the hell, so *Catholic* – I can't even say it.

Vito, *seriously*?

A Do Si Do With Death. The last book. It's a good read, a fun ride. Stanley sniffing out the bad guys and irritating the hell out of simply everyone while he's doing it. I hate that it's the last book, but I'm grateful to ReQueered Tales for giving us one last chance to visit with Stan.

I wish Grant Michaels had had more time. Time for himself, and time to take Stan on new adventures. But as long as there are readers, Michaels is still around. And so is Stan, doing what he does best. Cutting hair, solving crimes, and copping Nicole's cigarettes.

And, I suspect, giving Vito Branco a lot of sleepless nights.

— Leigh Ann Wallace,
February 2022

Leigh Ann Wallace is an aspiring writer and inveterate fangirl.

For Vidalia, the sweetest li'l gal in town.

And in memory of Kris Benton Anderson.

1.

FRIDAY MORNING, MEMORIAL DAY weekend in Boston, and the weather forecast says no snow.

So far, so good.

The sun is shining, the air is pleasantly cool, and I'm enjoying the shady sanctuary of my backyard, the ultimate status symbol in Boston's South End.

The house itself is another story. I got the original place through a technical loophole. It cost me a song, and I sang in cash. But that structure was burned to the ground by an arsonist. (Not hired by me.) Fortunately, I'd insured the building for market value, which paid for the new construction ... almost. It's a dream-domain come true – from the outside, anyway. But the final budget turned out to be farcical. Everything cost more – way more – than estimated, and the insurance money ran out just as the last roof tile was laid. (Hand-fired, imported.) So basically I live in a brand new four-story Victorian-style single-family dwelling with plumbing, HVAC, triple-glazed windows, and most of the flooring. The supporting studs and beams are all there, ready for soundproofing, drywall, plaster, and paint. But that's it. Except for two of the bathrooms, when you're inside my new house you can pretty much see forever.

It's a look I can live with, since finishing things the way I'd like will deplete whatever other wealth I've managed to accumulate. It's even a joke to hear myself use the word "wealth". Considering how I got the stuff – my husband died – you'd think I'd have blown it on mind-numbing pleasure long ago. But instead, I developed a peculiar need to hold onto it, as I've tended to hold onto his memory. It's as though investing the money and watching it grow will assure me a safe and secure trip along the nebulous path of life. Some joke, since that's never been my style. To me, security is a middle-class affliction, something I never contemplated when I was a Working Joe. But now, with my few millions invested, things seem different. I may be living without interior walls, but who cares, as long as I have the means to continue making those critical decisions of *Buy! Sell! Hold!*

Could be I've lost my compass.

Meanwhile, I sit in my backyard like a thirty-something retiree, sipping coffee and watching the birds, thinking of my recently departed Sugar Baby, the cat who never saw the house or the yard, and who would have taken over both as Queen Of All She Surveys. I can imagine the torturous favors she would have bestowed on every creature out here, but Sugar lies peaceful and harmless beneath the rose arbor. (Rose bushes to come.)

It's especially quiet this morning because most of the neighborhood left town yesterday morning, Thursday, if not Wednesday night. Post-holiday, they'll roll back horne sometime next Tuesday and return to work late on Wednesday. In yuppie parlance it's called a long weekend; in Olde English it still means a week off.

And why am I home? Because I decided to have a cookout – to host it actually – a real Memorial Day barbeque, the first one ever in my adult life. I'll be The Hostess With The Mostest, as long as it remains an outdoor event. (Indoors here means really roughing it.) The guest list is small but elite: There's my best friend Nicole, who runs Snips Salon the way a precocious child might run a dot-com; then there's my adoring and adorable friend Benjy, who still thinks of me as The Man Who Got Away; and finally, in a place of honor worthy of Valhalla, is Lieutenant Vito Branco of the Boston police. Ever since I saved that cop's life, we maintain what might be considered friendly terms.

Hang on. There's the kitchen phone.

"Stan?"

It's the god himself.

He says, "You sound out of breath."

"I was outside."

"Still no wireless phone?"

"Still considering it. Hey, Lieutenant, you're not going to cancel, are you?"

"Cancel what?"

"My cookout on Monday. You're still coming, right? No last-minute plans? No sudden urge to take off for places unknown?"

He says, "What are you talking about?"

"I know how unpredictable things can get once you're married. How is married life these days?"

He pauses, so I'll fill you in. Yes, Branco got married a few months ago. How else would a paragon of virility solve a chronic case of uncertain sexuality? He found a nice Italian virgin of legal age and married her in a church. It was a huge, all-day event. The girl's family – excuse me, the young bride's family – though frankly, she is young enough to be Branco's daughter – anyway, her family and friends filled the church, spilling over to occupy most of Branco's side as well. Since Branco has no family per se, it was basically me, Nicole, the Mayor of Boston, a representative of the Governor of Massachusetts, one actual U.S. Senator, and a good number of Boston police, all on his side of the church. The blushing bride wore white, which only amplified her extreme state of fertility. You could almost sense her ovulating as she walked down the aisle. Those few minutes at the altar next to Branco was all it took. After the service, on the way back up the aisle, she was flushed with the fiery glow of conception. For his part, Branco looked a bit embarrassed. A newbie to public sex, I guess. I occasionally wonder – like every hour on the hour –

if they still do it, now that she's pregnant. They must, right?

Branco's voice comes over the phone.

"I'll tell you something about marriage," he says. "It's not all it's cracked up to be. So, what are you up to this morning?"

"Nothing much," I say. "Why?"

"You interested in doing a little work?"

"Work?"

"Right," says Branco. "Remember that? Isn't that why you got that license? To work as a private dick?"

Why is it when Branco says "dick", there's a certain tingle? Is it some inherent taboo of a straight man alluding to anything sexual with a gay man? Or is it Branco? All I know is when he says "dick", I wish I'd been that blushing virgin he married.

Branco says, "Are you there?"

I answer, frog-like, "I'm here."

"Are you interested?"

"In what?"

"In working!" he snaps. "What is it with you? Did I wake you up or something?"

"No. I got distracted."

"By what?"

"The birds outside."

"Sounds more like the birds and the bees," he says. "You got company there or something? Did I get you at a bad time?"

Vito, Darling! There is no bad time. Don't you know that? I wish you'd call me every day, every hour, and say "dick" to me.

Now that Branco's married, I can admit things like that to myself.

To him I say, "What's this work?"

"You know about a cowboy convention in town this weekend?"

"Over at the Park Plaza Hotel," I say. "It's a big deal, first one of its kind in Boston. Lots of dancing."

"That's the one," says Branco. "Apparently they had a little trouble over there this morning, some guy claims his jewelry was stolen. He's making quite a noise about it, so the hotel called us to take a report."

"Called you?" I say. "In homicide?"

"Stan, why would I take a report on missing property?"

"Then how do you know about it?"

I hear one of Branco's trademark grunts over the phone. Amazing, the fidelity you get with these old-fashioned wired jobs.

He says, "I got wind of it, okay? And I thought it might be something up your alley."

"My alley?"

He hesitates. "Since the incident occurred, so to speak, within your community, I thought of you."

"So you're calling me because something happened to a gay guy at a gay event?"

"There's more to it," says Branco.

"I hope so."

He says, "You want to investigate as a professional, right? And I helped you get your license, right?"

"Yeah ..."

"So, here's a chance to get some experience. And if you come up with anything the hotel's insurance company misses, they'll even pay you for your time."

"But nobody's really hiring me."

Branco pauses. "That's right."

"So how do I explain my presence?"

Branco says, "That never stopped you before."

Touché.

"And now you have a license," he says. "If anyone asks who you're working for, just tell them you're not at liberty to say."

Whom, goes my recurrent grammatical tic. *Whom* I'm working for.

I say, "And you're not that client?"

"Absolutely not!" says Branco. "You and I aren't even having this conversation. This is all off the record, Stan. It's missing property. I have no business even knowing about it."

"But you do," I say, "by some mysterious wind."

Branco grunts again.

I ask, "Are you by any chance trying to drum up work for me?"

"Why would I do that?"

Do I say it? To thank me for saving your life.

I gaze out the kitchen window, I heave a sigh, then I say to him, "So my first case as a licensed investigator is contingency work to recover some gay caballero's lost jewelry."

"It's always tough when you're starting out."

Some people get a mentor, I get Branco.

He says, "The claimant calls himself Paladin."

"Paladin what?"

"That's all," says Branco. "Just Paladin."

I tell him, "My grandfather used to watch an old TV western with a character named Paladin."

"Mine too," says Branco.

The shared memory catches me off-guard. How can Branco's life have a single moment that resembles one of mine?

He says, "If you're going to do it, you ought to get over there soon. I don't know how long these folks are in town."

"I think it ends on Monday with a big cookout. Speaking of cookouts, you're coming to mine, right?"

"If it's in the book," he says, "then that's the plan."

"What book?"

Grunt. "My wife keeps track of the social calendar."

"Give my regards to Costanza."

"She was asking about you."

"What did she want to know?"

"Nothing," says Branco. "Just asking about you."

"Well now you have something to tell her."

"Right," says the cop, and he hangs up.

Two sips of now-tepid coffee and the phone rings again.

"Did I wake you?"

It's Nicole, Ms. Bizz-Blitz of the Millennium, also my adopted Big Sis and best friend.

"No, doll. I'm already up."

"Too bad," she says.

"What, just because you have to work today, I should be up at dawn too?"

"That's right, darling. Besides, it's hardly dawn."

"Branco just called."

"Vito? How is he? And how is that darling Costanza? What a lovely girl."

"Good thing I took my Dramamine early."

"What's the matter, dear? Are you still secretly hoping the marriage doesn't work out?"

"Where'd you get that idea?"

"From your behavior ever since the wedding."

"Like what?" I say.

"Like never acknowledging that they are a couple."

"Nikki, I invited them both to the cookout, didn't I?"

"Yes, darling, but as I recall, with an exceptional lack of enthusiasm. It was obvious you'd rather have Vito come alone."

"Wouldn't you?"

"No," she says. "Unlike you, Stanley, I am genuinely pleased that he's found someone he can be happy with."

"More Dramamine!"

"Can't you be happy for him too?"

"I am happy, Nikki. Happy, happy, happy. But if marriage is such a good thing, then why doesn't Branco seem settled and content? Aren't you supposed to be settled and content when you get married?"

"You weren't," she says.

"I wasn't married either."

"What was it then, between you and that handsome devil?"

"I was lost in lust."

"Maybe that's what Vito is."

"Branco lost?" I say. "That doesn't sound like him."

"And that's precisely why he can't get his bearings. He's never been in this situation before, with a young woman controlling him. But that doesn't mean he doesn't like it."

"Nikki, I would never do that to him. I would never try to control him or let him feel lost. Branco would always have a safe and secure haven with me, a sanctuary from life's trials."

"Sounds like a church," says Nicole.

"Better than mindless, tawdry sex."

"I'm sure they have a lovely time together."

"I'm certainly no match for a girl-wife."

"So you *are* jealous," she says. "How unlike you. Well, if it's any consolation, dear, I do agree with you somewhat."

I sense a change in Nikki's voice as she capitulates to my side of the fence.

"Vito's marriage could be construed as just a bit out of line for someone in his position."

"*Construed*, doll? Have you been reading again?"

"It's a perfectly good word, Stanley. But if Vito felt it necessary to marry, for whatever reason, he might have chosen someone older –"

"Like you, for example?"

"– and then," says Nicole, not missing a beat, "and then, if he found himself enthralled with a younger woman, well, then he could have explored that situation separately."

"Outside the marriage."

"Yes," she says. "Let's face it, Stanley, the girl, lovely as she is, is young enough to be his daughter."

"Doll, biologically speaking, she's almost young enough to be *my* daughter, which relegates *you* to the ranks of grand –"

"That's enough."

"As for that impending baby, that's going to put you up there with the great-grand –"

"You've made your point!" snaps Nicole. "Now, what did Vito call you about?"

"Back to business, are we?"

"*I'm* at work."

"So to speak. Here's the deal with Branco."

I tell her how miffed I am that Branco has called me about some missing gay baubles, when previously we were connected by homicide – real man's work.

"And this isn't?" says Nicole.

"Sounds frivolous to me."

"Well, darling, it will help you pass the time until Monday. I'm so looking forward to your gala event."

"Don't expect too much, doll. It's just an old-fashioned cookout, nothing fancy."

"Don't be modest, Stanley. It's a formal sit-down affair."

"At my place? Nikki, in case you haven't noticed, I don't have a dining room. I don't have *any* rooms."

"But it's outdoors, isn't it? Candlelit? Crystal, linens, sterling? It sounds lovely."

"Nikki, where are you getting these ideas?"

"From your friend Benjamin."

"Benjy?"

"Benjamin, yes."

"You talked to him?"

"Yes."

"When?"

"Excuse me, Stanley?"

"Who called whom?"

"What does it matter?"

"It matters to me. This is my cookout, Nikki, and I'm the one who'll decide how it's going to be."

"Well, well," she says. "And I thought you wanted to show your friends a good time."

"I do."

"Maybe it will rain on Monday, and it won't matter."

Then, as is her wont, without another word, Nicole hangs up.

Okay, maybe she's right. Maybe I don't have enough to do.

Maybe forcing some structure on my life is good, even if it means investigating a gay jewelry heist. So I douse myself with fairy dust and pull together an outfit worthy of a preppy dick: pink button-down cotton shirt, gray pleated chinos, and black penny loafers. It's certainly not cowboy garb, but it is reminiscent, colorwise at least, of some fabulous, high-finned, two-tone convertible from the bygone days of Gene Autry and Roy Rogers.

Attired like a retro "gay blade", I leave my sanctuary to cruise the hustle and bustle of the outside world.

2.

THE PARK PLAZA HOTEL is a short walk from my South End digs. It's nearly eleven o'clock, and the sun is approaching its daily zenith. I take Berkeley Street north to Columbus Avenue, then turn north on Columbus. (In Boston it is commonplace to turn north while traveling north. Likewise for any other compass point. Blame the cows. Their grazing paths became the city's first street plan.) My goal on Columbus is Arlington Street, one block away. At that intersection sits The Castle.

The Castle was built in 1891 as the armory for Boston's First Corps of Cadets. Its erection – you'll appreciate the word – was funded in part with monies garnered by a group of young men from Boston's upper class. They earned the money – a remarkable feat in itself for Boston's elite – by selling subscriptions to amateur musical productions written and performed by themselves. Historic photos from those halcyon days show many of the young men cheerfully and convincingly attired to play the roles of ravishing females onstage. There is even documentary evidence of stage-door-Johnnies courting these young "actresses", fully aware of the anatomical truths that lay beneath the greasepaint, the crinolines, and the padding. But it was all done for the erection of the armory, and whatever sacrifices those boys of yesteryear endured in pursuit of their grail, it was worth it, for here stands the fruits of their loins, er, labors: a magnificent granite castle, complete with moat and turrets, right in Boston's Back Bay – a National Historic Landmark, no less, now owned by the Park Plaza Hotel.

As I approach The Castle, I hear the muffled thump of music with a definite and lively beat. The closer I get, the more the music takes form, and I recognize the twang and energy of gen-yoo-wine, yee-haw cowboy music. Three huge vertical banners blaze outside The Castle:

<pre>
M
U   M
C   A   H
H   C   O
O   H   N
         O   C
                  H
                  O
</pre>

The gigantic block letters vary in color within and across the banners to create a colossal billowing rainbow, the standard of gay identity. This is definitely the place.

The main door is open, and music comes at me like a storm, a midsummer thunder-boomer whose lights and sounds are so extreme that, instead of being scared, you find yourself amused and laughing from the sheer immensity of it. The party going on inside The Castle is like that – all lights and noise and commotion. I enter the foyer and glimpse into the cavernous hall. The place is packed, a mass of bobbing heads – colorful hats and hairdos – all shifting and moving and changing directions like one gigantic organism responding to the music. My own head and shoulders start bob-bob-bobbing along too.

Above the din I hear a voice to my left, calling to me in a squawky, forced falsetto.

"Do you have your pass?"

I turn to see someone seated at a table in an alcove, a vision in pink who can best be described as apparently female.

"Pass, please," she says with a genial smile, but with lots of strain in her voice. (*His* voice? What *is* the proper way to address a man in drag? Does it depend on the sincerity of the ruse?) Whichever it is, the falsetto is taking its toll.

"Please show your pass," she says curtly.

Her big flouncy dress is pink, her heavily smeared eye shadow is pink, her long polymer fingernails are pink, and her hair, a beehive-styled wig of awesome height, is also pink. Her teeth, thankfully, are not pink, but they are so dazzlingly white they can't be real. And despite the monochromatic excess through which she attempts to convey femininity, it is too, too obvious there's some kind of man lurking under all the pink.

Once more she speaks in that harsh, strained falsetto – what opera singers call *stracciatta della voce*, but what regular folks might describe as Julia Child with a lump of *foie gras* stuck in her throat.

"Do you have a pass?" croaks the lady in pink.

"No," I say, and go to the table where she sits. There's a sweet floral scent about her, pushy but pleasant, almost generic. It's a pink kind of smell, probably all the makeup.

"Are you here for the convention?" she says.

"Actually, I'm here to investigate a theft."

"A theft?" she says. "*Here?* I don't think so. You probably want the hotel." Her smile is less friendly now. "Across the street," she says, and makes a firm and unmistakable gesture toward the door with her hand – a hand bejeweled with rings and bracelets and sheathed with an over-the-elbow pink glove.

I tell her, "I'm sure this is the place."

"You're certainly not with the police, not dressed like that."

"I'm a private investigator."

"Do you have credentials?"

I show her my license.

She looks at it carefully, then does the same to me. I notice that her eyes are not pink, but lavender – maybe pink contact lenses over pale blue eyes.

"Interesting name," she says, "but I still don't see how we can help you."

I tell her, "The theft was reported by a cowboy dancer, and by the looks of what's going on in there –"

The pink lady clucks her tongue. "My dear young man, what is going on in there is *square* dancing, not cowboy danc-ing."

"Well, whatever they' re doing, I'm sure this is the place."

"And how do you know that?"

"Because of the music," I say, "and because of the rainbow flags flying out front."

"Ah," says the lady in pink, suddenly softening. "And do you wave that particular flag?"

"If I waved a flag, it would probably be that one."

"In that case," she says, "you are very welcome here." To emphasize this about-face of her regard for me, she winks co-quettishly. But her false eyelashes are so stupendously long – are they pink too? – that she has a bit of trouble getting that eye open again. With one lid at half-mast she goes on.

"And since you say you're here for professional reasons, I think I can arrange for one our special press passes."

I tell her, "I don't mind paying. It seems like a good cause."

"It is a good cause, but I wouldn't dream of charging you admission, not if you're here to work." She rummages around behind her table and finds a press pass for me. I take it and start to clip it to the pocket of my shirt, but the lady in pink says, "You don't have to wear it. No need to spoil the fresh, crisp look of that nice pink shirt. You see, I like pink too. Just keep the pass handy. Then you can come and go as you please."

"Thanks," I say.

Then she puts out her pink-gloved hand. "I'm Fannie Mae," she says. "Fannie Mae Knox ... *Miss*."

I take her hand. "I'm Stan Kraychik."

"Yes, I know," she says. "From your license. Pleased to meet you, Mr. Kraychik. They'll be resuming the competitions soon, for the special dance categories. That's fun to watch. Some of the dancers are professional level. And be sure to stay on and enjoy yourself when you're done working."

"Thanks," I say, "but first I have to find someone, a guy named Paladin."

"Oh?" says Miss Fannie Mae Knox.

"He's the person whose jewelry is missing."

"Oh," she says again, "I see." Then she makes a little *humph!* I'm sure her throat is irritated from all the squawking. "I would say your best chance of finding Mr. Paladin would be in the dressing room downstairs. That's where the contestants get ready. Just go inside and follow along the wall to your left until you come to the stairs. Frankly, though, I'd wait until after the semifinals. If you go down there now, you enter at your own peril. They are quite a high-strung group of dancers."

"I know about high-strung dancers," I say. "But thanks for the warning."

"You're very welcome," says Miss Fannie Mae Knox from within her parapet of pink.

I wander inside the main hall where everything is in full swing, as in "Swing yer partner!" The music is loud and the beat is strong. The super-amplified voice of an unseen man is half-talking, half-singing in a strange language I don't understand, though the words are clearly English. In a deep and sultry voice, he drawls out terms like "glide through", "pass through", and "ride through". The allusions are suggestive, but there is absolutely nothing erotic happening on the dance floor. The steps and formations are executed smoothly and coolly, with detached, almost military precision.

The costumes, however, are totally playtime. Lanky, lollipop-colored cowboys are linked arm-in-arm with pastel-petticoated dames flashing masculine calves. It's as colorful and random as a kaleidoscope. And the hairdos? Some of those wigs have taken yards of hair – bales, probably – to reach such heights and to occupy so many cubic feet of the earth's atmosphere. Sequins are everywhere – on fabric, hair, and skin – and there is enough leather and fringe adorning torso and limb to foreshadow the extinction of domesticated cattle. And finally, how many versions of Annie Oakley, Dale Evans, and Dolly Parton do you see? Boston's First Corps of Cadets would be pleased that their trailblazing spirit continues with the he-men and fe-men of today.

The music comes to a rousing finish and the dancers applaud themselves, along with hoots and hollers and whistles, real rodeo-like. Then they shake hands with one another, real downhome-like. I still cannot locate the man who's been giving the orders, the disembodied square-dance caller.

The music starts up again, and I remember that I'm here to work, supposedly. Following Fannie Mae's directions, I make my way along the nearby wall to the stairway, then descend. It's quite a different world down here. It may be the dressing room, but from the sound of things, the drama is worthy of the Greek stage. I hear two men yelling at each other. One voice is machismo-infused, an aggressive baritone; the other is feline, but feisty and defensive. I move quietly to the open door and look inside. It's a large open area with makeup tables and mirrors all around the perimeter. There's quite a crowd of guys in there, some of them fussing with their costumes, some with their makeup, others are stretching their muscles. One couple tries to rehearse a dance move, but they keep bumping into other people nearby. Snarls are exchanged, but no one seems to notice or care that two of the men are arguing loudly. Maybe hot tempers are part of the culture. Fannie Mae did warn me.

"I know you have them, you bitch!" accuses the more manly-voiced. I can see him now, and he's a young god clad in haunch-hugging black leather jeans topped with a silky shirt, also black. His lush black hair is slicked down, like a matinee idol from the silver screen days. "Where are they?" he demands. The sparkling sequined filigree on his sleeves counters his aggressive stance.

The softer-voiced man protests. "I told you, Paladin, I don't have them!"

Well, I've found Paladin, at least.

The other guy is Asian, small and delicately built. His clothes are tight-fitting as well, and from what I can see, it's all sinewy, quick muscle that drives his compact body. He says, "Maybe you put them in with your tampons."

Paladin makes a lunge for him, but the smaller one dodges the attack, quick as a cat. Paladin falls to the floor roaring, "I'll kill you, you little bitch!"

The sudden crash draws everyone's attention to the argument. There's a moment of relative quiet in the big room, though the dancing and music continue overhead in seismic volume.

The smaller guy says to Paladin, "You're the bitch." Then he moves cautiously toward the open doorway where I'm standing.

Meanwhile a third man steps in to help Paladin to his feet. "Never mind," he murmurs quietly to him.

But I hardly hear him speak. His gentle and inviting face has usurped my senses, and I am overcome with a memory of my very first true love, a boy in fifth-grade. Even back then in the Pleistocene Era, before I had any notion of homosex, even then I had wanted to run off and live with him forever in perpetual grade-school bliss.

I feel a nudge and I am back in the real world. The slighter, catlike fellow is standing next to me at the open door, ready to flee if necessary, but also, like any good feline, lingering to admire the havoc he's just created: felling a stallion through sheer wiliness.

Paladin sees him and bellows, "Get him out of here!"

Naturally, the little cat doesn't leave, but continues to provoke his prey. He steps back into the room but stays close to the open doorway. "I wouldn't touch your holy trinkets," he says. "It's bad enough I have to handle your clothes."

"That's exactly when you took them," says Paladin. "When you came in last night to get the laundry. You were the only one in my room last night."

"What about Chester?" says the cat-boy. "He was there."

Chester? The cuddly, sandy-haired cowboy, my boyhood dream of bliss incarnate, is called Chester?

Paladin says, "Chester didn't take them. Why would he?" Paladin glances at Chester.

Chester smiles back.

Of course he didn't. Chester couldn't steal a thing, except maybe someone's heart.

Paladin says, "So that leaves you, Kitty."

Kitty? The three guys involved in this little tempest are named Paladin, Chester, and Kitty?

Kitty moves further into the room. "I happen to know –" he says.

But Chester interrupts him, and coos to Paladin, "Maybe you left them in a shirt pocket."

Paladin says, "I didn't *leave* them anywhere! I always put them away. It's a ritual." Then to Kitty, "What did you do with them?"

"I didn't touch them!"

"You came in last night and took them."

"I took the laundry! Maybe someone else came in and you didn't hear them because you were so busy in the Jacuzzi."

"Shut up, you little bitch!" screams Paladin and he makes another lunge for Kitty. Chester holds him back. Paladin seethes. "You get back to your shop and get my collar tips!"

Kitty blows him off. "I'm not chasing after your missing trinkets. I have three other clients to fit here this morning."

"I'll go," says Chester.

"How can you go?" says Paladin. "We're on soon."

"Then you'll have to dance without them."

"I can't," says Paladin. He actually sounds desperate.

"I don't have time for this shit! Maybe they can delay the semifinals until I get my collar tips back. And you, Kitty, you can arrange for a courier to go to your shop and bring them here."

Kitty says, "I'm not letting a total stranger into my shop

when I'm not there."

"Then I'll call the police to do it."

"Go ahead," says Kitty. "It'll be your funeral, because I don't have them, and I'll sue your ass so fast you won't have anything left to hang my fabulous costumes on."

Did I mention that Paladin has a fabulous ass?

"Then fuck you!" says Paladin. "Fuck you and everybody and everything!"

That's certainly one solution to a problem.

Kitty says, "Looks like you won't need your usual fluff-up before you go on, since you're already full of hot air."

Kitty then turns and struts out of the room, his head held high, moving as noiselessly as his namesake.

The PA system springs to life with an announcement: "Dancers, this is the three-minute call for semifinalists for the category of Most Together Couple. Please report to the dance floor. Three-minute call for Most Together Couple."

There's a sudden bustle in the dressing room as the dancers realize they've lost precious minutes to Paladin's drama. They race about making frantic, last-minute adjustments to face, hair, costume, boots, and psyche. My best bet is to get out of there now, before the frenzied rush upstairs to the dance floor.

Topside, another square dance is in progress, and I find myself a decent vantage point for the imminent competition. Then I feel a soft but purposeful nudge against me. It's Kitty again. He seems to nudge a lot. He looks up at me from under the brim of a black suede cowboy hat, an added accessory since the brawl downstairs. His dark eyes are intense. They seem ready to weep for love, or else to eviscerate a rival without mercy. He lifts his chin slightly, as if inviting me to say something – or to use my mouth at least. I choose the safer route.

"Where's the caller?" I ask.

His eyes are eager to get familiar, but he answers idly, as if my stupid-assed question isn't worth the bother.

"It's a CD."

"But isn't there a live person making the calls?"

He scowls now, like a young tiger uncertain of his quarry.

"Not at this convention."

"Why not?"

"Because that's the way they want it."

"Who?"

His eyes say, How stupid can you be? His mouth says, "Her." He looks toward the stage at the far end of the hall. "There's number-one-in-charge now."

A female voice cries over the PA system with amphitheater volume: "Thank yew, dancers, one and all!"

She pronounces the word like the bush: yew. Thank yew.

Everyone turns toward the stage. A woman bounds onto it like an animal released from confinement. Her hair is pixie-cut and dyed in various hues of blonde. She holds a wireless microphone dangerously close to a mouthful of teeth that flash like a Nantucket lighthouse. She's wearing a suit – very red, very virgin wool, very Italian. No cowboy clothes for her, but high-echelon bizz drag. Her one concession is a neckerchief worn jauntily off her shoulder, but even that looks like hand-blocked Italian silk. Maybe Giorgio Armani has a western-wear line called *Quasi un uomo di vaca*. Or maybe he should. The woman is chic-to-death thin, yet her feet – shod in hand-fashioned Italian boots – pound the platform like cloven hoofs. A nod to bovine awareness, I guess.

"In case any of yew out there still don't know me, I'm Bistany Evans, your mistress of ceremonies."

Did she just go *tee-hee?*

"Don't yew boys love the sound of that? Mistress of ceremonies?"

The audience makes no response.

"I'm Bistany Evans," she says again, "no relation to Dale." *Tee-hee.* "And I can't tell yew how thrilled I am to be here and doing this, at the very first Mucho Macho Honcho Dance Convention in history. This is a big day for all of us, and I am so thrilled! Aren't yew all so thrilled out there?"

There is a slight rustle through the audience, but little

enthusiasm, nothing like the manic act onstage.

Another moment passes and Bistany says, "Well now, ladies and gentlemen ... and others ..." She pauses again for a laugh that never comes. "Okay, well, I have to ask yew all to clear the dance floor one more time. Yes, I know, yew've been doing it all morning – go away, come back, go away, come back – but that's how it is with competitions. Yew all know that once the contest is over, the dance floor will belong to all yew ever-lovin' dancers again. But for now, please clear it all the way. Thank yew!"

The people on the dance floor shuffle about – grumbling with their bodies, as it were – until finally the floor is vacant. Then Bistany announces, "And now I am so very proud to present the semifinalists for the category of The Most To-gether Couple. I want yew to give them all a nice warm welcome! Let's hear it!"

As the audience applauds, twelve male couples – *all* male, no drag among these guys – charge onto the dance floor like it's a one-day sale at Filene's Basement. The handsome hunks take numerous bows – mind you, they haven't danced yet – and they finally settle down and strike their starting poses. There is a moment of silence. Then the music begins. It is "Stand By Your Man" sung by the one and only Patsy Cline. Standing by *me* is Kitty, pressing himself ever-so-surely my way. He looks up at me with such longing – or need, I still can't tell which – that I lean away. Was that me back in fifth-grade, yearning for a love that passeth all understanding with my boy-idol?

In the limelight of the dance floor, I see Chester and Pal-adin together. Without Paladin's demands and accusations, they appear to embody a dream of male-male love where words don't matter. Paladin leads, of course, and Chester follows in a satisfyingly masculine way. Doesn't he? I watch some more. Whom am I kidding? Chester's doing the girl's part, pure and simple. He's being led, no, dragged around the floor by Paladin. Then I notice that Chester has a limp. May-be he got hurt when Paladin fell down earlier. It didn't stop him from performing, though. Real dancers tolerate pain that would crumple a Marine.

Patsy sings another chorus, I gaze at Chester, and once more I see my fifth-grade dream of bliss eternal. That thralldom had persisted a full year – eternity for a ten-year-old. There was no reciprocation from him, not in the forever way that I wanted and needed. He was friendly to me, but he had also acquired his own special friend, someone whose last name was alphabetically akin to his, and so fate had place them at adjoining desks. He and this other boy would fling themselves into each other's arms upon arriving at school every day. They spent recesses and lunchtimes together, hand-in-hand, and would often go home together too. And no one once called them "sissy". That was reserved for me, the alphabetically-challenged one who was holding hands with *girls* back then. Then, suddenly, his family moved away, and he was gone. I thought I was desolate, but I was actually relieved. And until I laid eyes on this Chester fellow this morning, I never once thought of that other boy in the eons since he entered my life and taught me the facts of unrequited love.

The song is in its last moments. All the couples save one have finished their dance. As Patsy Cline's vocal directive to stand by your man fades away, Chester, the present specter of my own long-lost beloved, is hoisted overhead by his partner, Paladin, and held there on one arm in a fantastic airborne arabesque. It is a spectacular, incredible pose, combining sheer muscularity and grace. It would be thrilling in a Las Vegas club; in Boston it borders on the incomprehensible. Holding the pose, the men turn slowly, creating a romantic *tableau vivant*, with lights glinting off Chester's sequined jeans high in the air and Paladin's sequined shirt below him.

The audience roars its approval. Even Kitty, despite his earlier contest with Paladin, is applauding, though he continues to glance moon-eyed at me.

Paladin lowers Chester easily back to earth, and the applause increases. One good trick is all it takes.

And then ...

Bistany Evans is sucking the microphone again.

"Thank yew, thank yew all! Aren't they wonderful? Let's hear it for the twelve semifinalists for The Most Together Couple. I am so proud of yew all! Now, dancers, and now I mean everyone out there, not just our contestants, we're going to have another open dance for yew all, and this time it's a round dance. So set yourselves up with that special fella yew've been eyeing all mornin' and give him a whirl!"

She gives a cue to the DJ, who is concealed in a small booth high above the dance floor. Then off the stage she goes – *clomp, clomp, clomp* – digging her heels into the floor like some agitated, dim-witted ungulate. Maybe that's the real connection between Bistany Evans and the Wild West – those killer hoofs.

The music starts, and as the dancing couples take to the floor, the pressure of the crowd slackens. Kitty lingers, as if I'm supposed to ask him to dance. But I see Paladin at the other end of the hall, standing to one side of the low stage and talking with Chester. Since I'm here to investigate Paladin's missing jewels, I'd better get to work. Besides, it will give me a good chance to see Chester close up. Maybe they're just friends. Can't "just friends" dance together the way they did? People don't have to be physically intimate to move together like that, right? So maybe after all these years I'll rekindle my fifth-grade dream of pure love, even though I know Chester isn't the same guy at all.

As I approach them, Paladin's features seem to get coarser with every step. Ironically, it explains why he looks so good when performing. To be distinguishable from a distance and under bright lights, facial features have to be somewhat exaggerated. Ergo, makeup. But close up is another matter. An impressive profile onstage can be snoutlike in real life.

Chester, on the other hand, is much more attractive close up. Big surprise. In fact, I just want to keep getting closer and closer until I can see how good-looking he really is. Maybe how he tastes too.

I stand there waiting for one of them to acknowledge me.

Finally, Paladin says, "You want something?"

Your boyfriend.

I ask, "Are you Paladin?"

He looks around himself, grins, feigns modesty. "Looks like you found me."

"Mind if I ask you a few questions?"

"What about?"

"Your lost jewelry."

He says, "Are you a cop?"

"I'm a private investigator," I say, and flash my license.

"Took you long enough to get here," he says. "I needed those collar tips before we danced, not now."

Chester soothes him. "It's okay, Pal. There's still the finals tomorrow."

Pal? Not a good sign. Butch nicknames imply carnal contact.

Paladin says, "Let's see how we made out today, Ches, before we assume we're in the finals."

Ches? Pal and Ches? They're definitely doing penile things.

Then Chester leans toward Paladin and whispers something. Paladin says, "Permission granted." They smile at each other, a leer that transforms Chester from wholesome to lascivious, the final proof of conjugal conjoinery. Chester gives me a cool nod – heartbreaker! – then goes away, leaving Paladin and me alone.

I watch him depart.

Paladin watches me watching Chester.

"Well?" he says. "You wanted to ask me something?"

Maybe not. The awful truth is that I want to know more about Chester. I'm as bad as Paul Drake falling for one of Perry Mason's sexy witnesses. Maybe if I focus on Paladin, I can get back to work. But with those skin-tight leather jeans, all I can focus on are his legs and butt, the hallmarks of a professional dancer. He's probably had some ballet too, given the apparent ease with which he maneuvered that lift. Paladin's face may be unrefined, but those peerless loins are utterly tantalizing at close range. I can almost see why Chester is interested.

"Hey!" he says. "Are you awake?"

"Sorry," I say.

"Who sent you anyway?"

"Nobody."

He considers this. "You telling me nobody hired you?"

"That's right," I say.

"So, what are you? Some kind of ambulance chaser?"

I grimace. "Not quite."

Paladin has taken control, leaving me the recipient of his rapid-fire questions. So what if he's got luscious loins?

I regain my professional footing and ask, "When did you last have the missing jewelry?"

"Last night," he says.

"Describe it for me."

"I already did that with the hotel people this morning."

"Once more for me."

"It was a pair of collar tips," he says. "That's two pieces, one for each collar, just in case you dozed off again."

"Thank you."

Bitch.

He says, "Aren't you writing this down?"

"If there's anything I might forget, I'll note it."

He says, "They were platinum set with jewels."

"What kind of jewels?"

"Diamonds, I think."

"You think?"

"Is there anything diamond-colored that's worth more than diamonds?"

"No."

"Then they were diamonds," he says.

"Do you have a receipt?"

"No, but I know they cost an arm and a leg."

From the looks of his arms and legs, the price was a regal ransom.

"How much?" I ask.

"I told you, I don't have a receipt, so I don't know exactly. Does it matter?"

"If you plan to file a claim, it definitely matters."

His jaw clenches nervously, like he's chewing his teeth.

I say, "Were they a gift?"

"What?"

"You don't have a receipt, and you're not sure what they're made of, so maybe they were a gift."

He eyes me warily. "Are you sure someone didn't hire you to come after me?"

"I'm sure."

"You don't have to name names," he says. "Just say yes or no."

"Sounds to me like *you* know someone who might have hired someone like me."

"Forget it," he says.

Meanwhile he's squirming, really nervous about something. Or maybe he's thinking about Chester, and that's making his tight jeans a little tighter. Paladin's not so bad to watch, with those good legs and rock-solid butt squirming in tight leather, even if the guy's a jerk.

"Okay," he says, "look, you're right. The collar tips were a gift. And I know they're insured, but I can't tell the person who gave them to me, because ... well, he wouldn't be too happy to know where I was when I lost them. You get the picture?"

"I think so."

"So if I can make it sound like it all happened here at the hotel, they're responsible, right?"

I tell him, "Hotels routinely decline any responsibility for valuables kept in a guest's room."

Paladin says, "You sound like a fucking lawyer. Can't you help me?"

"Help you?"

"Can't you say you saw someone suspicious near my room, something like that?"

"You mean lie?"

He says, "I'll give you a share of whatever I get."

"I'll help you find the missing goods, but I won't help you file a bogus claim."

"It's not bogus," he says. "They're really gone."

"Then tell the person who gave them to you that they're lost, and let him file a claim."

"I told you, I can't do that!" says Paladin. "I've got to get the hotel to pay me."

"And I'm telling you, unless that jewelry was in the hotel safe, you haven't got a legitimate claim against the hotel."

My first professional interrogation is a dead-end battle of limited wits.

I say, "Good luck to you," and turn to leave.

He says, "Just don't get any ideas about Chester."

"Ideas?"

"I saw you looking at him."

"He's a nice-looking guy," I say.

"Just make sure that's where it stays – with the eyes."

As the music concludes I see Chester talking with Kitty at the opposite end of the hall, in the shadow of a balcony.

I ask Paladin, "By the way, what happened to his foot?"

"What?"

"I thought I saw him favoring it while he was dancing."

He says, "Maybe you were seeing things."

Then Paladin notices Chester and Kitty talking covertly as well. He mutters, "Why is that little bitch buzzing around Chester so much? That's the second time this morning I turn my back and they're together." He starts to head off, then turns back to me. "Y'know," he says, "the same goes for you. Chester is spoken for, so settle your petticoats." He pulls himself up tall and sticks out his chest. "Meaning me!"

On these last two words, Paladin jabs his thumb into his inflated bosom.

Meaning you what, doll? Settle my petticoats? Or yours?

In perfect echo to those two chest-thumps come two heavy *clomp-clomps* on the stage. Bistany Evans is back, and she's blasting us with another announcement.

"Hi, yew all! Did yew make a date for tonight with that special someone? Good, *good!* Now folks, we have a very special situation here, and I have to ask for some very special cooperation. In the category of Best New Moves, which we ran earlier this morning – remember? – well, we have one more semifinalist, and they are so unique there's just nothing like them. And for reasons of general safety, we are making an exception to the rules of competition, and we are giving this group the opportunity to perform on an absolutely clear floor, with no other competitors dancing along with them. So! Now I need yew all to step way far back from the dance floor. So could yew all do that please? Now? That's right. Yes, all of yew, please step back ten paces. I mean Texas-sized paces. Those dainty little Boston steps aren't going to do it. Stretch those legs out, fellas, and really step back. Come on now! One! Tew! Three! ..."

And on she goes up to ten.

Meanwhile, Paladin is making his way around the edge of the floor to where Chester and Kitty are still talking. As soon as Kitty sees him approach, he flees. Scaredy-cat! And me, with the crowd pressing against me, I can't move anywhere.

Our now sardine-like condition satisfies Bistany, who announces, "Thank yew all. Thank yew! And now, let's welcome the Loco Moto Mavericks!"

The PA system gives off a series of rhythmic ground-shaking thuds, a sensation that in the real Wild West means *Earthquake!* The thudding progresses to include off-beats, then quickly develops into complex syncopation, a high-tech percussion track. When the instruments come in, it is a fully synthesized orchestra that coincides exactly with the Loco Moto Mavericks' entrance. Thirteen men in wheelchairs catapult themselves onto the dance floor – catapult, as in airborne.

The audience gasps, then cheers wildly.

And the Loco Motos' high-action show begins. They spin, they do wheelies, they hop, skip and jump. They create formations – real Busby Berkley stuff – pinwheels and kaleidoscopes and exploding stars. As the "dance" continues, they escalate their tricks, like skateboarders whose ultimate goal is to spend more time hanging and spinning midair than on the ground. All the while, whether earthbound or airborne, the bright rhodium spokes of the Loco Motos' wheelchairs shimmer and sparkle in the lights. As for the guys themselves, their arms and shoulders are massive and solid. How else could you expect to launch your rocket repeatedly? Yet their lower limbs appear frail and delicate. In two cases they're nonexistent. This is an astonishing new vision of dancing, and the thirteen men of the Loco Moto Mavericks finish their act to an explosion of cheers and whistles and boot-stomping. The Castle walls reverberate as though the original Corps of Cadets has been resurrected for the occasion.

Amidst the din Bistany reappears on the stage. The applause for the Loco Moto Mavericks masks her hoofs, even at my close range. But now a wave of unbreathable air follows in her wake and shrivels my olfactory bulbs. Bistany Evans has resorted to aroma warfare along with sonic assault. Moments later her voice comes blasting over the PA system.

"Hello again, yawl!"

What happened to *yew*? Probably died of poison gas.

"How yawl doing? Fine? Good! Well, I'm back with the judges' decisions. What'yawl think about that, huh?"

The voice, the hoofs, and now the fumes are too much for me. I squeeze my way along the wall to the other end of the hall. I've got to put as much real estate between me and Bistany Evans as possible.

Her voice continues booming through the PA system. "What a thrill it is to be here, isn't it? Show me how happy yew are!"

The audience gives her a reasonable wave of cheering. Easy enough, since they're still buzzed from the Loco Motos' show.

"That's more like it, gang! I am so proud of yawl! Well, the judges have made their decisions for the finalists in the categories of Most Together Couple and Best New Moves. Now, before I announce the finalists, I want to share some personal feelings. May I do that? Thank yew!"

Who said yes?

"This event is the culmination of a whole year of dreaming for me. When I saw the lack of a commercial venue in Boston for cowboy lovers and dancers, I went out and created it. Of course, it wouldn't be possible without all of yew. Yew should be proud, every one of yew, that yew have helped me achieve my dream, the first all-inclusive celebration of who *yew* really are, your similarities and differences alike. This is the inaugural moment to confederate your diversity and to empower yew toward the ultimate goal – a unified *in*clusivity that resonates for everyone. Thank yew!"

Sounds like the fumes have invaded Bistany's language center.

"So, now," she says, "without further *adew* ..."

Doll, I think you mean *ado*, of which you make far too much.

"... I am pleased to announce that in the category of The Most Together Couple, our three finalists are couples number one, number sixteen, and number thirty-nine. Would yawl come up here so everyone can see yew?"

A wave of cheering brings the three couples to the stage. Paladin springs up onto the stage first, then turns around to pull Chester up after him. But there is no Chester. So, where is my tousle-haired fifth-grade cuddly-boy with the puppy dog eyes?

"Oh, great, *great!*" squeals Bistany, and she applauds like a circus seal on amphetamines. "Aren't they the best?"

She looks at the three couples, or what should be three couples, and asks Paladin, "Where's Chester?"

Paladin seems confused as he looks out over the audience.

Bistany says to him, "Did yew lose something?" *Tee-hee.*

Paladin scowls at her, then steps to the edge of the stage and calls out, "Chester!"

Various people in audience also call his name, as if calling a fifth-grade boy in for supper. "Chester!"

"Chester!"

"Chester!" Then someone else yells, "Get your butt out here!"

When Chester doesn't appear, Bistany shrugs. "I guess nature called, or something. I'll just keep going. And now for the three finalists in the category of Best New Moves, couples number eighteen, number twenty-three, and, one of our special, special favorites, couple number thirty-five, the Loco Moto Mavericks." The Loco Motos were actually thirteen, not a couple.

This announcement causes a huge wave of cheering.

The lead Loco Moto Maverick propels his wheelchair up onto the low stage with a dramatic leap, like an arm-powered Evil Knievel. That move brings a roar from the audience. He wheels over to Bistany and asks her for the mike. As he speaks, his voice quivers, and he seems on the verge of tears.

"I want to thank my brother, Theodore, for composing the original soundtrack we used today. Thanks, Teddy! And I want to thank all the people in charge of this convention for letting the Loco Motos enter this contest, and for helping us come this far. I can speak for every member of our group and say we are honored to be here, especially since we are not a gay group, per se. In fact, we're mostly *not* gay. But I want to let everybody out there know that we accept anyone into our club, even walking people. So, I'm inviting you all to come on down to our place and join in and have some fun!"

The roar of the crowd following this speech proves one thing: The guys at this convention are here for a good time, if only the Mistress of Ceremonies would let them.

Then, out of nowhere it seems, a big buffed cowboy appears onstage. His buzz-cut hair is salt-and-pepper, and he wears levis and a red plaid shirt. He goes and says something to Bistany, and she shakes her head no. Then the cowboy goes and takes the mike from the Loco Moto Maverick who is still onstage.

"Hi, there," he says. His voice is super-controlled, low and gravelly, the way you'd expect the Marlboro Man to sound if you didn't know he was a countertenor. "I'm Colt Remington," he growls. "I'm your DJ today, although the booth is kind of hidden, so you probably haven't seen much of me."

There's plenty to see now. This guy is tall and broad and muscular. The tight jeans and fitted shirt reveal that every muscle has been disciplined and trained to perfection. He could be a poster-guy for a gym, or even sex-for-hire.

He says, "I'm also the resident DJ at Gunsmoke Saloon, which you local guys know about."

Random cheers and applause from the crowd.

"Thanks," says Colt. "I'm also a certified square dance caller, but the powers-that-be at this convention didn't want any live calling, which is why we've been using pre-recorded steps. How do you all like that?"

Boos from the crowd.

"Right," says Colt. "And you want to know why that is? To save money. Pure and simple. Higher profits for the convention, even if it means less fun for you."

Bistany is moving toward Colt, but he puts up one massive arm to stop her. What can she do but stay? Colt's arms are each about the size of Bistany's thighs – put together.

"But that's not why I'm up here," he says. "The most important thing in my life is fairness. And I'm sorry to say we have a situation here that doesn't seem fair."

Bistany's screechy voice is audible without the microphone. "What are yew doing?"

"Just hang on," says Colt. "Now, some of you may be aware that Bistany herself is a strong supporter of the Loco Moto Mavericks. In fact, one of her own companies – Angel Wheels – provides funding for the Loco Motos, which is good, since their club has a lot of extraordinary expenses. Still, I put it to you all, doesn't this sound like a conflict of interest?"

The crowd is silent, which unsettles Colt just enough for Bistany to step in and grab the mike from him.

"That's enough, Colt. Thank yew!"

He grabs the mike back. "I'm not finished!" he says.

Then, to the crowd, "Now, along with Bistany's personal interest via Angel Wheels come the possibility that she swayed the judges' decision to put the Loco Motos in the finals for Best New Moves."

There is a sudden rush of boos, jeers, and hollers from the audience, but it isn't clear if the dissent is against Colt himself, or the supposed unfairness he is trying to expose.

When it all quiets down, he says, "Didn't you notice how fast the judges made their decision? Those guys just about got out of the spotlight and *boom!* – they're in the finals."

There's an instant outcry from the crowd.

"Easy," he says, trying to calm them. "Look, I know we all agree that the Loco Motos deserve every chance to compete and win a prize like the rest of us. In fact, it was my own club, the Boston Bobbie Boxers – which I'm sorry to say is no longer in operation – that sponsored the very first fundraiser that got the Loco Moto Mavericks started, long before Bistany and her Angel Wheels came to town. So the Loco Motos know that I am behind them one hundred percent, all the way. But the question remains, in the name of fairness, how can we walking people compete with those high-tech machines they dance with? There should be a separate competition with a separate prize for Best New Moves, one for walkers and one for wheelers."

Bistany rushes Colt and grabs the mike from him. "Thank yew for your remarks, Colt, and I'm sure we all appreciate what yew shared with us. But let me counter your position by saying that one of the founding principles for Mucho Macho Honcho Conventions is that we promote inclusivity at all times and at all events. That is the crucible of our mission: In-clu-si-vi-ty. We do not alienate. We inclusivate."

She pauses, as if jarred by some vestigial sense of language.

Meanwhile, the audience seems as shuffled up as I do. They're here for fun, I'm here to work, and instead we're subjected to petty politics and mutilated language.

Bistany says to Colt, "Now would yew please go back up to your DJ booth and do the job yew were hired to do? Thank yew."

Colt glowers at her, then sulkily leaves the stage.

Bistany continues brightly. "Now! I want to invite yew all to a special party at Gunsmoke Saloon tonight. Our benefactress, the lady with the big bucks, Miss Fannie Mae Knox, is hosting the event. Could we get a spotlight on Fannie Mae, please?"

A megawatt spotlight scans the crowd until it comes to rest in a faraway corner near the main entrance. There in the harsh glare of light stands the vision in pink who greeted me at the door. She looks pallid and two-dimensional now, as though she's been caught unawares in a tabloid expose. But Miss Fannie Mae Knox quickly recovers her composure and takes a regal bow – much practiced, obviously – to the approving hoots and hollers of the crowd. Standing beside her is none other than Kitty the costumer. That little puss sure gets around.

Bistany says, "I just want yawl to know that refreshments are on the house tonight, except for alcoholic beverages, of course, and it's all thanks to Fannie Mae's generosity. But yew must be wearing your convention badge, no exceptions. Okay? And now, gang, there'll be open dancing here for the rest of the day, and then tomorrow, the finals! Now I'm going to turn this mike off and go have some fun myself. Whoooh! What a morning, huh? Let's hear one more round of applause for our finalists! Yay!"

The audience cheers and applauds, and Bistany gives a signal to the DJ booth. But the music doesn't start. Moments pass. She grabs the microphone again. "Colt?" she says. "Where are yew? Don't yew start playing your power games with me."

Silence.

"We're waiting, Colt."

More silence.

"Damn yew, Colt! Don't yew make me come up there."

Still no music.

Bistany throws the microphone onto the stage, causing a

loud *thuk!* over the PA system. Then she storms off.

Is this how the West was won?

Suddenly the music comes blasting over the PA system, launching the cowboys and their "ladies" into dance.

It's my cue to get out of there.

3.

OUTSIDE, I DECIDE TO CALL Branco and tell him that Paladin's lost jewelry is just a scam for insurance money. I know the case isn't his department, but maybe he can blow that wind back where it came from. But first I need a phone. (I'm still not wireless. Is this how the dinosaurs felt?) I'll use the public phones in the Park Plaza Hotel, across the street from The Castle.

On my way into the hotel, I see Miss Fannie Mae Knox and Kitty crossing the great carpeted lobby together and heading toward the elevators. Probably a costume fitting.

Before I phone Branco, I decide to try one more "official" move before dropping this dopey case. I find the hotel's security office, introduce myself to the chief, and ask him what he can tell me about Paladin's missing jewels. He asks to see my license, and from then on he's very cooperative, which surprises me, given the reception I've gotten from everyone else so far. Maybe the fact that I'm not in cowboy gear helps, or the fact that we're in related lines of business. Whatever the reason, he takes me into his office where he informs me beyond any doubt that Vaslav Paladin (quite a first name!) had definitely not returned his jeweled collar tips to the hotel safe on the previous night, and that the hotel assumes absolutely no responsibility for his alleged loss. As a bonus, the guy snickers quietly and refers to the collar tips as "glass and rhodium plate."

"Not diamonds and platinum?" I say.

"Not what I saw. It's a spurious claim."

As I said, a dopey case.

I thank the guy and leave his office. I consider going back to The Castle to confront Paladin with the facts at hand, but then I figure, Why waste any more time? I'll give Branco a piece of my mind instead. But as I'm heading back to the lobby phones, I catch a whiff of familiar poison gas in the corridor. Through the open door to another office, I overhear the unmistakable voice of Bistany Evans, Miss Bovine Booties herself. She's arguing about some contract technicality with the hotel management. A second woman is telling Bistany about "nonexistent insurance coverage for that circus act with the wheelchairs."

Bistany replies, "But nothing happened."

The other woman insists. "Ma'am, you waived all insurance for special contingencies, yet you are sponsoring an event which poses great risk to everyone attending. We cannot allow you to continue that reckless behavior unless you agree to amend your contract with us. Or else show us proof that you are covered for any and all liabilities as defined by us."

"Meaning you want more money," says Bistany.

Offstage, *yew* has become *you*.

"We want insurance!" says the hotel woman. "You can't expect us to assume liability for a situation like that. The site is not equipped for it, and you never mentioned such risky events."

"And if I don't buy the insurance?"

"We'll close you down."

"You do that," says Bistany, "and I'll have the folks at City Hall on you so fast you won't know what hit you. Haven't you heard about equal access for people with disabilities?"

"It's not a question of access," says the woman. "We provide full and safe access for people with motion limitations. It's what your people are doing once they're in there. And since this is a holiday weekend, there's not much *you* can do at City Hall until Tuesday. Meanwhile, your little rodeo will be terminated. Have I made myself clear?"

"Shit!" says Bistany.

I take a deep breath, then move toward the open door and look inside. Bistany is getting a credit card out of her wallet. The hotel woman takes the card, thanks Bistany cordially, as if no ultimatum was ever uttered, then runs the transaction. As I stand there, I also realize that Bistany has "refreshed" her perfume – Why would anyone wear bug spray? – and there's probably not enough air in the entire hotel to dissipate it. How does the rep breathe at ground zero?

She returns the credit card, and Bistany says to her, "Next year we'll take our event elsewhere."

The hotel rep answers coolly, "As you please."

Bistany gets up and heads out of the office.

Fearing asphyxiation, I flee to police headquarters.

4.

NEW POLICE HEADQUARTERS IS IN West Roxbury, a Boston borough. I'm sure someone did tons of studies – or claimed they did – to determine the best location for the new digs. From the cops' perspective, it probably means a more efficient operation. But for a carless urban dick like me (the Alfa is in the shop again – the Alfa is always in the shop again), it sure feels like the cops' new house is too far away from my new house.

The building is a sprawling monstrosity of glass and steel. The glass is dark blue – gun-metal blue – and the whole place is frightfully sleek and clean – all business – exactly the way someone like Lieutenant Branco likes things.

I get to his office, and he's on the phone. He gestures for me to come in and sit down while he keeps talking. From his posture and his voice (he's speaking in monosyllables), I know it's a personal call. I try to look away, give him privacy, but he seems oblivious to me. So, I study him in the relative safety of psychic distance. His gray-blue eyes are cool and unnerving, like thin ice. His wavy black hair shines with bluish highlights, like Superman's. (The random strands of silver only enhance the sheen.) His skin still has that olive-hued, Mediterranean glow. But there's a change too, the beginnings of a crease over his brow, the first hint of a passage to maturity. Is it a result of his recent marriage and the growing daily reminders by his girl-wife that a little Branco baby is on the way? He seems a bit thinner too. He's probably working out less – at the gym, anyway. Sex-on-demand can keep the strongest stallion lean and hungry.

He hangs up the phone and says to me, "Hey, there, Stan. What brings you here?"

His casual tone disarms me. His greetings were always attacks. Maybe it's another sign of the improved and married Branco, who now begins every social situation bland and neutral. Well, to hell with marital niceties. I'm not married to him.

"What brings me here," I say, "is you."

"What did I do now?" he says.

You, you, you, Vito, it's always you. You are the sun, the moon, and the stars, and the rest of us all scramble around you in some eccentric orbit.

"You sent me out on a bogus jewelry theft."

"Hold it right there," he says, both of his palms signaling halt. He gets up and closes the door to his office. Then, back in his chair, he says firmly, "I never sent you anywhere."

"Didn't you phone me this morning?"

His mouth tenses up. "What I did," he says, "is happen to get wind of a situation, and then I happened to mention it to you. That's what happened."

"You didn't *happen* to suggest that I –"

"I thought you could use the practice," he says. "If you didn't want the work, you shouldn't have gone. But don't come in here complaining about it."

"I felt like a fool."

He says, "I can't help how you feel."

Is that what you tell your wife?

I say, "That guy Paladin doesn't even want his jewelry back, just the money. A lot of money, for diamonds and platinum. He even wanted me to help him with a fake claim. But when I checked with hotel security, they said the stuff he'd been putting in the safe was costume jewelry. Meaning I spent my time for nothing."

Branco says, "That's how most investigating goes, *real*

investigating. You strike out a lot. If you want recipes, Stan, go be a cook."

"I'd probably do better, considering the bones you throw me."

Branco's eyebrows shoot up, his beautiful, tapered, lush black Mediterranean eyebrows.

"Is that how you see it?" he says. "A bone?"

"It's fraud, clear as day, and I had no business being there."

"Then shut up and leave it!"

The phone rings. Branco picks it up, answers fiercely. Then his voice softens immediately. He listens a while, replies in monosyllables – must be his conjugal vernacular – then he says quietly, "I'll remember."

He hangs up the phone and writes on a notepad: ice cream.

He takes a deep breath then says to me, "Look, Stan, after what's gone down between us, I have no right to make the rules and call the shots for you. I can't even ..." He hunts for words, fails, shakes his head. "Never mind."

"What?" I say.

He struggles a bit, then says, "It's none of my business, but the fact is, now that you've got a little money, you keep quitting when things don't go your way. And in my book, quitting is for losers. I'd hate to think the guy who saved my life is a loser."

"Fate can play some weird tricks, Lieutenant."

"You are not a loser!"

"Whom are you trying to convince?"

Branco shakes his head. "I'm sorry I brought it up."

"But you did," I say.

Grunt. "I got wind of another theft this morning."

"Twice in one day? Sounds like this new office is kind of drafty. Or else you really are scouting work for me."

"Do you want to hear this or not?"

"Go ahead," I say.

Branco tells me, "A guy named Colt Remington phoned this morning to report a missing belt buckle."

"Colt Remington? He was at the convention, made a big speech, caused quite a stir."

"What kind of stir?" says Branco.

"He's some self-proclaimed Lone Ranger in the local cowboy culture. His credo is fairness in all things. This morning he was arguing about the unfair treatment of people in wheelchairs."

Branco says, "What's the problem with that?"

"Colt Remington thinks the guys in wheelchairs got special treatment, and the balance of fairness was violated."

"Cute," says Branco. "But the fact remains that there are now two thefts at the same event."

"You want me to go talk to Colt Remington?"

"Stan, I don't want you to do anything. I'm just telling you what I heard, off the record. You do what you want with it. It's what you usually do anyway."

"So it's all sub rosa between us."

"Not even that," says Branco. He opens his desk drawer, pulls out a gray envelope, business-sized, sealed, and he hands it to me. "I never saw this," he says, "and I don't know how you got it. After you read it, destroy it."

I take the envelope and start to open it.

"Not here!" he yells.

I quickly slide the envelope inside my shirt.

The air settles.

I say, "How'd you know I'd be coming here?"

"I didn't," he says. "I got that ready just in case." He gets up and opens the door. "Time's up," he says. I take my cue and leave.

I return to town the same way I came – via the T, which, by the way, is short for MBTA, which stands for Metropolitan Bay Transit Authority. There is an age-old question of exactly where the authority ends and the transit begins. So, while waiting for Godot in the Ruggles Street station, I read the police report Branco slipped to me. It's a standard form, barely filled out, since this preliminary report was taken over the phone. It turns out that Colt Remington lives near me in the South End. In fact, he's in a building I can see from my roof deck. (Rather, the beam-and-plank framework that will eventually be my roof deck.) Colt phoned the police early this morning as soon as he discovered that his prized Civil War belt buckle was missing from its display case. He'd hosted a party last night for twenty or so people and their guests. He would not provide a complete list to the police since many of the invitees were also his clients, and he is obligated to protect their privacy.

Fairness in all things, that's Colt. But who are these clients? And what kind of party was it?

Colt does provide the name of one person he believes is the culprit, a local cowboy costume designer named Wang Chu. (That's got to be Kitty.) Colt and Mr. Chu are "known associates", though not on friendly terms. Mr. Chu's appearance at the party was unexpected and made brief. Despite Colt's accusation, the theft could have been accomplished by any of the people present last night, since the buckle wasn't noticed missing until early this morning, long after the last guest left.

If you can believe any of Colt's report.

The train arrives. It's a few minutes' ride to the South End, and I head home to make some phone calls. Now, if I had a mobile phone, I could make my case-related calls anywhere, not just from Kraychik Central, or from some sticky, germ-laden public phone – provided it's even in service. But am I ready to make the techno-social leap of using a wireless phone in public? Will I ever feel comfortable walking down the street yakking away in full voice? People tell me you get used to it. Hell, you can get used to anything. But should you?

At home, with neither *felis* nor *homo domesticus* to greet me at the door, my wall-less house feels even emptier than it appears. I call my friend Benjy, former CEO of Hairnet, the Hairdressers Gossip Network.

When he hears my voice he squeals, "Penny!" which is his nickname for me, thanks to my coppery red hair.

I tell him I need his help.

He says, "For you, Pen, anything."

Like I said, The Man That Got Away.

"It's about some work I'm doing – a case actually."

"A case?" he says. "Like, with a cop?"

"Like, as a dick."

"*As* a dick?" he says. "Or *with* a dick?"

See? No tingle. Not like Branco.

"Both," I say.

Benjy says, "So now I know the Italian is involved." Benjy's heard about Branco, though he's never met him.

I tell him, "I need some research, and I thought of you, Wizard of the Information Age."

"What kind of research?" says Benjy. "Dick research?"

Is this how Branco feels when I provoke him?

"Research like this," I say. "First some guy's collar tips are missing, then someone else loses a Civil War belt buckle."

"Collar tips?"

"At that big cowboy dance convention in town."

"Mucho Macho Honcho," says Benjy, who is alert to everything social. "Penny, if these things were lost at the convention, I think you need the lost and found, not the Internet."

"But they were allegedly *stolen*."

"Then call the police."

"They did. And now I'm on the case."

"Wow," he says. "Are you working for the police now?"

"No," I say. "I am absolutely not, in any way, affiliated with the Boston police."

"Yeah, right, sure," says Benjy. "Oh-Branco-swoon! is more like it. Big, burly, brutish –"

"Married."

"Yes, Penny, I know he's married. I'm the one who told you, remember? I saw the announcement before it hit the papers. And now how many times have you told me? I almost wonder if you keep saying it to remind yourself that it's true. Like maybe you're in *denial* about it. Hmmm?"

"Let's get back to business, Benjy."

"Touched a nerve?"

"Since the collar tips and the belt buckle were allegedly

stolen –"

"You keep saying allegedly. Were they stolen or not?"

"Facts not in evidence yet."

"Jeez, Penny, you sound like a dick."

"Or a dick-brain," I say. "But if I assume they were stolen, it might help to know where a thief might try to unload them. Aren't there places on the Internet where people sell stuff?"

"Penny, Penny, Penny," he says. "The net is one giant flea market. You can buy and sell anything."

"So, then, maybe I – I mean, maybe *you* – can find this stuff out there."

"But it doesn't work like that. You can't just ask the net, 'Where are the stolen objects?' and expect an answer. No computer can do that."

"You told me once you could find anything out there."

"Almost, Penny. But I'm sure I was talking about information and entertainment, not the whereabouts of stolen property. Anyway, tell me about the stuff."

"They collar tips sound like costume jewelry, but the belt buckle might be real. The owner claims it was Civil War era."

"Does he have the provenance?"

"It wasn't mentioned in the police report."

Benjy says, "I thought you weren't working for the police."

"I'm not."

"Then how did you see the police report?"

"They're not secret, Benjy. Anyone can see them." Can he hear me tap-dancing?

"That's news to me," he says. "Are you sure you don't get special privileges since you saved that cop's life?"

"Maybe," I say.

"If I saved your life, would you give me special privileges?"

"Business, Benjy."

"Sure, Penny. Okay, well, depending on the condition, something like a Civil War belt buckle could be valuable."

"How valuable?"

"Sky's the limit with some collectors. But you know, Penny, right here in Boston we have a world-renowned repository of Civil War relics."

"The Federal Reserve Bank?"

"The Vade Mecum," says Benjy.

"Sounds like a medical condition."

"It might as well be, it's so old. The Boston Vade Mecum Society is the oldest circulating library in the United States. For most of its life, membership was by invitation only. But eventually they had to open their doors to the rest of society, so now riffraff like us can join too."

"Sounds kind of calcified."

"Lots of old bones," says Benjy, "and lots of old dough."

"And how is a moldy old library going to help me?"

"Because, my dear Penelope, they are also a museum of sorts. In fact, when their original collection grew too large, back in Medieval times, they spun off a separate organization that became the Museum of Fine Arts."

"I'm impressed."

"They're impressive," says Benjy. "And since the Vade Mecum Society still has its Civil War collection in-house, someone there might know of places or people who buy and trade related objects."

"Even stolen ones?"

"Uh, Penny, I think I'd couch my queries more diplomatically. For all you know, the Vade Mecum Society may be the recipient of that very buckle. And try to say 'antiquities' or 'relics', not 'memorabilia' or 'stuff', okay?"

"Sure, Benjy. Marketplace colloquialism will not penetrate my vernacular."

"Are you trying to talk dirty again?"

"There is one other thing I'd like to, uh, discuss."

"Sure," says Benjy.

"It's kind of serious."

"You want to discuss something serious with me?"

"Yes," I say.

"Well, start talking."

"I'm not sure how to start."

"Just say it, Penny." He sounds eager, as though I'm about to propose marriage, along with a full church wedding, outdoor garden reception, and month-long Caribbean honeymoon.

I ask him, "Have you been talking to my friend Nicole?"

"She is an absolute doll! You are so lucky to have her!"

He sounds as though he's just met his future sister-in-law, and they *really* like each other. And so it must follow, as the night the day, that Benjy and I will marry.

Benjy say, "How did you meet her?"

"Nikki and I just happened to meet each other."

"Oh, I love her!"

"Then maybe you ought to propose."

He says, "You know there's only one man for me."

"I guess it's not Nicole. I was kind of surprised when she told me this morning that my Memorial Day cookout was going to be a formal, sit-down affair, very fancy. And since that was never my idea at all, I was wondering where she got the notion."

"From me, Penny. She and I were talking about it, and how nice it would be to do a formal outdoor setting in your garden with silver and crystal and linen and candles and –"

"And just where is this vast array of tableware coming from?"

"From me, Penny. It's my housewarming present to you. Except for the silver. That's my grandmother's, so it would be on loan. For now, anyway."

"Are you choosing the china and crystal patterns too?"

"I thought we could do that together. Nicole really likes the idea."

"She's got great taste, Benjy."

"I meant you, Penny. I want to go shopping with you."

"Look, Benjy, it's a nice idea, but this is a cookout, not a wedding reception. I want to do the kind of thing my family did – with paper plates and plastic utensils and napkins that blow away, and hamburgers and hotdogs and potato salad.

And beer in a cooler. That kind of thing."

"Beer?" says Benjy. "You drink beer?"

"My father did."

"Oh," he says. "That was close. Well, your idea sounds okay too, but aren't you pandering just a little bit to your cop?"

"Pandering?"

"With the beer, I mean, and the hot dogs. Maybe you ought to have a few touches of refinement, just in case there's a side to your cop you don't know yet."

"And you do?"

"All I mean, Penny, is that you're trying really hard to please him, and you're not letting any of yourself show through."

"It's not any trouble, Benjy. It's what I want to do."

"But I thought you liked formal dinners."

"I do, but I also want Branco to be at ease. This is the first time I'm actually entertaining him."

"Sounds like this whole thing is for him."

"It's for everybody."

"His wife's going to be there too, right?

"Yes," I say.

"Will she be all right?"

"Why not?"

"She's preggers, isn't she?"

"Probably as big as a house by now."

"That's not very nice, Penny."

"Maybe I'm not very nice."

"She can't be that big," says Benjy. "It's only three months, right? Unless they did a little premarital test drive."

"Not Branco, not with a virgin."

"She was a virgin?"

"That's probably what snagged him."

Benjy says, "How do you know?"

"Nicole told me."

"How does she know?"

"She can tell."

"Still, Penny, don't you think a formal dinner would impress Branco's wife?"

"His wife?" I say. "I don't care about his wife. I saved his life. Isn't that enough?"

"But they weren't married when you did that."

"All the more reason. Without me she wouldn't be married to him now."

"You're right, Pen. It's all thanks to you that every night, while you and I are lying alone and chilling between our respective sheets, she's with that big, brawny Italian, wrestling with his big, brawny Italian –"

"Benjy! Are you having a teen-age meltdown? Look, I just want a cookout – nothing fancy – just a simple, comfortable cookout. If Branco is at ease then maybe I'll be at ease."

"Maybe," says Benjy.

"I said *maybe*, didn't I? And wouldn't that be nice for everyone else?"

"I still think Nicole would enjoy it more my way, and Branco's wife too. We're gay men, Penny. Women expect this kind of thing from us."

"It's my party, Benjy, and I want it simple."

"Okay," he says with a sad little mew. "Even if the silver is all polished. It's so beautiful, Penny. It could be yours too, you know, someday ..."

"Yeah, well, there's still time to decide."

"Take all the time you need."

"I meant about the cookout, Benjy. One thing about doing it formal – it would be fun to see Branco fumble with the tableware."

"The offer's there, Penny, along with my grandmother's silver."

When would Benjy realize he was squandering precious metals trying to woo someone with a stainless steel heart?

He gives me directions to the Vade Mecum Society, and we say goodbye. Thus informed, I set out to discover where a stolen Civil War belt buckle might be unloaded in Boston.

5.

BENJY'S DIRECTIONS LEAD ME directly to the Boston Vade Mecum Society. It's on the uppermost elevation of Beacon Hill, almost across the street from the State House. I've walked by the place countless times and never noticed it, and now that I do see it, I can't imagine how I ever missed it. It's an old stone building – the kind of thing you'd call an edifice – imposing yet discreet, like the Brahmin aristocracy that built it.

Two gargantuan bronze doors lie open, as if inviting passers-by to enter. But just within the massive metal framework are two additional doors clad in burnished red leather with brass accents. The leather doors are closed – they looked sealed, actually – which somewhat tempers the first invitation, maybe to dissuade all but the most determined souls from entering the hallowed halls.

But I'm on a mission and can't afford to be a shrinking violet, so I push my way in. Once through the bronze and leather entranceway, I'm in a palatial vestibule with marble flooring, surrounded by four bigger-than-life portraits of four bigger-than-life men, probably the guys who built the place. There's also a statue of George Washington signifying the dawn of civilization.

I pass through the foyer and go up a few steps into a small chamber, a bottleneck that forces you past a security guard. I tell him I'm there to do some research. He has me sign in as a guest, then lets me enter.

The place is silent as a tomb, the way the privileged class goes to the library. Directly ahead is a huge circulation desk, solid mahogany and about twenty feet long. The backdrop for the desk is a Palladian window as big as a movie screen. Sitting on top of the enormous desk and aligned with the window is a porcelain vase about two feet high. From the top of the vase bursts an entire botanical garden that adds another three feet. For a conservative bunch, these Brahmins sure like drama. Or else their florist is gay. The flowers are mostly lilies, roses, and carnations, and they fill the air with a soothing nondescript scent, a potpourri of tranquility. Behind the circulation desk sits a refined looking woman in her fifties. She smiles my way.

"Can I help you?" she asks pleasantly.

I ask her, "With whom would I speak regarding Civil War antiquities?" I sound like some idiot trying to pass for British, but isn't that how people talk in a place like this?

The woman struggles to contain her laugh. "Are you an actor?" she says.

"No."

"I thought you might be rehearsing."

"No."

"Sorry," she says, then gets her mirth settled down. "We do have a fine Civil War collection, but I'm not sure if the curator is here today. Let me check." She dials her phone. "F.L.? So you are here. I must have missed you. There's a young man asking about Civil War antiquities ... Yes, at the desk now ... I don't know." She looks up at me. "Are you a scholar?"

How do I answer that?

She says into the phone, "No," then asks me, "Collector?"

I shake my head.

Into the phone: "No, not a collector." To me: "Tourist?" I whisper to her, "What do I say to get him to see me?" She speaks into the phone: "He says it's a personal matter ... Yes, I'll tell him." She hangs up and says to me, "Mr. Newbegin will be down in a few minutes."

"Thanks for your help with that 'personal matter'."

"Don't mention it," she says.

A few minutes later a man appears at the big circulation desk. He's medium height, around five-ten, and in good shape for a guy in his fifties. His hair is thinning, but still a fine silvery crown. His face is ruddy, the skin looks clear and well-scrubbed. He's got pale blue eyes – very alert – and he's wearing wire-rimmed glasses. He smiles cautiously toward me, then quietly addresses the woman behind the desk.

"Where is the young man with the personal matter?"

Mind you, I'm the only one in the place.

"Right here," I say.

He turns to me and extends his hand. "How good of you to come. I'm F. Lloyd Newbegin."

His handshake is vigorous but restrained, and there's a faint fruity scent from his mouth – pleasant.

"I'm Stan Kraychik."

"That's Czech, isn't it?"

"Yes," I say.

"A fine nationality to be."

Like I have a choice.

He eyes me directly. "You look familiar. Have we met before?"

"This is my first time here."

"Well, that won't happen again, will it?" Then he laughs, a discreet *har-har!*

Some joke.

He says, "How can I help you?"

"I have a question about a Civil War relic."

"Then you've come to the right place, young man. Shall we go up to my office?"

In the elevator Mr. Newbegin says, "It's lucky you arrived when you did. Any earlier and I wouldn't have been here – I took a long breakfast. Any later, and I'd be gone, since we're closing early today. It's not a usual thing, but with the holiday and all, it's nice to get a head start on the weekend."

His large office has the same soothing floral scent as the

area near the circulation desk. Maybe the whole building is aromatized for tranquility. Then I notice a vase of flowers on his desk – again, mostly lilies, roses, and carnations.

Mr. Newbegin suggests that we sit in the two leather club chairs in an alcove off to one side. A Persian carpet – cream figuration on an indigo ground – defines the area. The chairs face each other diagonally, with a small table between them. I half-expect him to offer me a drink, but he doesn't.

"Now," he says, "what is this personal matter you'd like to discuss?"

I tell him, "I'm investigating the loss of a Civil War belt buckle, and I was wondering, if such a thing went missing, where would be a likely place for it to turn up?"

"You choose your words carefully, young man. You say 'loss of' and 'went missing'."

"It's not clear what actually happened to it, and I'm trying to find out where a person might start looking for it."

He chuckles, then says, "Are you the person who might start looking?"

"Yes."

"Does the buckle belong to you?"

"No."

"I see," he says. "You are merely looking for it."

"That's right."

"And you'd like me to suggest where you might start?"

"That would help."

"I see," he says again, then thinks a moment. "Might I ask, do you work for an insurance company?"

"No."

"But you are investigating."

"That's right."

"Privately engaged, then?"

I hesitate. "Yes."

"That's always best," he says. "Well, where to start, where to start, let me see ... There are private collectors, though certain objects never come to light with them."

"Because they're stolen, you mean?"

My candor flusters him slightly, but he recovers quickly.

"Well, yes," he says. "Though not all collectors are of that ilk, young man."

"What about places like this?"

He chuckles. "We have no interest in changing our collection, even with legitimate pieces. As for other museums, they'd verify the provenance of every object they acquire."

He smiles at me, and I smile back. There's a pause while we sit there smiling at each other. His teeth are white and sound, but they haven't been forced into alignment. Maybe cosmetic dentistry wasn't proper for a Brahmin male of his generation.

I break the silence. "However ..."

"However indeed!" he exclaims, suddenly animated. "Yes, yes, *however*, young man! Now we come to the facts. There is no denying that in the real world, as opposed to some idealized world of museums and private collectors, that the source and provenance of a item can be utterly irrelevant. And so you are quite clever to say 'however'. Now when did this piece go missing?"

"This morning."

"So you've lost a bit of time already."

I say, "I was only just called in."

"And tell me again what the missing piece was."

"A belt buckle," I say. "A Civil War belt buckle."

"Union or Confederate?"

"I don't know."

"Come, come!" he says. "How can you not know something like that? The first point of valuation on a Civil War piece is knowing which side it's from."

"Actually, I never saw it. I'm just part of the effort to recover it."

"Privately engaged," says Mr. Newbegin.

"As I said."

"Yes, well," he says, "things move so fast in this world of ours, there's no telling where this buckle could be, even as we speak. It wouldn't surprise me to see it turn up on

The Antiques Roadshow tonight." *Har-har!*

I tell him the show is pre-recorded.

"Is it?" he says. "I wouldn't know. But I have heard about the program – apparently an unqualified success."

"It started in England."

"Is that so? Surprised I didn't know that." Then he adds, "If it's *true*." *Har!* "Sorry, young man," he says, "no offense."

"None taken."

"And if that's all you have to ask me, I'm going to excuse myself. You understand, with the holiday and all."

"Sure," I say, and stand up.

He stops at his desk and offers me a fruit pastille from a small tin.

"Opera singers use them," he says. "They're from England, like the original *Antiques Roadshow*."

That's when I notice a large poster, mounted and framed, hanging behind his office door, announcing a past exhibition at the Vade Mecum Society. The print shows two cowboys in the desert at sundown. One stands tall, with legs apart and arms akimbo, his long-barreled pistol hanging low and glistening off one hip. The other cowpoke lies on his belly, propped on his elbows, with his long legs spread open behind him. He polishes his revolver with a red kerchief, the barrel pointing upward. Both men are lit by the soft glow of a campfire, while two horses graze quietly nearby.

Mr. Newbegin says, "You've noticed the work of Mr. Bryce Timothy, a young master in the tradition of the great Will James."

"And with a very definite message."

"Message?" says Mr. Newbegin.

I hesitate. "I mean with the guns and the fire and the position of their bodies. It's almost ... romantic."

"Romantic?" he says.

"Like George Quaintance with clothes."

"George Quaintance, indeed!" says Newbegin. "You betray your naivete, young man. I never saw anything like *that* in Bryce Timothy's work."

But the twinkle in his eye tells me he means exactly the opposite.

He says, "I curated an exhibit of Bryce's recent work here at the Society last year. It broke all records for attendance. The Beacon Hill matrons returned again and again, and the catalog sold out before the first week." He looks at his watch. "And now, young man, if you don't mind ..."

"I was just leaving," I say. "Thanks again."

"Good luck," he says. "Here's my card, in case you want to call on me again."

I leave the Vade Mecum Society somewhat reeling, as though I have imbibed an elixir I am ill-equipped to assimilate. I'm sure it's my background, both genetic and cultural. Mr.

Newbegin did comment on my name. If I'd been born Stanley Coleridge instead of Kraychik, would he have treated me differently? He was cordial enough, or was it mere tolerance, expertly expressed? What if my bloodline was the same as his? Then what might have happened in F. Lloyd Newbegin's office? An actual drink poured for me? Wading through this miasma of class consciousness, I wonder, What *did* I learn about Civil War belt buckles? Answer: naught.

It's after four o'clock, and the afternoon sun invites me to take the long way home, through downtown Boston's green acreage – the Common and the Public Gardens – where I can enjoy some natural urban potpourri. Then I head over to Newbury Street to see Nicole at Snips Salon. She won't be busy today, not on the Friday afternoon of Memorial Day weekend. Everyone's gone, right?

Wrong. The place is jumping.

The new receptionist at Snips doesn't recognize me. She actually stops me as I go sailing by her desk, and asks if I have an appointment. I tell her I don't need an appointment. She promptly activates the buzzer under Nicole's manicure table, and within seconds Nicole is at the front desk.

"Oh, it's you," she says, then turns to the receptionist.

"It's all right, Belinda. He's a former employee."

Ouch.

Nikki used to be a model, and though the years have thickened her figure a bit, she always looks great. Today she's wearing a suit of gray wool crepe piped in scarlet, and her auburn hair is styled in a classic chignon, a holdover from her modeling days.

I say to Nicole, "What are all these people doing here on a holiday weekend?"

"The same as you, Stanley. They are trying to imbue their lives with some semblance of pleasure."

"*Imbue*, doll?"

Nicole smiles.

I ask, "Have you got a minute?"

She replies, "Let me check," even though she always knows her schedule – and everyone else's too. "As a matter of fact," she says, "I'm free at the moment."

We walk together to the back office. Or, rather, I walk and Nicole struts. I'll bet she had that strut before her modeling days. She probably took her first baby steps with a Dior turn.

"All right," she says, once we're seated, "I really do have a customer coming, so you might as well get to the point and tell me what's on your mind."

"Like what?"

"Stanley, you only drop in here unannounced when you have something on your mind, so talk."

"Nikki ..." I'm eyeing the liquor cabinet.

"It's too early," she says.

"Since when?"

"Since I have a customer in seven minutes. But help your-self if you must."

"I don't need a drink."

"But you want one," she says.

"Don't you?"

"No."

"Liar."

She says, "You must be having problems with that investigation Vito asked you to do."

I tell her, "Branco never asked me to do anything. He's made it very clear. All he did was mention a theft in passing, and it's all off the record, and anything I do is on my own."

"So where is the problem?" she says.

"Branco isn't behind me."

Nicole arches an eyebrow.

"I mean standing behind me."

The other eyebrow goes up.

"Do you mean, darling, that you want Vito to recognize your work in an official capacity?"

"You're patronizing me."

"Then tell me what's wrong."

"What's wrong, Nikki, is that the whole thing is a joke, and I'm going to give it up."

"Again?" she says.

"What do you mean, again?"

"You usually give up when things become difficult."

"Branco said the same thing."

"Vito is usually right about you. Not in the superficial sense, of course."

"Of course," I say. "Branco deals only with the profound. Still, Nikki, this whole idea to become a PI was stupid."

"Then stop doing it and go back to the other things that keep you busy."

"Like what?"

"Like cat-sitting for friends, watering plants, picking up mail, things like that."

"Whoopee."

She says, "And you still have the occasional client here."

"Double whoopee. Nikki, I want to do something useful. I thought being a PI would be useful. But when I finally get a lead on a case, it's some flimsy gay rhinestone theft. Is this what the future holds for me? Being a gay dick?"

"First thing," she says, "you ought to come up with a better term."

"I'm getting tired, Nikki, tired of trying to find a new career."

"Then come back to the shop."

"You'd like that."

"So would you," she says.

"But it's going backwards."

"Backwards from where?" says Nicole. "You were doing fine until you got that money. Then you started questioning your life, and now look at you. You're like a leaf in the wind."

"Not a puff on the pond?"

"You need to work! You are too idle!"

"Look who's talking."

"I may indulge myself, Stanley, but I earn the right to do it."

"Earn?" I say. "What does that mean?"

"It means I come to work, and you've become lazy."

"Maybe I should go to law school and become Perry Mason. Then I could solve serious crimes, not find lost trinkets."

"But darling," says Nicole, "you're not the ingenue type."

"Nikki, Perry Mason was not an ingenue."

"Then what was he?"

"Broad in the shoulders and light in the loafers."

"Loafers like yours, you mean?"

"Yes, doll. But ingenues, real ingenues, are always young women."

"Are you sure?" she says.

"Yes."

"Well, emotionally they're the same."

"As what?"

"As you, dear. Now tell me, are you free tomorrow morning?"

"Depends."

"Mrs. Haffenreffer needs a color and cut, and the last time she was here she told me that she prefers you to Ramon."

"Me? Or my work?"

"Isn't it the same thing?"

"Not with Ramon."

"Stanley, do you want the appointment or not?"

"What time?"

"Ten."

"I can manage that."

"Much obliged," says Nicole.

"The old gal tips well, that's for sure."

"Not according to Ramon."

"That's because he just stands around *deserving* his tips."

"You have to admit, Stanley, Ramon is quite a looker."

"I'll admit it, Nikki, but I don't have to admire it."

Nicole stands up. "Time for my five o'clock. What are you up to?"

"I'm going to talk to someone who lost a belt buckle."

"That could be interesting, depending on how he lost it."

"At home," I say.

Nicole gives me a quizzical look. "Perhaps you're right, Stanley. That kind of work does sound a bit dull."

Then she leaves me alone in the back office. I eye the liquor cabinet, but then I realize it's only out of boredom and frustration that I'm considering a drink. The fact is, I still have work to do. I still have the impending thrill of meeting Colt Remington face to face.

Maybe just one shot before I go?

6.

ON THE DIRECTORY OF Colt Remington's building, I find his name followed by some odd letters:

C. REMINGTON, PIC & PPS

I press the code that rings his condo, and he comes on the intercom.

"Yes?"

There's some static on the thing, so I yell into it.

"Stan Kraychik to see Colt Remington!"

"Top floor," he says, and buzzes me in without another word.

Does he know who I am? Doesn't he care whom he lets in?

I take the elevator up and find his apartment. I'm about to knock on the door when I see that it's slightly ajar. I hear two voices inside, one male, one female, both arguing loudly. I can't see the two people but I hear their voices clearly. Fortunately – or un – I also catch a whiff of something anti-tranquil and anti-bug: Bistany Evans's pungent perfume.

She says, "And don't you ever pull another stunt like you did today!"

Yew is gone, so apparently we're backstage here.

"Or else what?" says Colt.

"It was totally inappropriate."

"Why should I care now? You're not going to keep your promise."

"What promise?" says Bistany.

"You said if I didn't protest the pre-recorded steps here in Boston, you'd take me on the national tour."

"I never said that."

"Poster boy," says Colt. "That's what you told me. National Poster Boy for the Mucho Macho Honcho Conventions, including an executive compensation package."

"Baby," she says, "I'd remember if I promised you anything like that."

Baby?

"But you did," he says.

"Look," says Bistany, "I'm under a lot of stress – stress you can't even imagine. This convention is going to make or break the corporation. It's that serious. So I don't have time for everyone's petty little issues and agendas. I just hope we can get through the next few days without killing each other."

Colt says, "Is that a threat, or a warning?"

"You know what I mean," she says.

"The only thing I know," he says, "is that you replaced me with Chester Wright as your new poster boy."

Chester Wright? That's his full name? As in, Mr. Right?

Colt says, "Don't I deserve an explanation for that? I'm a better caller than Chester. I could do more for Mucho Macho than anyone else in Boston. So what happened to change your mind?"

"I had to, Baby."

"Had to?" says Colt. "That's not your style. I think you needed something to boost your pathetic all-inclusive campaign. And along came Chester with that bad leg, and you couldn't resist. You could have had me up there on your poster, and instead you're using a crippled guy. Is that why you did it? For inclusion?"

"*Inclusivity*," says Bistany. "And it was more than Chester."

"Then what else?"

"That fight club you used to run – you've got a smudge on

your reputation, Baby, a smudge I can't afford to have associated with me or the convention."

"But the club is closed. You and Heather saw to that."

"People still know about it."

"So because of something I did in the past, and which *you* made me stop, you changed your mind about me."

"That's right," says Bistany. "You were encouraging women to beat each other up. The idea is just too dangerous."

Colt says, "So you're afraid of an idea."

"I'm afraid of what someone like you could do to my plans."

"But what about me?" he says. "What about us?"

"There's no more *us*, Baby."

"Just like that."

She says, "What we did was totally inappropriate."

"Sounds like everything about me has become totally inappropriate."

"That pretty much sums it up," she says. "So, can we just get along?"

"Go to hell," he says.

"You go to hell yourself, you bastard!"

From baby to bastard in mere seconds.

Colt says, "Maybe we'll get along better down there."

Then Bistany comes storming out through the door. She crashes into me, spreading noxious bug repellent onto me.

She brays, "Who are you? Another one of his boys?"

Close up she looks older than the Mistress Chickie she tries to portray onstage. Fine lines around her eyes and mouth indicate she's of a certain age, and the slight sag around her jaw and neck implies that she's lost a lot of weight recently, long after the salad days of resilient young flesh.

"Figures!" she mutters, then clomps down the hall to the elevator.

The backstage Bistany, she is not so nice.

I go into Colt's apartment.

He says, "Where's my pizza?"

"Pizza?"

"Aren't you the pizza guy?"

"No."

"But I just buzzed you in."

I tell him, "You buzzed me in, but I'm not the pizza guy."

"Who are you then?"

"I'm an investigator. Stan Kraychik."

"ID?" he says, snapping his fingers.

I hand him my license. While he looks at it, I do a quick make on his apartment. It's a duplex, spare and fastidiously clean, everything screaming, "Designer! Trendy! Expensive!" I do a quick make on him with the same results.

"Christ!" he says, "it's your name. On the intercom I thought you were some foreigner delivering my pizza, but it's your name." He returns my license and asks, "How long were you out in the hallway?"

"Long enough to know that you and Bistany Evans aren't kissing cousins."

He sniggers. "Not tonight. So what do you want from me?"

"It's about your belt buckle."

"My belt buckle?"

"You called in a report for stolen property with the police."

He says, "But you're not a cop, not according to that ID."

"That's right."

He stares at me, observing, making judgments. I do the same for him. I was impressed with his body this morning when he made his big accusatory speech, but now, in real-life and away from the stage lights, Colt Remington is even more startling. He's tall and broad, with big heavy bones. The rest of him is meat – dense lean meat, like a natural fullback or a heavyweight fighter. His hair is pepper-and-salt, cut brutally short, military style, and it's thick as a bristle brush. The look is "standard issue" for certain guys of his age and physical shape, meaning around forty and hunk-like. As much as I don't want to admit it, the sheer bulk of his muscles is fascinating. Not sexy, but fascinating.

He says, "Are you with the insurance company?"

"I'm freelance. Gives me more variety, keeps the work interesting." I'll convince myself eventually.

"Variety is the spice of life," he says. "But I can't give you any time right now. I'm expecting a client."

"And a pizza."

"Huh?" says Colt. "Oh, right."

"Does your client like pizza too?"

"It's for me," he says.

"Sounds like you got Bistany out of here just in time."

"Hey, look," he says, "whatever it is you want, make it quick."

"Sure. Tell me about your missing buckle."

"First tell me who hired you."

"Like I said, I'm freelance."

"But someone had to hire you, unless you're working on spec."

"Something like that," I say.

"All right," he says. "The buckle was very old, very rare, very valuable."

"When was the last time you saw it?"

"Last night."

"Where was it? I mean, you obviously weren't wearing it when it vanished."

He arches an eyebrow. "Why obviously?"

"Someone would have to get it off you."

Colt smiles. "That could be interesting."

"But you weren't wearing it."

"No. *Obviously.* It was in a display case, but I don't keep it locked. What's the sense of having something if all you're going to do is protect it?"

"Doesn't sound like you're very careful with your toys."

He says, "And it sounds like you use humor as a weapon."

"It's a defense against massive insecurity."

Colt smiles again. "I doubt that," he says. "Look, there were a lot of people in and out of here last night. Any one of them could have taken it. Now how about asking me something you really want to know?"

"Okay," I say. "Why was Wang Chu the only name you gave to the cops?"

He's surprised but he recovers quickly. "You saw the police report," he says. "Is that how you get your leads?"

"Close enough," I say.

He considers this, then says, "I gave the police Kitty's name, I mean Wang Chu's, because I think he took the buckle."

"But you said there were lots of people here last night."

"Yes."

"How many?"

"I don't recall exactly."

"But you know whom you invited."

He smiles slightly. Maybe the objective case amuses him.

"Of course," he says, "but some of them brought guests, and others didn't show up at all."

"Guests," I say. "So there were strangers here too."

"Some, yes."

"And one of them could have taken the belt buckle."

"Possibly," he says, "but not probably. It was Kitty, er, Wang Chu. I'm sure of it."

"Why would he take it?"

"Who knows?" says Colt, and he shrugs his brawny shoulders.

"You'd know," I say.

"Then who cares?"

"Don't you want to recover the buckle?"

He smiles. The guy smiles a lot. "I'll probably get more from the insurance claim than what the buckle is worth."

We look at each other.

He says, "So maybe we should quit this little dance."

"The police may not be so obliging. You did file a report, after all."

Colt shifts his weight. His tight jeans creak a bit.

"Look," he says, "I really don't have time."

"With that nonexistent client coming, you mean?"

He tries to unnerve me with a smoldering Theda Bara

look, but I've seen better.

"What kind of party was it?" I say.

"What kind do you think?" he says coyly, then he winks at me.

Who is he trying to be now? A flirtatious Sophia Loren?

"Take a guess," he says, "about my party."

"Okay," I say. "How about the obvious? How about a sex party?"

"Why is that obvious?"

"Because you look like the kind of person who has an active sex life."

"Why is that?"

"Because of your body."

"That's a fair assumption," says Colt.

"You know what you've got."

"I do," he says, "and a body like this comes with responsibilities."

"So, in other words, it *wasn't* a sex party last night."

He's intrigued. "How do you figure that?"

"Because if it *had* been a sex party, either you'd deny it, assuming you have something to hide, or else you'd brag about it, assuming you celebrate group sex. But you did neither. Instead you directed my attention to your body."

"And why do you think I did that?"

"To make sure that I noticed the goods. And that I appreciate their attendant responsibilities." Now I wink at him, but ironically, like Rosalind Russell.

Colt faces me head on. "You know something? I think I like you. It seldom happens, but I have a feeling that you're exactly the kind of person I could genuinely get to like."

"Well, thanks," I say, suddenly sheepish. But really, what do I care what he thinks? I don't find this guy attractive in the least. It's only muscular fascination.

Fascination.

Music, maestro, if you please.

We waltz around his fastidiously clean living room. His fascinating muscles guide me the same way Paladin guided

Chester this morning. We even do that same triumphal lift, and Colt's heroic strength supports me effortlessly – no mean feat, given my insistent, persistent avoirdupois. The song ends and the audience cheers. The entire world approves.

Meanwhile, Colt is munching a slice of pizza – mushrooms, extra cheese. Apparently real-world events have continued during my hallucinatory dance sequence, probably a delayed reaction to Bistany's lingering fumes.

Colt says, "Are you hunting down Paladin's collar tips too?"

"How do you know about that?"

"I saw you talking to him at the hall this morning, from up in the DJ booth. And now you're here talking to me. So maybe you're some kind of ambulance chaser, but with stolen property instead of injuries."

Never mind that, Baby.

"Speaking of Paladin," I say, "did you know he attacked Kitty this morning? That is, Mr. Chu."

"Sounds like he found him then."

"Who?" I say. "Who found whom?"

Colt smiles again. He does like the objective case. Or else he's just plain cocksure of himself.

He says, "Paladin created a big row when he came into The Castle this morning, something about missing jewelry. He even had me page Kitty – I mean, Mr. Chu. Sounds like he found him. Where did the attack happen?"

I tell him, "In the dressing room."

"Was Kitty, er, Mr. Chu hurt?"

"He got out of Paladin's way. He's pretty fast."

"He's lucky," says Colt, "and luck runs out eventually. Kitty –" He starts to correct himself again, then shrugs. "Kitty relies on defensive tactics, but you need a good offense too, if you're really going to protect yourself."

"You ran that fight club."

"Are you interested in fighting?"

"I'm a congenital wimp."

"All the more reason," says Colt. "Aren't you tired of being afraid of other people? Wouldn't you like to know you could beat the shit out of the next asshole who bothers you?"

"I never really thought about it, not in those terms."

He says, "Besides great protection, fighting is an honest means of self-expression. It can also be an effective form of therapy. *Mano à mano* combat can help you find the origins of your essential self. Internal dynamics result from external stimuli."

"You sound like a shrink."

Colt says, "When I'm not calling square dance steps or being a DJ, I'm a therapist."

"Those letters after your name ..."

He says, "PIC is Personal Inventory Counseling, and PPS is Personal Person Services."

"Sounds like organizing closets and doing errands."

Colt smiles. "Your aggressive-defensive humor again. Fact is, humor was *my* aim in choosing those names for my therapies. I help people recognize and identify their personal baggage. That's the Personal Inventory part. Then I help them face their issues and unload the baggage. That's the Personal Person part. Isn't that what life is really about, facing your issues?"

"What's your degree in?"

"Does it matter?" he says. "What's important is having a natural and disciplined intelligence coupled with the responsibility to know when and how to apply it."

Like with that body.

He asks, "What's your degree in?"

"I thought it didn't matter."

"It doesn't," he says.

I tell him, "Clinical psych."

"No kidding," he says. "What happened?"

"I didn't like the clinical part."

"Some people get knowledge, but they can't use it."

I say, "And others treat people by getting them to fight."

Another shrug from Colt. Lots of shrugs and smiles from him. He says, "Some therapies use art. Some use sex or some vague concept of love. Some even use religion. I eliminate all the decoration and use hand-to-hand combat. It's a lot more honest than talking."

"We're talking now."

"So far."

"But fighting hurts," I say.

"Not as much as lying. When you get hurt fighting, you know why it happened – because you made a mistake somewhere. And you know something about the mistake because the injury tells you, so you can do something about it. Can you say the same about all the talking people do about love and religion?"

"But you can't just go and beat someone up when you have a problem."

"Some people do," says Colt, "but that's too simplistic. It's also wrong. You have to learn how to fight properly, with discipline. It's a lot more efficient than trying to reason a problem out. Logic is a good mental pastime, not much else. Where we all really live is in the instinctual part of our bodies. And that's exactly the part that can be awakened and developed by disciplined fighting."

I say, "If fighting is so fabulous, why did you make such a ruckus at the convention this morning?"

"That was an act of assertion, not a fight."

"It was combative, all that inflammatory language."

"You sound like a textbook," he says. "I didn't hurt anybody by getting up there and talking."

"You might have hurt some feelings."

"What are feelings?" he say. "Show me where they are." Colt points to different muscles on his fascinatingly muscled body. "Is there a feeling here? Or here? How about one here?"

I'd like to know what *that* muscle is feeling.

"Feelings are just a form of thought," he says. "Same goes for emotions. It's all happening in your brain."

"But you feel emotions in your body."

"Not quite," says Colt. "What you experience as an emotion is actually your brain interpreting signals it receives from your body. The fact is, your body alone can't feel a thing without your brain telling it so. And here's the payoff: If you can discipline your mind to change how you think, or at the very least what you're thinking about, you can change the way the brain interprets the signals it receives from your body. Ultimately you can train yourself to experience a completely different reaction to a longstanding, familiar situation. And all the old feelings and emotions? *Pfffft!* Out the window."

"Just like that?"

"Right," says Colt.

"But what about instinct? Didn't you just say it's all based in the body?"

"It is," says Colt, "and therefore it's totally controllable by the brain."

He looks at his watch.

I say, "One more question."

He smiles. "You'll always have one more question for me."

"You said you saw Paladin at The Castle this morning, from up in the DJ booth. And he was upset over his collar tips."

"That's right," he says.

"Was his dance partner around?"

"You mean Chester?"

"Yes."

Colt says, "You know how I feel about Chester, right? You overheard Bistany and me talking just now."

"Yes," I say. "But I don't care about that. I want to know what Chester was doing this morning. Was he upset? Did he talk to anyone? Did anyone talk to him?"

Colt grins at me. "That's a lot of questions."

"I need to know."

"You need to know?" he says with a laugh. "Do you know your eyes light up when you talk about him? I'd say you're smitten with him. Do you know where that word comes from? Smitten? It's the past tense of *smite*, which means to hit or to strike. To love and to strike – see how close they are?"

"That's too Biblical for me."

"I say what I see," he says. "Take it or leave it. You guys do what you want."

"We guys?"

He grins again, and now I'm tired of it.

"I'm not like you," he says. "Yes, I encourage and condone anything people do to express themselves sexually. But personally, for me, man-to-man sex just isn't my thing."

"You mean you're straight?"

"Are you surprised?" he says.

"I somehow got a different impression."

"Lots of people do."

"I wonder why."

"Personal baggage," says Colt. "People make assumptions based on what they hope is the truth."

"So you think man-to-man fighting is okay, but man-to-man sex is wrong?"

"No, no," he says. "You didn't hear me. Men having sex together is a good thing – all sex is a good thing – but man-to-man sex just isn't for *me*. Fighting is something else entirely. I'll fight with any man, gay or straight. I'll even fight with a woman. But I never hit anyone who isn't ready to hit back."

"What about your clients?"

"What about them?" he says.

"Are they all gay?"

"For some reason," he says, "they are."

I'm counting to ten. To hell with fascination.

Colt goes on. "Now, I'm not saying that I don't have homosexual tendencies. I'm honest enough to own up to that. Almost any man who's alive has at least wondered about it. But I'm not an active participant. I appreciate what you guys do. I really do. In fact, I'm fascinated by homosexual expression. But I don't get it on with men. And that," he says with a shrug and a smile, "is my sex life in a nutshell. Now, does that put you more at ease?"

"About what?" I say.

"About having sex with me."

"I don't want to have sex with you."

All right, sure, so I imagined us dancing around the room in that fume-induced fantasy, but there was no sex. Maybe some frottage, maybe a lot of frottage, but nothing more. Besides, the music has stopped now, and the fascination has vaporized.

Colt says, "I'm being completely honest with you. Can you say the same about yourself? Are you being totally honest?"

I say again, "I don't want to have sex with you."

"Don't you find me attractive?"

"You're ... fascinating ... but I don't want to have sex with you. Nothing personal, Colt."

"I don't take anything personally. It's a waste of time."

"Except when Bistany changes her mind and dumps you for Chester."

What? No smile? No shrug?

Colt glowers. "What Bistany did is stupid, but it isn't against me, per se. She's trying to force her business model to work. Personally, I think her ideas are shit, but it's all valid to her. And I don't take it personally. But with you I'm talking honesty. I have this theory that most people vary their level of honesty according to whom they're talking. And I'm not like that. I am dead-on, straight-ahead honest with every person I meet, all the time."

"I still don't want to have sex with you."

Colt looks at his watch again.

"Well," he says, "since my new client is obviously a no-show – and a loser – I'm going to grab a quick workout before my gig tonight."

He starts to leave the room, then turns back to me.

"You want to watch?"

"Watch what?"

"Me," he says. "I've got a setup in my bedroom. It's called The Interim Gym. Gives you a decent workout when you don't have time for the real thing."

"In your bedroom."

"That's right," says Colt.

"And you're inviting me to watch?"

He shrugs. "Up to you."

"No thanks."

He smiles. "Just testing you."

Or yourself, doll.

He says, "You ought to come by Gunsmoke Saloon tonight. You'd see me with my other hat, and maybe you wouldn't have such a bad opinion of me."

"I don't have a bad opinion of you."

"But you don't want to have sex with me."

"You know, Colt, for a straight guy, you seem preoccupied with having sex with me."

"No," he says. "With *you* having sex with *me*."

I try to figure that out and fail.

He chuckles. "If you were a woman, the situation would be totally different."

That's some relief.

"Right now," he says, "I've got a date with myself. No more time for you."

I leave Colt's place and walk back to my house feeling dazed, as though he has punched me around physically, not just with words. Is this what he does to his talking clients? Maybe hand-to-hand combat *is* more honest.

7.

BY THE TIME I GET HOME it's around eight o'clock. There's a message from Benjy, all apologies: Of course the cookout should be according to my original idea. It's my party, my guest list, my menu, and all me, me, me. He doesn't say it like that – Benjy is incapable of bitter sarcasm – but that's what I hear, maybe because sarcasm is *my* native vernacular. But the focus on everything *me* makes me wonder if I'm becoming more of a creature like Colt than I am comfortable to admit. Maybe I already am.

I call Benjy. "I got your message," I say, "and there's no need to apologize."

"Sometimes I barge in where I don't belong, Penny."

"You belong, Benjy. It's just me being stubborn."

"I wouldn't know you otherwise."

We've kissed and made up, so I ask him, "You know a place called Gunsmoke?"

"The Gunsmoke Saloon," he says. "Sure. Why?"

"I think I have to go there."

"*Have* to, Penny?"

"It's for that case I'm on."

"Your first case," says Benjy, "the gay jewelry heist."

"Thanks for reminding me."

But if I really believe the case is bogus, why am I going to Gunsmoke Saloon? Just because Colt said, "Come up and see me sometime"? Or because action is better than idleness? Or because I might get to see Chester Wright again?

Benjy says, "I'll come with you if you think it will help."

"Help what, Benjy?"

"Help you, Penny. I always want to help you."

Am I Benjy's unrequited fifth-grade love? Am I his Chester?

I tell him, "It's better if I go alone."

He says, "Wear a cowboy hat or something. Otherwise there's a cover charge."

"Will a lariat do?"

"Depends what you do with it."

"I'll pay the cover," I say. "But I have another question, something only you can help me with." Suddenly my mouth goes dry. "I'm not even sure I can say this."

"Yes?" says Benjy, with that expectant, hopeful tone.

My voice is hoarse. "I think it's time."

"For what, Penny?"

Seconds pass. My heart is racing. "Benjy, I think maybe I ought to ... uh ..."

"Penny, you mean ...?"

Can I say the words?

"Benjy ... I think it's time to go wireless. Or mobile or digital or whatever it's called."

"Oh!" he squeals. "I'm so happy for you!" His voice is atremble. "What convinced you? The cop?"

Now that I've said it, my heart rate returns to normal. "No," I say. "More like running home to make phone calls, or looking for public phones that work. Besides, where would styling salons be if we stuck with henna and curling irons?"

Benjy is breathless. "So you're finally doing it."

"Yes," I say with a moan.

"I have an extra one you can have."

"An extra?"

"It's too big for me," he says. "God, I never thought I'd live to say that. I can set you up with a calling plan too. If there's one thing I know, Penny, it's the best phone deals."

"Thanks, Benjy."

"So, you want me to bring it by now?"

"Let me think about it."

"But you said you needed it."

"It's a big step," I say. "One more day and I'll know for sure."

"Don't wait too long, Penny. The technology changes fast." We say goodbye.

So why am I stalling about the phone? I've made critical, life-altering decisions faster than this. Maybe the wireless phone is a metaphor for Benjy, and some part of me believes that by taking on the phone, I'll also be accepting him into my life exactly the way he'd like. We'll begin to enmesh with each other until we end up as one personality in two bodies. *Cathexis*, the shrinks call it, though some people call it love.

What would Colt Remington make of these mental gyrations? Probably suggest I beat Benjy up, and that would solve everything.

Unlike Colt, I don't squeeze in a quick workout, but instead mix myself a mogul-sized martini, parched, then throw together a quick supper – a spinach and cheese omelet with a side of buttery hash browns. Along with another martini. (It only *looks* like breakfast.)

Sated and buzzing, I head out for the Gunsmoke Saloon.

8.

ONCE AGAIN BENJY'S DIRECTIONS are simple and direct. (Is he my lost compass?) Turns out the Gunsmoke Saloon is just a few blocks from my South End digs. It's amazing what you can find in your own neighborhood if you're willing, just once, to turn left where you always turn right.

The place is on the ground floor of an old warehouse. The building is large and looming, and at this hour – 10:00 P.M. – mostly in darkness. But that darkness is dispelled by a mammoth electric billboard over the entrance. Two fantastic cowboy boots, each over six feet tall – standard cowboy height – are animated by a gazillion tiny lights within the immense sign. I watch from the sidewalk as the boots dance gaily overhead, kick up their heels, crisscross each other, pirouette, then come to a full stop while the spurs spin and sparkle and send off dazzling rainbow fireworks. The fabulous contraption looks like it arrived direct from Las Vegas, and now it's causing energy brownouts throughout Metropolitan Boston.

The sidewalk pulses with the beat of music from inside. I open the door and darkness draws me in, away from the bleaching glow of the electric billboard. The loud, lively music shakes the floor, and my feet start dancing on their own, just like those quick-stepping electric cowboy boots out front.

Benjy was right about the hefty cover charge for people

who aren't "showing western", but the lanky cowpoke at the door is such a rascally looking varmint, who cares? I pull out my wallet to pay, but a voice calls out above the noise and music.

"No, no, Travis! He's a *guest*."

It's the castrato-like caw of Fannie Mae Knox. Even in the diminished light of Gunsmoke, her color scheme reflects the myriad intensities of a single hue – pink, pink, and pink.

She scolds me. "Where is the press pass I gave you this morning?"

"I guess I, er, plumb forgot it."

"Naughty knave," she says, then, "never mind. Come along." She grasps me with her pink-gloved hand and leads me into the saloon. "Welcome to my domain," she says with a chortle. "Or is it my dominion?"

Unlike The Castle, with its day-bright, out-in-the-open sideshow, Gunsmoke Saloon is dark with drama. The atmosphere is ... what? ... amorously predatory? The people dance only in couples, with none of the cool detachment of square-dancing. Every person holds someone else close, and they cover the floor like that – pressed together. Also, there's no female drag here. Faux femme couture is reserved for the campy fun of daytime square-dancing. At Gunsmoke Saloon, the men are men.

Except for Fannie Mae Knox.

She steers me to the far end of the bar, an ideal corner spot where some pink concoction sits on the bar top, half-consumed and glowing in a martini glass.

"This is my coign of vantage," she says, patting her pink-gloved hand on a special barstool upholstered in pink velvet. "And you, Pumpkin, are my next subject."

Pumpkin? Who's Pumpkin?

"Now," she says, "you sit here while I go freshen up."

She indicates the neighboring barstool – not pink velvet, mercifully – and I do as instructed. Maybe I will be deemed important sitting next to her, or else just another courtier.

The bartender comes over. She's a big blousy gal with a

pile of curly red hair that, even in the dimness, is obviously bottled. She looks like she's trying to play the last of the red-hot mamas.

"Hi, there," she says with a big smile. "What's your poison?"

In a place like this, best to order something masculine.

I say, "A Black Russian, dry."

"You trying to get laid, darlin'?"

"Not that I'm aware of."

She says, "Guys usually drink Black Russians when they want to get laid." Her twang is slightly erratic, as if she's still learning how to do it.

I say, "I'll have a beer then."

"Beer?" she says. "Darlin', you're not the beer-drinkin' type. You want to get laid, Little Heather's going to help you."

Little Heather? Is that like Baby Huey?

"I'll make you my own special version," she says. "Called a Russian Revolver. Gets you a lot more playful than a regular Black Russian. More like Russian Roulette." She laughs.

"I'm not sure I want to get that playful."

"Don't worry, darlin'. I'm just kidding you. I always kid people their first time here. It's my special kind of welcome, and you seem kind of nice."

Me? Nice?

"A Russian Roulette, then," I say.

She corrects me. "A Russian *Revolver*, darlin'."

I watch her mix the drink. She's awkward with the setup, not a natural bartender. Otherwise, it looks like a standard Black Russian. That is, until she takes a small plastic squeeze-bottle from the well and adds a squirt to the drink.

"What's that?" I ask.

"Secret ingredient," she says.

"The one that makes me more playful."

"That's right, darlin'." She puts the drink on the bar.

"Go on. Try it."

I do. "Lemon," I say.

"That's right, darlin' . That's all it is. Fermented lemon."

"Why is it in a plastic bottle?"

"Because I can't show the bottle it comes in."

"Why not?"

She leans close to me. "Because it's bootlegged from Italy. Jeez, I hope you're not undercover with the ATF."

I tell her, "Alcohol, Tobacco and Firearms wouldn't have me."

"Well, that's a good thing, darlin'." Then she pulls back, no more secrets. "So, what brings you round these parts?"

Round these parts?

I tell her, "I was at the convention today, and I figured I'd keep on with the festivities tonight."

Heather says, "Glad to hear you're having such a good time, but don't you think you ought to get yourself some gear?"

"Gear?"

"Western duds," she says.

"I'm new to the scene."

"No kidding," she says, "but even a heifer gets something to wear, just to fit in."

"I, er, haven't had time."

She says, "Maybe I can help. What'd you say your name was?"

"Stan. Stan Kraychik."

"Pleased to meet you, Stan Kraychik. I'm Heather Blossom. And welcome to Gunsmoke Saloon."

I pull out my wallet to pay for the drink, but she stops me.

"First one's on the house," she says.

"Are you sure?"

"I ought to be," she says. "I own the place."

"Thanks," I say.

So if Heather Blossom owns Gunsmoke and tends bar, is that like Nicole owning Snips and doing manicures? But Heather has already blown her cover with me, while Nicole maintains hers, even with her longest-standing clients.

"This is quite a place," I say. "How long have you been open?"

"Almost a year now, and we just put up that new sign out front. How do you like it?"

"Incredible."

"Me and Fannie Mae weren't sure about the extra expense right now, but it seems like a good time, with the convention and all."

"You and Fannie Mae?"

"We're partners," says Heather.

"Meaning?"

"Meaning business," she says. "Some folks say partner when they mean a husband or a wife, y'know?"

"Sure, but Fannie Mae is really a man, right?"

Heather smiles. "Yes, darlin', but I *like* men. I just can't seem to nab one. People think I'm gay 'cause I run a place like this, but I'm not. What about you?"

"It's Ken-dolls for me."

"Well," she says, "don't corral yourself too close. You could pass for straight."

Me? Straight? And nice?

Heather says, "But as far as Fannie Mae and me are concerned, we are best, best friends. Although ..." She leans close to me. "There are some things you can't even tell your best friend."

"Why not?"

"Why, because of who *her* friends are!" She laughs and goes off to her other customers.

From atop my barstool, I look around the place. A slow old-fashioned waltz is playing now, a change from the up-tempo, drive-your-baby-home kind of music that was shaking the place when I came in. Guys are now swooping gracefully around the floor with other guys, and gals with gals. There are some mixed couples too, actual real ones. But, save that singular pink vision, there's no female drag in Gunsmoke. As for me, I'm in blah-drag. Maybe that's why Heather thinks I can pass for straight.

I look upwards and see Colt Remington in the DJ booth. He's wearing a black leather vest tonight, and under that, his skin. A leather band around his left upper arm enhances the bulge of recently pumped muscles. The shiny studs on the arm-band flash and dance as Colt moves in the booth. He's even got a small Halogen spot aimed on it to guarantee the special effect. Otherwise, the booth glows softly, giving his angular face the look of a sorcerer casting a musical spell on the crowd.

Did Colt just wave at me? I wave back, and sure enough, he waves again and smiles. But he's straight so it's okay. Apparently Colt can see pretty much everything from up in his control tower here at Gunsmoke, same as at The Castle. His attention goes back to the dance floor and stays fixed on something out here. I try to follow his gaze into the crowd. I look and look, scanning the many heads and hats that are swaying to the sentimental music, but it's all just a bunch of people playing cowboys and cowgirls.

And then I see what might be intriguing Colt Remington so much. Mr. Wang (aka "Kitty") Chu is hanging on the arms of a big cowboy – a towering palooka probably named Tex – who is basically sweeping the floor with him. Delicate Kitty, connected in some nebulous way to Colt, now looks as pleased as the town belle who's just corralled the mayor's son.

Heather returns with another Russian Revolver.

I tell her, "Those go down pretty easy."

"Be careful," she says. "And look what else I brought you."

With her other hand she produces a cowboy hat.

"Put it on, darlin'."

The thing looks a party favor.

"No thanks," I say.

"Go on. Have a little fun."

I take the hat. It's made of some kind of fake crunchy material. I put it on.

She says, "Don't you look sweet!"

Sweet? I don't want to look sweet. I want to look tough, like Colt in the DJ booth, or the hunk who's waltzing Kitty around the floor, or even that guy Travis at the door. I see my reflection in the mirror behind the bar. I don't look like any of those guys. I look like a three-year-old trying to be Hopalong Cassidy. I start to take the hat off, but Heather reaches across the bar and pushes it down on my head.

I say, "Can I still pass for straight?"

"Keep it, darlin', as a souvenir of your first time." She laughs loudly. "Get it? Your first time!"

She leaves me just as Fannie Mae returns.

As Her Royal Pinkness resettles herself in her pink velvet throne, she mutters, "The line at the ladies' was impossible."

"Why don't you use the mens'?"

"Because, Pumpkin, a lady doesn't do such things."

"It's only a costume."

"*Only?*" says Fannie Mae. "If you're going to denigrate costumes, Pumpkin, you should consider that ridiculous thing on your head."

"Heather gave it to me."

"Please remove it."

"Why?"

"Because I don't like it," she says.

I'll bet it's all the pink. That's probably what makes her the way she is. It's the years of pink-on-pink. It's destroyed her color perception, and along with it, her grasp on reality.

Fannie Mae continues. "How else can I see your hair? And why else should I dub you *Pumpkin* but for your hair?"

My hair? With its brilliant coppery sheen? It's hardly the color of some sludgy old gourd. I guess I ought to be relieved she's not referring to my physique.

Fannie Mae says, "So, Pumpkin, please remove the hat."

"My name is Stan."

"You are Sir Pumpkin," she says. Then she raises her chin slightly and looks down her nose at me. "And in the presence of a lady, a gentleman removes his hat."

I push the hat up slightly so it rests on the back of my head, like a real-world ranch hand might wear it.

"Recalcitrant knave!" she says.

I sip my drink nonchalantly, then say to her, "Heather

says you and she are business partners."

"Oh?" says Fannie Mae.

"Is it true?"

"In a way."

"What way?"

"Pumpkin, business talk is so tedious."

"What about Bistany? Is she a partner too?"

"In a way, yes, in a way, no," she says.

"I'm kind of surprised Bistany isn't here tonight."

"Oh, she's here," says Fannie Mae.

"I don't see her."

"The world does not turn through your eyes alone, Pumpkin. Now, tell me, what is it that *you* do?"

"Do?" I say.

"Yes, Pumpkin. You wake up every day, and then you do what? Besides provoke people, that is."

"I, er ..."

"Oh dear," says Fannie Mae. "This doesn't sound at all sparkling."

"Pumpkins don't sparkle much, especially in the morning."

"They do if the light is right."

I ask, "What do you do?"

"Me?" she says with that fey chortle. "I give away money."

"How sparkling."

"It can be, Pumpkin. But that's not all I do. Obviously, one must do more. There's love after all. I do things for love. Do you, Pumpkin? Do you do anything for love?"

"I, er ..."

"Oh dear!" says Fannie Mae. "Have I erred in acquiring you?"

"Maybe you should tell me what *you* do for love."

"What I do for love, Pumpkin, is to act."

"You act."

"Yes," she says.

"For love."

"That's right."

Sparkle, sparkle.

I ask her, "Where do you act?"

She says, "In this town – I won't grace Boston with the appellation of city – but in this *town*, if one is going to act for love, one must act every day, everywhere, and at every moment."

"Are you with a theater company?"

"The world is my stage," says Fannie Mae Knox.

Still sparkling.

Heather appears with a fresh pinky-drinky for Fannie Mae, who takes it, then raises the glass toward Heather.

"To the convention," she says, "and to our future." She downs the potion at once, then places the empty glass on the bar and says, "Another one, please, Heather dearest. And freshen up whatever Pumpkin is having."

Meanwhile, out on the dance floor Kitty is still lost in the arms of Towering Tex, and Colt is still watching them.

"See something interesting?" says Fannie Mae.

"Depends," I say.

She follows my gaze out into the dancing crowd, and makes that little *humph* again, common among deposed royalty. Then she says, "Do you have any money, Pumpkin?"

"I have about fifty bucks on me."

"No, no," she says. "I mean money-brokerage accounts, income instruments, property. Anything like that?"

"I have a bit."

"How did you acquire it?" she asks.

"Life insurance."

"Is that what you do?" she says. "Sell insurance? No wonder you were so reluctant to tell me."

"Someone died," I say, "and I was the beneficiary."

"Oh," says Fannie Mae. "Well, that's better, but still unpredictable. You could wait forever."

"I didn't have to wait."

Fannie Mae says, "That's some relief."

Is that what Rafik's death was? A relief?

Heather approaches with our fresh drinks.

Fannie Mae says, "If you are a very good Pumpkin, I may tell you how I got *my* money."

As Heather sets the drinks down, she leans close to me and murmurs, "You're really going to need this one."

I tell her, "These Russian Revolvers are great. Kind of like espresso with a twist of lemon."

"Just go easy, darlin'," she says. "You got all night and that's your third one already."

"Who's counting?"

"I am," she says, then she leaves us.

Fannie Mae leans toward me and speaks low. "Heather is my best friend, Pumpkin, but it's sad when people lack the natural graces." Then she sits up and lifts her glass toward me. "To Pumpkin!" she says, and once again drains the thing in one smooth swallow. Then she raises her pink-gloved arm and snaps her fingers to get Heather's attention, but it comes out a muted *thup!*

One of the natural graces?

The music changes abruptly. The tempo is up again and the rhythm is sharp, as if to convey the message: "You've been courting sweetly, and now it's time for some down and dirty." There's also cheering and applause near the saloon's entrance. I strain to see, as does Fannie Mae.

Chester and Paladin have just arrived and are being feted like homecoming heroes. That one-armed lift this morning made its impression. And tonight, despite the reduced light of Gunsmoke – perhaps because of it – Chester's face appeals to me even more. Fifth-grade love imprints itself deeply.

I feel a touch on my arm.

Fannie Mae says, "Lost in a fog?"

"These drinks are strong," I say.

"Do you find that young man to your liking?"

"Which one?"

"Which one, indeed!" she says with a chortle. "The one who came in with Paladin. If your wish came true, Pumpkin, you could have the young man, and Paladin would learn a lesson."

Is she reading my mind?

I say, "It sounds as though you don't care for Paladin."

"He could be taken down a notch," says Fannie Mae, "but I don't know him enough to care."

Chester and Paladin look troubled about something. How can they be? They are The Most Together Couple, almost. How can there be turmoil anywhere in their lives?

Paladin leaves Chester and makes his way through the crowd toward us. But he passes by and doesn't stop. He doesn't even notice us. Instead he goes up the metal stairway that leads to the DJ's booth. Colt lets him in, and they greet each other like old Army buddies. (Anything goes in a foxhole, right?) With Paladin preoccupied, maybe I can steal some time with Chester. He's still standing out there, and he seems to be looking for someone. I want to call out, "Chester! Over here! You're looking for me!"

But I don't.

Fannie Mae says quietly, "Pumpkin is enthralled."

Meanwhile Paladin emerges from the DJ booth – that was fast – and jogs down the metal stairs. For all his dancer's muscularity, he makes no sound. Again he passes by Fannie Mae and me without acknowledgement. Paladin is a man on a mission.

Fannie Mae makes a disgruntled little *humph*, definitely not one of her chortles.

Then Colt's voice comes over the PA system. "Hey, fellas – and gals – it's me up in the control booth, Colt Remington, your Gunsmoke DJ." He makes the simple message sound sexy and insinuating. "It's time for my break, so I'm turning on the presets to keep you dancing till I'm back in control. The first number is one of Paladin's favorites, Alan Jackson singing 'My Own Kind of Hat'. So why don't you all clear the floor for the first verse and chorus, and let him show what he does best."

The music starts and Paladin takes to the dance floor. It's a solo, but there's an invisible partner out there with him. Every turn, every pose, every silent leap is all done for that person. His arms caress and embrace the air; his legs and hips overpower the space around him; his face wins the heart of his invisible beloved. Lucky the recipient of physical expression like that. My man was a dancer, and the only times I ever thought I understood him was when he used his body. Then I'd realize it had all been practiced to death in a mirror.

I glance at Fannie Mae. She is so enraptured with Paladin, her eyes are moist. I don't go that far, even with Chester.

She senses me watching her. "Will you excuse me, Pumpkin? Damn bladder!" She smiles brightly, valiantly. "Don't go away now." It sounds like something a talk show hostess says just before a commercial break. "And have my drink freshened, would you? There's a good Pumpkin."

For the second time Fannie Mae Knox snakes quickly down the corridor where the rest rooms are. With Paladin on the dance floor and Fannie Mae taking care of business, the coast is clear for me to go and talk with Chester. Except that Chester is now engaged with someone else – Kitty. It all seems friendly enough. Even Kitty's dance partner, Towering Tex, is smiling and chatting with them. I'll go join them. The more the merrier.

But no sooner do I stand up than the second verse of the music starts, and all the other dancers – the ordinary mortals – are migrating back onto the dance floor, ending Paladin's solo spot. At the same time, the rest of the saloon crowd – the part that watches and doesn't dance at all – mobs the bar. In short, I am trapped. If I want to get to Chester, I've got to stagger through them all to get to the other end of the saloon where he and Kitty and Towering Tex are talking. Well, what is love for, but to be tested? I down the rest of my drink à la Fannie Mae, then make my way slowly and deliberately through the crowd.

On the way I feel the ever-increasing and inebriating effects of fermented lemon. I've somehow lost track of time, and I've definitely lost sight of Chester. I strain to see through the tangled mass of bodies ahead of me. Kitty is now standing alone near an exit. Chester and Tex are not with him. When

I finally get there, Kitty seems to be cowering, as if afraid to be seen.

I say, "Where did Chester go?"

"Who?" says Kitty.

"Chester Wright. Paladin's partner. You were just talking with him."

Kitty says, "I don't know any Chester."

"I just saw you with him. Did he go off with your cowboy?"

"Who?"

"That big guy you're dancing with. Or don't you know him either?"

"He's in line," says Kitty. "The men's room is always mobbed when Colt takes a break."

No comment on that.

Suddenly Paladin is standing there with us, and Kitty quickly moves toward me, as if for protection. Talk about fickle.

Paladin barks his accusation at Kitty: "Exactly what is going on between you and Chester?"

That's the guy you claim not to know.

"Nothing," says Kitty, now trembling.

"The two of you are up to something," says Paladin, "and I'll find out one way or another."

Kitty says, "Maybe you should ask him."

"I'll ask who I want!" says Paladin.

It's *whom*, doll. But never mind.

Then Towering Tex appears, and Kitty rushes into his arms. Tex says, "Is there a problem here?"

Even Paladin's godlike proportions are undermined by Tex's monolithic height and breadth.

Tex says to Kitty, "You want to go?"

Kitty nods without word.

Tex says, "What about your friend? Should we wait for him?"

Kitty shakes his head and says, "Never mind."

"That's it then," says Tex. "We're going home."

And they push open the exit door and vanish into the night.

Paladin then turns toward me, and he recognizes me from earlier today. "You! What are you doing here? Trying to pass for gay or something?"

"You mean it doesn't show?"

"I mean it doesn't matter," he says. He looks around impatiently. "Where's Chester?"

"Why ask me?"

"You were here with Kitty, and Chester was talking to Kitty."

"And they're both gone," I say.

"I only care about Chester."

"Squirms out of his tether, does he?"

Paladin says, "Do you know what those two are up to?"

"No," I say. "By the way, did you ever find your collar tips?"

"I don't care about them."

"After all that ruckus you made this morning?"

Paladin says, "Chester and I got into the finals without them, so who needs them now?" All the while he's looking anxiously through the crowd. He mutters angrily, "Where did he go? I told him to meet me here after my solo."

"Maybe he took a little walk."

"Maybe that's what you ought to do," he says.

Then he turns to go, but he's blocked by the crowd.

You're not in the spotlight now, pal.

But unlike Fannie Mae, who seems able to part the Red Sea waters, Paladin has to push and jostle his way through the crowd.

I'm ready to leave too. In fact, why did I ever come here? To test my infatuation with Chester? That's waning fast, especially since he's not made one sign in my direction. But why should he? He doesn't have an inkling of my foolish feelings. Maybe staying at home alone isn't such a bad idea. Maybe it's time to get another cat.

Suddenly the room changes. The dimensions switch, and I lose my balance, my legs feel empty and my body totters.

I grab onto the nearest person to keep from going down. He looks at me like I'm a disgusting drunk. I make a lunge for the bar, then scrabble along, stool by stool, pawing my way to the far end, to Fannie Mae's reserved royal corner, still discernible to my delinquent eyes. I get to the courtier's stool and climb into it, exhausted. A bartender appears in seconds – a slender guy, definitely not Heather – with a huge glass of water. I gulp it down, but my mouth is like cotton.

He says, "You okay?"

"More, please," I croak.

He refills the glass and I drink it. My mouth is wet again, but I feel more and more removed from everything around me.

The bartender says, "Looked like you were going down."

"Thanks," I say unsteadily.

"It's okay," he replies, "but I'm cutting you off for a while. Just water."

"Whatever," I say, and thank him again.

I try to get my bearings by watching the crowd and listening to the music. But it doesn't work, and suddenly I need fresh air. I've got to get out of here. In the glass of the saloon's front window I see giant reflections of the dancing electric cowboy boots on the billboard outside. I imagine those boots are on my feet and they're dancing me home. If I just keep watching the reflections from that neon treadmill out front, with the spurs twirling and spewing those rainbow-colored sparks, maybe I'll actually *be* home, automatically, safe and sound.

Beside me someone says, "Are you okay?"

It's Benjy. Despite my skewed vision and the dimness of Gunsmoke, Benjy's blond hair shines and his eyes sparkle happily.

He says, "I had a feeling you might need a tour guide, Penny. Are you all right? You look funny."

"I feel funny."

Heather appears behind the bar. "You boys need anything?"

I say, "You're back."

"I never left, darlin'."

"Someone else just waited on me."

She says, "Your friend need anything?"

Benjy says, "Just water, please."

Heather smiles. "You taking care of him?" Benjy nods.

She leaves us.

"What," I say. "I'm fine."

"You sure, Penny?"

"Where's Chester?"

Did I just say "Whersh?"

"Who's Chester?" says Benjy.

"I want to dance with Cheshter."

"Penny, I think you'd better sit this one out."

"I wanna dansh."

"Okay, I'll dance with you, Penny."

"You? Dansh?"

"A guy from Oregon showed me some neat tricks."

"Oregon?"

Benjy says, "He was straight but he liked to dance with men."

"Wasn't it shtrange danshing with a shtraight guy?"

"There wasn't any sex, Penny. We just danced."

"Well, if thesh no shexsh, lesh go!"

I put my water on the bar, almost topple it. The hell with it. The hell with everything. I'm going to have some fun. So maybe it feels kind of weird putting yourself front-to-front with a friend and moving around the floor, mashing your stuff against his. Maybe it even feels kind of like sex, but it's not, right?

Benjy leads. Yup. He, the shorter, blond, frisky guy is leading me, the taller, full-figured wench who could pass for straight, if you could believe Heather Blossom.

Then suddenly, there's a loud buzz and the lights get very bright, so bright they hurt my eyes and my head. Then the buzzing stops and the lights go out.

My lights, that is.

9.

THERE'S A GENTLE NUDGE, and the sun hurts my eyes.

Then there's pain, a heavy, depressing pain.

It takes me a moment to figure out where I am.

I'm at home. I am in my bed. I am naked. And it is … What day is it?

I roll my head to see the bedside clock.

Ouch.

I hear Benjy's voice. "Penny?"

"*Whror?*" is my first sound.

Benjy says, "It's all right. I'm here, and you're okay."

I hesitate. "What happened?"

"You don't remember?" he says.

"Did I do anything I might regret?"

"Regret, Penny?"

"How did I get naked?"

"How do you think?"

"Did I make a pass at you?"

"Would you regret that, Penny?"

"Sometimes after a few drinks I get affectionate."

"I know," says Benjy. "I think it's cute." Then he leaves me and heads downstairs.

I yell after him. "I don't want to be cute!"

Ow!

From down in the kitchen he calls up to me. "But you are cute, Penny! And don't worry – as far as I'm concerned, whatever happened last night, nothing has changed between us."

I put on my robe and stumble downstairs. Slowly, softly.

Every step I take causes a thumping in my eyeballs, in my whole brain. Benjy is in the kitchen fixing coffee. Rather, cappuccino. He's working it all to perfection, brewing the brew and steaming the milk. He hands me a mug-sized portion. I take a sip. It's as good as any in an Italian *caffè*.

I notice a crumpled cowboy hat on the kitchen counter.

"What happened, Benjy?"

"You blacked out."

"After three drinks?"

"Is that all you had?" he says.

"Three, I'm sure of it."

Benjy makes a disbelieving shrug.

I say, "Step-by-step, what happened?"

"Step-by-step," he says. "That's cute."

"Benjy!"

"No, really, Penny, step-by-step, we started dancing. That's all I meant. You're a natural dancer. You really ought to get out more."

"Right, and maybe I'll meet a straight guy from Oregon who dances with men."

Benjy says, "You remember that?"

"That's what you told me. Are you changing your story now?"

"No," he says, "but if you remember that, maybe you really weren't drunk last night."

"I'm trying to tell you, Benjy, I had only three drinks."

"You started out fine – twirling like a top – and then suddenly it was like you lost your gyroscope. You said you were thirsty, very thirsty. Then you got kind of panicky, so I got you off the dance floor, and you kept saying, 'I'm fine, I'm fine,' but you didn't look fine. So I was getting you some water, and you said, 'I want to go home.' I said, 'Okay, I'll get a cab.' Then you said, 'Huh?' And that was it. Lights out for Penny."

"I wonder if someone slipped me a mickey."

"A Mickey Finn?" says Benjy. "Why would someone do that?"

"Maybe I was asking too many questions. Or maybe someone wants me to appear unreliable."

"Like who's going to believe a drunk, you mean?"

"Exactly," I say. "But I'll get to the bottom of it."

Benjy smiles. "I got to see your bottom. Very cute."

"Stop with the cute!"

"Look, Penny, I know you and I are going nowhere that way. All the more reason you should get out more. Widowhood doesn't become you."

"Who's a widow?"

Benjy heaves a sigh. "By the way," he says, "Nicole called about your ten o'clock appointment. I told her what happened, and she said Ramon would fill in."

I look at the kitchen clock: quarter past nine. There's just enough time to pull myself together and get to Snips. (It was one of the paradoxes between my late lover and me: For all his quick-change stage experience, he needed hours to prepare for ordinary social occasions, while I could transform myself from stubbly to semi-spectacular in less than half an hour.)

I stand up and declare, "Ramon will not steal my special clients!" I lurch toward the stairs, grab the banister, and turn back to Benjy. "Thanks for taking care of me."

"What are friends for?" he says, but he looks a little sad. I head back upstairs with my coffee, slowly, carefully. Benjy calls out, "We'll talk later, okay?"

"Roger!" I say, then, "Ten-four."

The walk to the salon clears my head a little, and I come to a decision: Once and for all, I'm going to drop the case. In fact, I don't even have a client, so what's to drop? It's just possible insurance fraud by Paladin and Colt. In fact, maybe they're trying to put Bistany Evans out of business by faking two thefts at her first convention. They might even be hiding each other's "lost jewels". But then why did Heather – or somebody – spike my drink? Was I hearing things that someone wanted me to forget? Or maybe something happened while I was dazed? If that was the plan, it worked, since I recall so little after that third drink. And with the morning sun on my back, I feel very lucky that Benjy showed up and saved my sorry ass. Otherwise where would I be now? Stumbling home from some hospital emergency room?

On the other end of the experiential spectrum, Snips Salon is humming like any other Saturday morning. You'd never guess it was a holiday weekend. Nicole sees me come in and shuffles me quickly to one side, away from the front desk.

"Should you really be here," she says, "in your condition?"

"The morning sickness has passed, doll."

"Consummation with Benjamin, finally?"

"No, doll. I'll pick my own amorous poison."

"One man's meat ..." she says with a smirk.

My client, a Mrs. Haffenreffer, is very pleased to see me.

Ramon, who is waiting in the wings and salivating at my near no-show, is not so happy. It takes me a few moments to jump-start the brain circuits that will spew forth idle chatter and flattery as required, but once I get going, it's as though I've never taken time off. At the shampoo sink – yes, I wash the hair of my longtime special customers – I tell Mrs. Haffenreffer how much I want to "keep my hand in, but only for my best clients." She titters contentedly. I almost believe it myself.

On the way back to the styling chair we pass Ramon. He slouches idly against a wall, his slim Cuban hips gyrating to unheard music. He grins at me. "You doan look so good, baby."

I reply, "Don't you have some sweeping up to do?"

Some time later, as I'm applying the last of the color to Mrs. H's hair, I see Nicole's reflection in the mirror. She's hanging onto the arm of none other than Lieutenant Branco.

"You've got a visitor," she says.

Branco's eyes are intent and curious, as if he really wants to understand what I do here. At one point he leans toward Nicole and says something, and she replies, "Do you really think so?" Then she lets out a bubbly little laugh and struts off.

I ask Ramon to escort Mrs. Haffenreffer to a heat lamp. He grumbles, but does it. As he leads her past Branco he pauses and lets his gaze rove up and down the cop's body, taking in every swell and plane of Branco's physique. I want to scream, *He's mine!* But such adolescent tactics are for Ramon, not me. When it comes to Branco, I am a sensible, responsible adult. And like a sensible, responsible adult, I take Branco to the back room – I mean, the back *office* – where we can have some privacy.

The cop seats himself opposite me. He leans back in the chair, crosses his arms over his chest, and sets his thighs open wide. It's just like old times, except now he has a wife.

Branco says, "Any progress with those thefts?"

"I've dropped it all, Lieutenant."

Grunt. "Did you ever get around to questioning a fellow named Chester Wright?"

"Not quite," I say. "Why?"

"What do you mean 'not quite'?"

"Chester reminds me of someone, and I can't quite –"

"Christ!" says Branco, shaking his head. "Don't tell me you're getting involved with these people."

"I'm not involved." My voice is whining, defensive.

Branco grunts again.

"What's this all about, Lieutenant?"

"You have no personal involvement with Chester Wright?"

"He's got a partner," I say. "That guy Paladin, who lost the collar tips, he and Chester are a couple. Okay?"

Branco exhales through pursed lips, like he's letting off steam. "Why didn't you tell me that before?"

"Because it's theft, not homicide. *Petty* theft, in fact. Nothing to do with you."

His eyes glitter angrily. "What else are you holding back?"

"Nothing," I say.

"How do I know that?"

"How do I know what you want to know?"

"I want to know everything!" he yells. "How am I supposed to do my job if you keep things to yourself?"

"Lieutenant, yesterday you made it very clear that whatever I did about the missing jewelry was my own choice, and that I wasn't working for you in any way. Now today you come here and attack me for *not* telling you about it."

Branco mutters, "Jesus!" and he runs one hand through his hair. "Okay, look," he says, "the situation has changed. We've got a homicide now, so every fact counts – everything."

"Who is it?"

"Chester Wright."

"He's dead?"

Branco nods.

My embodiment of naive fifth-grade love is dead?

Branco sits there silently, watching me. Then he mutters, "Not involved."

"When did it happen?"

"Sometime last night."

"How?" I say. "What?"

"Do you really want to know?"

I don't answer that.

He says, "Puncture wound with a pair of sewing shears, entered the chest and heart from behind."

"Stabbed in the back?"

Branco nods.

I say, "Some fucking coward killed him!"

"I thought you weren't involved."

"I *wasn't* involved, Lieutenant."

He stares at me dubiously.

"I didn't have time to be, okay?"

Branco says, "Sometimes it only takes a few seconds."

You ought to know about that.

"No kidding," I say. "Where did it happen?"

"He was found this morning by a Mister Wang Chu in his costume shop."

"Kitty," I say.

"What?" says Branco.

"He goes by the name Kitty."

"Who?"

"Wang Chu."

One corner of Branco's mouth makes a curlicue. "So you know Mr. Chu?"

"I talked to him, yes. But what was Chester doing in his shop?"

"That's what we're trying to find out," says Branco. "That shop is in the same building as the Gunsmoke Saloon."

"Where?" I say.

"Upstairs, one flight."

"Do you know when he died?"

Branco says, "Sometime last night."

"So anyone who was at Gunsmoke could have gone up ..."

"That's right," says Branco. "Which means I have a lot of people to question."

"And a lot of stories to hear."

Grunt. "Another thing," he says. "Those missing collar tips? They were on Chester Wright's shirt."

"Are you sure they're the same ones?"

"It's a fair guess," he says.

I tell him, "Chester wasn't wearing any collar tips when I saw him at the saloon last night."

"So somebody put them there," says the cop.

"I did see him talking to Kitty. The same thing happened at The Castle yesterday morning. Kitty and Chester were talking together."

Branco says, "What do you make of it?"

"I don't know. They seemed anxious about something."

He says, "Maybe they had some scheme going."

"You think Chester was doing something wrong?"

"Considering he turned up dead in Wang Chu's shop."

I tell him, "Innocent people get killed."

"I know that," he says. "But unlike you, I don't assume they're innocent just because I'm attracted to them."

No comment.

Branco shakes his head. "It's something, at least."

"What is?"

"What you just told me. Mr. Chu is consistently denying any personal knowledge or acquaintance with the victim."

"That's not true," I say.

"Obviously not," says Branco, "not if you've seen them talking together." He hesitates before going on. "Look, I could use your help."

"With Chester's murder, you mean?"

"With that missing jewelry."

"Still?" I say. "But you found the collar tips."

Branco says, "And I want to know how they got there. I want to know every hand that touched them."

"Aren't your guys on it?"

"Of course!" he says. "But it doesn't hurt to have an insider on the case."

"The gay lost-and-found."

"Christ!" he says. "You'll be helping me track the whereabouts of some critical evidence."

"Would I be working for you?"

"Absolutely not," he says. "You're still a free agent."

"More like an informant."

Branco says, "Better than that, I hope."

"Thanks," I say. "But if I can be a free agent with the jewelry, why can't I be a free agent with Chester's murder?"

Another hesitation. "Frankly," he says, "you can, and I can't stop you. That license gives you the right to investigate, as long as it doesn't interfere with our work."

"And I'm not obligated to tell you what I find, right?"

"No," Branco says uncomfortably.

"It's almost like old times, Lieutenant."

"Except if you do find anything, I expect you to tell me."

"For old times' sake, you mean?"

"For the law," says Branco.

We go back out onto the shop floor. We must look a swell couple, him swaggering, me mincing three paces behind.

I finish the color job on Mrs. Haffenreffer. Thanks to Branco's visit and the news about Chester, I turn off all my feelings and do the work on autopilot. Despite my zombie state, my magic touch remains absolute, and Mrs. H is thrilled. But Nicole senses something troubling me, and once I'm free, she hooks my arm and drags me back to the office. I try to tell her what happened to Chester Wright, but my voice comes out hoarse and husky, and my chin starts trembling, my eyes get watery.

Nicole says, "Stanley, you mustn't let Vito affect you like this. Really, darling, you've got to toughen up. This has gone on far too long."

"It's not Branco," I say, trying to control the wobble in my voice. "It's Chester."

"Who's Chester?"

"I ... in a way ... I feel responsible."

"For what?" says Nicole.

"For what happened to him."

"Who?"

"Chester!"

"What happened?" she says.

"Chester's dead and it's all my fault."

"You?" she says. "Why you? Is there something you're not telling me?"

How can I tell Nicole that maybe, if I'd spilled my guts to Chester and promised him undying love and devotion, that maybe he'd have left Paladin and come and lived with me in eternal bliss. How can I tell anyone that?

Instead I say, "I should have kept an eye on him."

"Who?" says Nicole.

"Chester! I should have known that he and Kitty were planning something."

"Kitty?"

"That's how it looks now. Oh, Nikki, how can it seem so complicated when none of it means anything?"

"You can't blame yourself, Stanley, unless you knew for sure that something was going to happen to this Chester person."

"Instead, I got loaded and danced around the floor with

Benjy. If I'd been paying attention to Chester the way I was supposed to –"

She says, "I hope you're not going to blame Benjamin for what happened."

"No, but with Benjy there, our four eyes should have been better than my two. Instead I lost sight of everything, literally, and now Chester's dead."

"There's nothing wrong with having fun."

"But I was supposed to be working, Nikki. And instead of questioning Chester, I was dancing with Benjy."

Nicole says, "Is that all you were going to do, Stanley? Question the young man?"

"Why? What do you mean?"

"Sometimes you can be obsessive."

"Me?"

"It's an observation, darling, not a criticism."

"I don't let personal things interfere with my work."

"No, of course, not," says Nicole. "But, Stanley, I've never met this Chester person. I have no idea who he is, or was. I have no objective correlative for Chester Wright."

"No what?"

"Objective correlative," she says. "It's a term from my creative writing class."

"What writing class?"

"My teacher says I have a natural ability."

"What did you call it again?"

"An objective correlative, Stanley. You see, all I know about this young man is his name and your – dare I say this? – your intense emotions when repeating it. Chester, Chester, Chester is all I've heard for the past few minutes."

"Well, none of it matters now that he's dead."

Nicole shakes her head and clucks her tongue. "Every hard-boiled novel I ever read, the PI falls in love with the femme fatale, not the murder victim."

"I'm not in love! It was something else."

"What exactly was it?"

I tell her, "An old dream."

"Dreams are dreams, darling. They go away when you wake up. You must live in the reality of the moment – you and me in this little office. That's what counts right now."

"Reality of the moment?" I say. "Is that another writing term?"

"My teacher says I have great stories in me, and I shouldn't waste my days at a manicurist's table."

"So instead you'll write sex-laden romance novels."

"I'll write my memoirs," she says.

"Same thing, doll."

"You're just jealous, Stanley, that my sex drive is robust and yours is moribund."

"Sounds like the literary lover boy has shown you his thesaurus."

She says, "I know exactly what I'm getting into. And the difference is, darling, there'll be no tears for me."

"I suppose I ought to follow your example then. Toss away the lace hankies and become an effective dick for Branco. *Grrr!*"

Nicole cringes. "I wish you'd find another word."

"Why, doll? Haven't you and the book boy got an objective correlative for *dick* yet?"

She extinguishes her cigarette – which for Nicole is akin to micro-surgery – then gets up and heads for the door. She stops there and turns dramatically to me. "I wonder what *your* first steps are going to be in that direction."

"In what direction?"

"Finding an objective correlative for yourself."

Alone in the office, I wonder, Where to now? Chester is dead – *boo-hoo!* (No tears for me either, Nikki.) Fact is, Chester never said a single word to me, so how can I have any feeling for him at all? But Branco – Mr. Reality Of The Moment – Branco wants me to keep chasing down the costume jewelry. (Talk about no objective correlative.) Forget that. I'm a free agent. I can investigate whatever I want.

So, once again, where to? Gunsmoke Saloon? It's probably closed at this hour. Besides, it's down in the southernmost reaches of the South End. The dramatic players – the ones who are still alive – are probably at The Castle, where the Mucho Macho Honcho Convention is still underway, maybe.

10.

ROUGHLY TWENTY-FOUR HOURS ago, The Castle was alive with cowboy music, audible and palpable from the sidewalk. Now, Saturday morning, it's just as lively, loud, and thumpy. Doesn't anyone know that Chester Wright is dead? At least one person in there does – some yellow-bellied, backstabbing, coward of a cowboy.

Twenty-four hours ago I was also clear-headed. Now I'm still woozy from last night's adventure with fermented lemons and other possible toxins.

Fannie Mae Knox, head-to-toe in the pinkest of all pinks, sits at her table inside the door, collecting money and checking people's convention badges. There's a short line, but she sees me and waves me in like I'm a VIP. But I want to talk to her, so I linger. We exchange polite greetings, then I ask her where she disappeared to last night.

"Me?" she says. "You're the one who left *me*, Pumpkin, alone at the bar, while you cut a caper with that little blond."

"You saw me dancing?"

"I see everything."

"Did you see who spiked my drink?"

"Did what?" says Fannie Mae.

"Someone put something in my drink to knock me out."

She lowers her voice. "Pumpkin, you know I don't make judgments about people, but I fear you may have just the eensie-weensiest little problem with spirits."

"No," I say. "There was definitely something wrong with one of my drinks."

"Then you should have sent it back." Fannie Mae flashes her stunning fifty-thousand-dollar smile. It seems to take a bit more effort this morning. Maybe Pumpkin the courtier is losing favor. "Now," she says in full voice, "if you don't mind, *young man*, there are people behind you waiting to get in."

Pumpkin is definitely deposed.

I tell her, "I've got to talk to you."

"Impetuous," she says and she lowers her eyes coquett-ishly. "I'll find you later then, inside, once my relief arrives."

She gestures me into the hall with a florid wave of her pink-gloved hand.

Inside, a song is just ending. It's a frisky two-step, and I catch the final lyric: *I never thought I'd find someone like you*. The singer is celebrating his newfound love, while the dancers celebrate each other with turns and twirls. Chester is dead, yet the air throbs with romance.

Bistany Evans appears onstage, heavily miked and prob-ably heavily laden with *stench du jour*. "Wasn't that just the sweetest li'l ol' song? Are yawl in love now? Let me hear it! Yay!"

Some of the dancers cheer limply along with her.

Bistany grins and says, "That's good. That is *so* good! Now, dancers, I'd like yew to get settled and quiet because I have something very important to tell yew. Can yawl do that? Just settle down and go into your quiet place for one little minute, okay? Thank yew. Now, I'm sorry to report that we have a situation here at the Mucho Macho Honcho Conven-tion, a very sad situation, to say the least. One of our contes-tants, unfortunately, had an accid– Well, what I mean to say is last night he met with an unpleasant situation, and now he is no longer with us."

Though that grin is stuck on her face, Bistany's eyes begin to stream alligator tears. Good thing her mascara is waterproof. There is an agitated murmur among the crowd as she soldiers on through the tears.

"Yes," she says, "it is very, very sad. But our convention producers, Miss Heather Blossom and Miss Fannie Mae Knox, did call a special emergency meeting this morning, me included" – Bistany allows a small, self-effacing smile through her tears – "to decide whether or not to go on with the convention, since there was this very sad situation. It was a difficult decision, and I, for one, had a very personal experience which will help yew understand our decision better, and which I would like to share with all of yew, if yew wouldn't mind. May I do that?"

"Thank yew," says Bistany. "Well, when I was preparing myself for our meeting this morning, while I was putting the finishing touches on my face, I saw a reflection in the mirror of a young man standing behind me. And do yew know who it was? It was young Chester Wright. That's the name of the young man who had this very sad situation happen to him last night. Chester Wright was standing right there behind me in my bathroom, but only in the mirror, see? And he was smiling. Yes, even though this very sad thing had happened to him, he was standing there in my bathroom mirror smiling at me. I think he wanted me to know that, wherever he is now, he could take the time to come back this morning and let me see that everything is all right with him."

I say quietly, "He's not all right. He's dead."

The guy standing next to me shushes me.

Bistany says, "And I saw that as a sign that he wanted us to continue with the convention. So I told the board this morning, and we decided that yes, we should go on, and so here we are. In fact, we are dedicating this first Mucho Macho Honcho Convention to the memory of Chester Wright, who brought such happiness into so many of our hearts. And to begin that celebration of his life, this next song is for him."

She gives a cue to the DJ booth. I look up there and see Colt Remington's face. He's smiling, like it's just another day for him. In fact, from the looks of him, it's a very good day.

The music starts. It's Emmylou Harris singing "An

Old-Fashioned Waltz". The bittersweet sentiment cautions you to hold on to that man in your arms, because things will change when you blink, and he'll be gone. The guys on the dance floor seem to understand, since they're holding onto each other for dear life.

Me? Alone on the sidelines as usual.

Bistany Evans is coming off the stage. I take a few deep breaths to prepare for the anaerobic minutes ahead, then intercept her – in cowboy terms, head her off at the pass. Her eyes show a flicker of recognition, but she can't figure out from where. She tries to push by me, subtle as a bulldozer. I introduce myself and tell her I'm an investigator. I try not to inhale. Maybe it's my clothes. Maybe she thinks I'm a reporter or something. Whatever it is, she uses my reluctance to breathe as a cue to advertise herself. She flashes her broad, alienating smile and launches into what sounds like a prepared spiel, a pre-recorded tape her story: How she has worked doggedly to create her own reality. How most people have no idea of what to do with their lives. How they just pass the time until they die. But not her.

"That's why I created Mucho Macho Honcho Conventions," she says. "It's the first corporate entity without boundaries of any kind. Inclusivity! That's our goal!"

I ask, "Then why are there only men at the convention?"

"Yes!" says Bistany. "Yew are so right! This convention is the first public testimony of that unity, putting us at a crossroads of attaining a balanced inclusivity that will impel us into a vortex of empowerment. We will impact a new paradigm of responsibilitizing equality and re-enfranchising our solidarity."

Her eyes are luminous, even though the tape got tangled and only gibberish came out.

Bistany goes on. "Mucho Macho Honcho Conventions will unseat Mary Kay and Avon combined."

"But those are cosmetic companies."

"I know," says Bistany. "But a product is a product is a product." She considers her words. "Isn't that powerful? And yew have to use your power to get the people of the world coming to yew for the goods. They show up with cash and hand it over."

"And what do they get?"

"They get the dream of romance and love," she says. "The market is infinite. Mucho Macho Honcho Conventions will change the world. It will be the most recognized brand name on the international square-dance, round-dance, and country-western dance circuit. I'm seeing a lawyer on Tuesday about registering the trademark. In fact, if yew want a hot tip, we may be going public, and yew might want to invest."

"Invest?"

"Yew can get in on the ground floor. *Below* it, in fact. Yew can invest in the ... the ..."

"Cellar?" I say.

Bistany squints her eyes. "I was going to say foundation," she says. "But that just gave me another idea. I'll set up a foundation too. One side can make the money and then donate it all to the other side, which can then distribute it to me. We might actually get away without paying a nickel in taxes, ever! But don't print that." *Tee-hee.*

"Print what?"

"In your article," she says. "When will it appear?"

"What article?"

"Aren't yew with a magazine or something?"

I tell her, "I'm investigating the death of Chester Wright."

Bistany stands there blinking and wordless. Now, if only the stench would go, she'd be almost bearable.

"Yew mean," she says, "this isn't about me?"

"No."

"But yes said yew were a reporter."

"Investigator."

She insists. "Investigative reporter."

"No." That's what yew heard, doll.

"Well, then," she says, quickly realigning her market strategy, "isn't it the saddest thing yew ever heard? I just can't believe that something like this could happen during an event like this. Here we are, all together to have a good time, but for that poor young man, it turned out to be the unhappiest time of his life."

I say, "And his killer is still walking around free."

"Yew don't think it was someone from the convention? That's not the kind of people who attend Mucho Macho Honcho Conventions – thieves and such."

What about the people who run them?

"This is murder," I say, "not theft, and I'm trying to get the facts. Were you at the Gunsmoke Saloon last night?"

"For a little while," she says.

"What time?"

"I don't recall exactly, I've been so busy."

"How long then?"

"I don't know," she says. "An hour maybe?"

"How well did you know Chester Wright?"

"Hardly at all. He was only a contestant."

"But he showed up in your bathroom mirror this morning."

Bistany looks at me blankly, smiles, shakes her head and shrugs. "I don't think I can help yew," she says. "I've got a convention to run, and if things weren't already hard enough, now we have a situation like this."

"A sad situation."

"Yes, very sad," she says.

"How are you and Colt getting along today?"

"I beg your pardon?" she says. The smile is glued on.

"You and Colt Remington. I heard you two arguing last night at his place. He was pretty angry about Chester getting something he thought should be his."

Bistany says, "I knew I'd seen you before!"

Where's the *yew*, doll?

I say, "Colt was supposed to be going on the national tour, but you changed your mind, and Chester was. going instead."

Bistany digs her hoofs into the floor. "I can't help what you think you heard," she says.

"And now Chester is dead, and Colt looks almost relieved."

"You say you're looking for facts," she says, "but you sound more interested in making judgments about people."

I ask, "How did you hear about Chester's death?"

"Heather told me," she says.

"When?"

"This morning."

"What time?"

"I don't recall exactly."

"Before you put on your makeup?"

"Must have been," she says smugly. "Otherwise, why would Chester have showed up in my mirror?"

To give you a heart-wrenching tale to tell, doll.

I ask, "How did Heather tell you?"

"What do you mean?"

"In person? By phone?"

Bistany says, "She phoned me in my hotel room."

"What did you do then?"

Bistany's eyes become cold, and she speaks solemnly. "I prayed," she says. She gives me a moment to appreciate her piety, then her repulsive smile returns. "Now," she says, "if yew don't mind, I have a convention to run." And off she goes to conquer and conjoin the peoples of the world.

Another song begins, another ballad of sweetheart love and devotion. I watch the couples dancing on the floor and wonder why I'm not out there with them, being held by someone and feeling included, instead of trying to get people to tell me things they don't want to and feeling outcast. Maybe it's the nature of PI work. Nothing like the styling chair, where interrogations are voluntary, and it's one big party.

I feel a light tap on my shoulder. I turn to see the pink-upon-pink diaphaneity of Fannie Mae Knox.

"The party has arrived, Pumpkin."

Has she read my thoughts?

"If I were more brazen," she says in her cracking falsetto, "I would demand the next dance of you."

"I'm not much of a two-stepper."

"That's not the impression I got last night. You were the

belle of the ball. Who was that leading you around the floor? A secret spouse, perhaps? Have you been leading me on, when all the time you've got someone special?"

I tell her, "He's a friend."

"Does he have a name?"

"Yes."

"Are you going to tell me?"

"No."

"Privacy at all costs, eh?"

"Just privacy," I say.

"Ah," says Fannie Mae. "Then there's more to it. That's a relief, Pumpkin. I was beginning to worry about you. You seem like such a nice person, and nice people shouldn't be alone. Now *nasty* people," she says with a definite disparaging tone, "they deserve to be alone. But they usually aren't. Have you ever noticed that, Pumpkin? Justice is so fickle. Now what was so urgent for you to ask me?"

"Did you know Chester Wright, the guy who was killed?"

Fannie Mae's large eyes gaze at me. What is going on behind that pretense of pink?

"Mmmmm, yes ..." she says.

"How?" I say.

"He was a contestant. I made it a point to meet all the contestants."

"That's all?"

"Yes," she says. "But really, Pumpkin, if we're going to play cat-and-mouse, I expect you'd ask me about Paladin."

"All right," I say. "What about him?"

"Paladin," says Fannie Mae, "is nowhere to be found. Don't you find *that* intriguing?

"How do you know?"

"Because the executive committee has been trying to phone him all morning, to discuss the competition. But he has vanished."

"The executive committee being you and Heather and Bistany?"

"That's right," says Fannie Mae.

"When did you first find out that Chester was dead?"

"This morning."

"What time?"

Another wide-eyed look from her. "Pumpkin, aren't you working for the police?"

"No."

"Ah," she says, "then you *don't* know."

"Don't know what?"

"That I received an anonymous phone call this morning, in my hotel room, telling me that Chester Wright was dead."

"Come on!" I say.

"It's true, Pumpkin. And I immediately telephoned the police to verify the facts, and they told me that yes, indeed, Chester Wright was dead."

"What time was it?"

"Around eight o'clock."

"Did you phone anyone after that?"

"I called Heather, and she called Bistany, and here we are. It's very, very sad."

I say, "So someone called you anonymously and said Chester was dead."

"That's right," says Fannie Mae.

"Who do you think it was?"

"You mean, who called me?" she says. "Or who killed him?"

"Either," I say.

"It's obvious to me that Paladin killed Chester."

"Obvious?"

"Pumpkin, what kind of sign or symbol do you need? Why else would Paladin disappear? I told you, he's nowhere to be found."

"Maybe he's afraid of something."

"Afraid of being caught."

"But why would he kill Chester? They seemed very together."

Suddenly Fannie Mae lets out a loud shriek, and as she does so – how can I put this delicately? – she breaks a bit of wind.

"Oh!" she exclaims at the outburst. Then she snaps open her pink fan and flutters it quickly. "Hoisted by my own petard," she says. The crisis past, she continues. "But yes, Pumpkin, in a way you are absolutely correct. From all appearances, Paladin and Chester were a most together couple. Wasn't that the prize they were going to win, after all?"

"Which is why it makes no sense that Paladin would kill Chester, not if they were about to win a big prize."

Fannie Mae clucks her tongue. "Dear dim Pumpkin, will you never see beyond the surface? Let's suppose, just suppose, that Chester is still alive right now. He and Paladin compete and go on to win first prize as The Most Together Couple. Fine. Lovely! Cheers, dancing, flashing medals! Hooray, hooray!"

"Okay, I get the picture."

"And then, later, what?"

"What?"

She says, "Would handsome, virile, and able Paladin be content to remain partnered with a not-so-able Chester?"

"What do you mean?"

"Come, come, Pumpkin! What would any two dancing champions do? They'd take their show on the road. And I put it to you: Would that have worked?"

"Why not?"

"Oh, Pumpkin, you are too nice! Nice, nice, nice. And where did *nice* ever get anybody? Look, Paladin may have pretensions to Fred Astaire, but Chester; let's face it Pumpkin, Chester was certainly no Ginger Rogers. How could he be?"

"They seemed fine together."

"As long as Chester's feet weren't on the floor."

In my mind's eye I see an instant replay of Chester and Paladin dancing in the semifinals.

"Oh," I say, recalling Chester's limp.

"Yes, Pumpkin. *Oh.*"

"I think I'm beginning to understand now."

"It's about time," says Fannie Mae.

"But that's so ... blunt."

"Apparently *blunt* is what it takes for you to understand anything, Pumpkin. But those are the facts, plain and simple."

"And cruel."

"There's nothing cruel about it. A fact has no feelings or intentions. It simply is. Chester Wright was lame from birth."

"And you think because of his limp, Paladin wasn't going to take Chester on tour with him?"

"It's obvious to me."

"And so he killed Chester?"

Fannie Mae pauses. "Perhaps that's not so obvious."

"Besides, Paladin really liked Chester."

"No, Pumpkin. It is you who really liked Chester. Paladin likes Paladin, and that's it. He was just using Chester."

"For what?"

"To win! My goodness, I thought you understood! Pumpkin, I can't decide whether you're too nice, or too dim."

"I still don't get it."

"Paladin assumed that dancing with Chester would give him a distinct advantage with the judges."

"But why?"

Fannie Mae looks heavenward for the strength to explain the facts of death to her dim-witted Pumpkin. "How many times," she says, "have you heard the term *inclusivity* bandied about here?" She shudders at saying the word.

"You mean Bistany –"

"I never said a name!"

"But that's her word."

"That is *not* a word, Pumpkin. At best, a neologism."

"So you think Paladin danced with Chester just so Bistany would vote for him?"

Fannie Mae sighs heavily. "Pumpkin, this *explication du texte* is beginning to tire me."

I say, "Then let's get back to cat-and-mouse."

"Eh?" says Fannie Mae.

"Maybe *you* have eyes for Paladin."

"Me?" she says. "Eyes for Paladin?"

"You seem to know so much about him, and how he thinks and connives. And I saw you watching him last night at Gunsmoke. It reminded me of how I used to watch my lover dance."

Fannie Mae rears up. "Oh, no, no, no, Pumpkin. Wrong, wrong, wrong. Besides, if I were attracted to a cad like Paladin, I would protect him, wouldn't I? Not accuse him."

"Depends," I say.

"On what?" says Fannie Mae.

"On whether you were jealous of him and Chester."

"You are not being very nice, Pumpkin."

"Which of us is really, truly, deeply nice?"

Fannie Mae says, "Perhaps you do have another side, a not so nice side, and it's beginning to show."

"Maybe you were so jealous over Chester that *you* killed him."

"Pumpkin!" she squawks. "Now you go too far. It is beastly to taunt someone of my age and background with ideas like this. Can't you see the futility of me 'having eyes' for anyone, never mind an Apollo like Paladin? And then killing my rival, a cripple no less! And at my age?"

"You're not that old."

"Oh!" she groans. "Struck to the quick! Pumpkin, you are cruel! You dare to call *me* cruel for speaking the truth about Chester, but now you prove yourself the far, far crueler man."

She admits she's a man?

She goes on. "At last, I see your tactics. You start off nice and sweet and naive and caring, but then you take what the other person gives you and you return it as a blow – a very low blow on a defenseless person."

"Hardly defenseless."

"And the words you use – *not that old!* Exactly how old must I be to be *that old?*"

"I'm sorry," I say.

"Sorry won't do it, Pumpkin. It's too late for that. In fact, I rescind your knighthood. You are no longer in my favor. Go now! Go and see if you can find Paladin. Then ask him if I ever had the temerity to look his way with hope and desire. You foolish, hurtful, heartless young man!"

Then off she goes, in all her regal pink imperiousness.

And so much for the nice little pumpkin she was cultivating. With any luck I'll never suffer that alias again.

The music ends quietly. The dancing couples embrace in the silence that follows, reinforcing the bonds of caring for each other. Meanwhile, I'm alienating everyone in my path.

The silence is shattered by mega-muscled Colt Remington, onstage now and giving head to the microphone. (Should a straight guy do that in public?)

"Hi, fellas! I'm Colt Remington, your convention DJ. I know you guys are waiting for the dance competitions, and I promise you that's coming up real soon, right after the judges make some last-minute adjustments to the contestant list. Meanwhile, I want to say a few words about the unfortunate situation we had with one of our dancers. The convention's executive committee has given me permission to talk to you about it. And so I'm extending this invitation to everyone out there. Effective immediately, I am offering my professional services – meaning one fifteen-minute session of quality personal time with me – on a pro bono basis for the rest of the weekend. That's right. I'll talk to anyone out there for free, for fifteen minutes. Just come and see me during the break, and we'll set up an introductory consultation."

But who here is bothered by Chester Wright's death? These guys are dancing and competing for prizes as though nothing has happened. How is Colt Remington going to help them? Maybe *I'll* get in line for a fifteen-minute one-on-one with him. And I'll ask him where he was on break last night, out of the DJ booth.

Colt says, "Now I'll hand the proceedings back to your convention director, Miss Bistany Evans. Let's have a nice round of applause for the exceptional and professional way Bistany is handling this difficult situation."

As Colt claps his big hands together, the heavy muscles

of his arms and chest bounce and quiver. He leaves the stage, handing the microphone to Bistany Evans on the way. She pauses and gives him a big hug. Her hands are all over his back, like she's surveying the fleshy terrain – measuring, squeezing, feeling. They separate with a quick peck on the lips.

Bistany is screaming, "Oh, thank yew, Colt! Thank yew, *thank yew!* He is just so big and generous, isn't he?"

I guess she came.

But what's come down between the two of them since last night, when they were at each other's throats, and yesterday morning, when they were challenging other in public, casting slurs in a verbal duel to the death?

Still breathless, Bistany says, "Be sure yawl take advantage of this opportunity. If yew think Colt *looks* good, just wait till yew *talk* with him. Yew will never be the same after fifteen minutes alone with Colt."

Ask me. I spent an hour with him yesterday.

The music starts, and we're back in the realm of canned square dancing. Near the stage, Fannie Mae Knox and Bistany Evans are talking with Heather Blossom. The three ladies – I use the term loosely – look my way, and I wonder what galvanizes their grotesque triumvirate. (A nice phrase to try on Nicole.) Might it be – I fear to look – the common presence of hoofs?

Heather breaks away from her cohorts and comes over to me.

"Hi, darlin'," she says. Her curly red hair is extra lively in the brightness of the hall. "How're you doin' this morning?"

"Surviving."

"Ain't that the truth?" she says. "Fannie Mae and Bistany tell me you're asking about Chester Wright. Maybe I can help."

A volunteer? "Sure," I say. "But isn't Fannie Mae mad at me?"

"Mad?" says Heather.

"She pretty much blew me off just now."

"Why, darlin', don't you know? That's Fannie Mae's way of showing she likes you. If she can't disagree with you, you might as well be dead. Now, how can I help?"

"For starters, did you know Chester?"

"Of course," she says. "He worked for me at Gunsmoke."

"Chester worked for you?"

"Sure. He called the steps on Colt's off-nights."

"Chester was a square dance caller?"

"That's right," says Heather. "Didn't you know? That's how him and Paladin know each other."

"But Paladin's not a square dancer."

"No," she says, "and neither is Chester. He just calls them. I mean, he *called* them."

"Then how did they hook up as dancers?"

"I don't know, darlin'. It just happened."

"It doesn't seem likely."

"No?" says Heather.

"Chester had that bad foot," I say. "Why would Paladin dance with a guy with a bad foot?"

She shrugs. "I guess it was more than dancing that brought them together."

Even a body-obsessed dancer can be blind to the physical flaws in his beloved.

I ask her, "Was there any trouble between them?"

"Not that I know of. Why?"

"They didn't seem too happy when they came into Gunsmoke last night."

"I didn't notice," says Heather. "Besides, who doesn't have some kind of trouble in love?"

"How long did Chester work for you?"

"Started, oh, about six months ago."

"Is that when he met Paladin?"

"No, that was more recent, not even a month ago."

"They've only been dancing together a month?"

"Not even," says Heather.

"Did they know each other before that, during the six months, I mean?"

"I don't know," she says. "You'd have to ask them." She frowns. "I mean, Paladin."

"So until this happened, Chester was still working for you?"

"That's right, darlin'. In fact, he's still got a paycheck coming. Can you take care of that?"

"I think his estate will handle it."

"His estate?" Heather laughs. "You think someone like Chester has an estate? That boy was a tumbleweed."

"Who would have wanted him dead?"

"No one," says Heather. "Absolutely no one. He was such a sweet young thing. Everybody liked him."

"Not everyone apparently. How did Chester and Colt get along?"

"Colt?"

"You said they were both callers at Gunsmoke. Maybe there was a rivalry between them."

"Well, sure," says Heather. "There was a little healthy competition, but not enough for Colt to go and kill the boy."

"Why did you hire Chester?"

"You sure are asking a lot of questions, darlin'."

"I'm trying to find out what happened."

"And I want to help you, but this is taking way longer than I expected."

"How long do you think it took Chester to die?"

Heather says, "No need to get morbid about it. How I hired Chester was that he just walked into the saloon one night and asked if he could call a tip. The kid looked like he needed a break, and I like to give people a chance. I mean, where would I be now if no one gave me a chance? So I said okay. And he got up there and introduced himself. He sure is sweet with a crowd. Ten minutes later the whole place got all warm and cozy. And when he finished the tip, you could see how everyone felt sad."

"Sad?" I say.

"Yeah. You know how that happens. You're having a good time, then all of a sudden you realize it's going to end, it can't go on forever, and so you start to feel sad even before it's over. That never happen to you?"

Nope. Not once. Ever.

I ask her, "Was that a problem?"

"Could be, when you're running a dance club. You don't want people feeling sad about anything while they're in your place, or they might not come back."

"So Chester was something of a problem for you."

"No, no," says Heather. "That's not what I meant, darlin'. Not at all. He made you feel a nice, quiet sadness – a sweet sadness. That boy sure knew how to make you feel sweet inside."

"Maybe Colt didn't like that."

Heather says, "Look, darlin', I'm just trying to explain the difference between Colt and Chester. Colt get a crowd all fired up and jumping around, like they're ready to go out and conquer the world. And Chester made you feel homey and sweet. Not too many people can do that. But it wasn't something that would make Colt kill Chester, or anyone. Now I'm sorry I even mentioned it. I need Colt around here. He can be ornery, but he sure brings in the crowds. Look at them over there, all lined up just to get fifteen minutes alone with him."

It's true. Anyone who isn't dancing – meaning about half the people here – is waiting in line to set up a one-on-one session with Colt.

Heather says, "That's about all I have to say, darlin'."

"Just one more thing, please."

She heaves a big sigh. "Kinda sorry I offered my time."

"But I really appreciate it," I say. "Tell me, when did you first hear about Chester's death?"

"Fannie Mae phoned me this morning."

"What time?"

"I guess around eight o'clock."

"And what did she say?"

"Say?" says Heather.

"The words she used."

"I don't remember, darlin'. Does it matter that much?"

"It might."

"All I recall is Fannie Mae telling me that Chester was dead, and we should decide whether to keep the convention going."

"And then you called Bistany?"

"That's right."

"Why didn't Fannie Mae call her?"

"Because I offered to do it," says Heather. "We try to help each other, darlin'."

At least this part of Heather's story jibes with Bistany's and Fannie Mae's version: The Executive Committee's Tale.

"So, now, darlin', if there's nothing else –"

"Just one more thing."

"How many one-mores?" she says, and grimaces impatiently.

I want to say, Be glad you're alive and can be irritated about something.

Instead I say, "Where did you go on your break last night?"

"What break?"

"After Chester and Paladin came in you left the bar."

She says, "I had to check on some stock."

"You were gone quite a while."

"Like you could keep track of time?" She laughs.

"Darlin', if you can't hold your liquor, maybe you ought to admit it."

"I think someone slipped me a mickey last night."

"A Mickey Finn? *Hah!* You'll excuse me for saying this, darlin', but I think what you might have is a little problem."

"I'm not usually unconscious after three drinks."

She shrugs. "Never knew a drunk who could keep count."

"I'm not a drunk."

"A lot of people have a problem, darlin', and it's nothing to be ashamed of. What's shameful is the denial."

"I'm not denying anything. Someone slipped me a mickey."

"Did you see it happen?" she says.

"No."

"Well, there you are."

"But someone did put something in my drink."

"Look," says Heather, "even if it did happen – and I'm not saying it did – but if it did happen, it could have been anybody in the place. So don't go blaming me or my staff for doing something you have no proof of. If you keep going on about it, I might have to call my lawyer. And I'd rather give you some referrals where you can get some help."

"The only help I want right now is finding out who killed Chester."

"And that's good," she says. "But if you're serious about your work, you ought to try and control the drinking."

"Heather, I do not have a drinking problem!"

"Blacking out is a bad sign."

"Who told you I blacked out?"

"Darlin', I called the cab. You're lucky your friend was there to take you home. Now, listen to me and put your pretty little head to rest once and for all. There's no way I could slip you a *mickey*, leave my bar, go upstairs to Kitty's shop and kill Chester, then return and still have a perfect alibi. What do you think this is, a bad movie?" She laughs.

"I've got just one more question."

"Time's up," she says and starts to walk away.

"Who is Fannie Mae, really?"

Heather stops, turns, and smiles. "*Now*, darlin', you really are getting way too personal."

She laughs again and walks off.

Three for three, and I am absolutely nowhere.

I go and stand in the line for my free quickie with Colt.

It will be fun to put him under fire in public. Although I'm beginning to wonder if I might need some real shrinking after all. According to everyone else here, I'm a drunk in denial. And if I'm losing touch with reality, it might be time to begin the descent back to terra firma.

Reality and terra firma are confirmed when Lieutenant Branco enters the hall with three other cops. They head directly to the table where Colt is sitting, way at the head of the line I'm standing in. Colt stands up and faces Branco belligerently. I can hear angry words, but not what anyone is saying. (The music and dancing are still going on, believe it or not.) One of the cops pulls out handcuffs, but Colt backs right down and goes willingly with them.

Afraid of a little bondage, doll?

As Branco leads the group away, he sees me standing in line.

"Good that you're here," he says. "Saves me tracking you down. I want you at the station."

"Sure," I say.

"Now," he says. "With me."

11.

AT POLICE HEADQUARTERS BRANCO takes me directly to his office and closes the door.

"I need a favor, Stan."

"Off the record?"

"No," he says. "This one is definitely *on*."

"Name it," I say.

Just as Branco is about to speak, an officer arrives with a large envelope. He hands it to Branco and mumbles, "ME's report."

Branco says, "Thanks."

The other cop gives me a cool glance as he leaves.

Branco pulls out the report. He ponders it a while. Then he says, "At least the kid wasn't raped. No penile, anal, oral –"

"Lieutenant, why are you telling me this?"

"This is what homicide is about, among other things."

"Do you have to start with that?"

"What do you suggest I start with?"

"Maybe how he died," I say.

"Sure," he says.

"And maybe just describe it, not read it from the report."

Branco says, "You mean soften it for someone who wasn't emotionally involved with the victim?"

"Just soften it," I say.

"Sure," he says, then tells me, "the victim was stabbed

with a pair of cutting shears. Very long blades. They were found next to the body."

I gulp. "Not in him?"

"No," he says. "In fact ..." Branco pauses, uncertain he should go on. "You know he was stabbed in the back, right?"

"Yes, you told me this morning." But knowing it doesn't lessen the awfulness. My Chester, stabbed in the back. That's the only way you could do it. You couldn't look into Chester's face and do anything harmful.

Branco says, "The odd thing is he was lying on his back."

"So somebody moved him."

"Right," says Branco.

"And then put the collar tips on him."

"Could be more than one person," he says.

"Any prints?"

Branco grunts, shakes his head. "The killer wore gloves." It sounds like the title of an old dime-store paperback.

"Whoever did this," Branco says gravely, "knew exactly where to strike. There was one direct hit through the heart."

"So death was instantaneous."

"Not quite," he says, "but fast."

"And only one wound."

"Yes," says Branco.

"So Chester wasn't mutilated at least."

"No," he says, eyeing me intently. "You want to stop?"

"No, why?"

"Just checking your emotional barometer."

"Holding steady," I say. "Was there much blood?"

"Plenty," he says. "Why?"

"I figure if his heart stopped, there was no way for the blood to get pumped out."

"With a wound that size," says Branco, "and the victim on his back, gravity pulls the blood out, but it's pooled, not splattered all over like you get with a severed artery."

"I think I get the picture."

"Do you?" says Branco, like I'm too much of a wimp for the awful truth, which I am.

I ask him, "What about that favor you want?"

"I'd like you to talk to Wang Chu."

"Kitty."

Branco arches one eyebrow.

I say, "Why him?"

"For one thing, I suspect he found the victim in his shop and then went to the hotel to phone us."

"All that way? Why?"

"To keep it anonymous," says Branco, "and also implicate everyone else in the hotel. But we got a positive match on his voice print."

I say, "Anything else?"

"When Mr. Chu arrived at his shop and saw my crew there, his reaction was over the top, like he'd rehearsed it all, just for us. There was nothing natural about it."

"Maybe he was in shock from what he found earlier."

"Or from what he did," says Branco.

"You think Kitty killed Chester?"

"I don't know, but he's sure clammed up on me."

"And you think I might pry him open?"

Branco says, "You're pretty good with the velvet gloves."

"If not the shucking knife. Will you be there with me?"

"That would defeat the purpose, wouldn't it? I told you, he won't talk to me. Besides, I've got Colt Remington to deal with."

"The real man."

Branco's lips tighten. "It was Mr. Chu who named Mr. Remington."

"I wonder how Colt feels about that."

"I intend to find out," says the cop.

"Turn them on each other."

Branco grunts. "There'll be a camera going in your room, so I can watch the tape if I need to, after I get your report."

Definitely on the record.

I ask, "Who'll be in there with me?"

"You'll be on your own."

"Alone?" I say. "But you suspect Kitty of killing Chester."

"Not really," says Branco. "Too soft."

"He's not soft," I say. "Especially his hands. Sewing on all those sequins, he's probably got a death grip. I know from cutting hair."

"Nah!" says Branco.

"Lieutenant, you may see Kitty as a harmless little butterfly, but stabbing someone in the back doesn't require –"

"Look," he says, "my sergeant and I survived in there, and I'm sure you will. And the little butterfly, as you call him, has no weapons. We did a quick frisk, took away his sewing kit."

"This doesn't sound like standard procedure to me."

"Nothing I've ever done with you is standard procedure."

"But why am I alone with him?"

Branco says, "Because that's how I want it. Now, do you want to help me or not?"

"Show me the way."

One of Branco's minions arrives and takes me to the room where they are holding Mr. Wang "Kitty" Chu, costumer to the stars of Boston's country-western and square-dance firmament.

I enter the room cautiously. The steel-reinforced door closes behind me, sealing us both in the small chamber. Kitty looks up from where he sits in total dejection. He sees me, then he leaps from his chair and throws himself at me. I have no chance to call out. He grapples me – engulfs me – in a stifling body lock. How can such a small man be all over me at once? I can barely breathe. I struggle to push him off, but he's glommed on with Superglue tenacity. He keeps moving his head in my face, and his dense black hair prevents me from calling out for help. It smells slightly of verbena, and I think of Cio-Cio-San (*Madama Butterfly* for you non-opera buffs). Calm in a crisis, that's me. That's also when I realize Kitty is not trying to hurt me. He's merely scared to death.

"Oh, oh," he whimpers into my chest, then he lifts his head to speak. "Take me out of here, please. Take me now!"

I look around the room. Isn't anyone watching the video monitor? Why doesn't some cop come to my rescue? Or are they all too busy laughing?

"Kitty," I say gently. "Okay, Kitty, that's enough."

"You have no idea!" he says into my shirt. "They're awful. Awful, horrible brutes!"

Well, after all, the poor thing has just endured his first encounter with Branco. Even hardened criminals are known to crack under his steely gaze. What hope does a sensitive, delicate soul like Kitty's have?

Correction: a sensitive, delicate, potential killer's soul.

"Kitty?" I say. "Kitty, you can let go of me now. It's all right. I'm here to talk to you, so you can let go of me."

"Oh," he says, "it was awful! You don't know! I can't go back there! Not now, not ever! I just want to burn everything! Burn the whole place down!"

"Burn what down, Kitty?"

"My shop! I can't go back!"

"Why not?"

"He was dead, just lying there dead. *Ohhhhhhhhhh!*"

So it's not just Branco who's driven Kitty over the edge. He's seen Chester too, and now he's in acute mental shock. That's what's really wrong with him, and he should probably be sedated.

Finally, Kitty lets go of me, and I can breathe again. He stands in front of me, head bowed slightly, eyes raised and looking up into mine.

He says, "I tried to tell the police everything, but that lieutenant, he's so cold. He has cruel eyes. And I ... I ..."

Just like the rest of us, Kitty. We see those eyes and we are lost.

Kitty continues. "He wouldn't believe me, so I started making things up. I didn't know what else to do. I told him Chester and I spent the night together in my shop, and that I went out early this morning for coffee for us, and when I came back, he was ... he was ... like *that.*"

Kitty starts blubbering again, and reflexively I put my arm out to help him, then realize it might instigate another deadly embrace, so I withdraw it.

I say, "But that's not what really happened, is it, Kitty?"

Kitty looks at me, sniffles loudly, and shakes his head no.

"Now," I coo softly, imbuing my voice with a hairstylist's earnest interest, "why don't you tell me what really happened."

Kitty whimpers. "What really happened?"

"Start at the beginning and tell me a story."

"Oh," says Kitty. "A story. Maybe I can do that."

You and Scheherazade.

"Good, good," I say and give him a few light encouraging pats, but very light, not too encouraging.

Kitty says, "It all started with the collar tips."

"The collar tips," I say.

"Paladin's collar tips. He thought I stole them, but I didn't."

"No, of course you didn't."

Or did you?

Kitty says, "I don't know if I can go through with this."

"You can, Kitty. Do it for me."

Kitty sighs. "I'm so confused. Sometimes I think it's all my fault."

"What is?"

"That Chester is dead. See, if I had given Paladin the collar tips when I found them, none of this would have happened."

"You found his collar tips?"

"They were in his laundry. I do his laundry too, along with making his costumes. I went to his hotel room Thursday night to get his laundry, but when I went in, he was in the Jacuzzi with Chester. It sounded like there were having sex, so I just took the laundry and got out of there."

"You didn't say anything?"

"Would you?"

"Maybe they weren't having sex."

"They were," says Kitty. "I could tell."

"So you took the laundry with the collar tips inside."

"Yes, but I didn't know that."

"Why not?"

"Because I never looked," he says. "There was too much

for me to do that night besides sort laundry. Everyone eats and drinks so much at these conventions, some of their fasteners don't connect anymore, and I have to move them. So I had a lot of hand sewing Thursday night."

"So when did you find the collar tips?"

"I didn't even know they were missing until I got to The Castle Friday morning. Chester grabbed me right after him and Paladin came in."

He, goes my tic.

Kitty continues. "Paladin went down to the dressing room, but Chester stayed behind. He was in a panic and wanted to know if I found Paladin's collar tips, but I didn't know what he was talking about. He kept saying it was a mistake and he had to get them back right away. He was desperate."

"But you knew the collar tips were in the laundry."

"No. And Chester never said that either. Then Paladin came back and saw us talking and wanted to know what was going on. But Chester shut right up, and so Paladin thought I took them. Then later, down in the dressing room … Well, you were there. You saw what happened then. That's when Chester mentioned the shirt pocket to Paladin. And then Paladin had that big hissy-fit about his sacred ritual and all that shit. I guess Chester was trying to give me some kind of hint about where the collar tips were. But how was I supposed to know that?"

"Didn't it occur to you that the collar tips might be in Paladin's laundry after that hint?"

Kitty says, "I didn't *know* it was a hint! Not then. I didn't know they were in the laundry until later on."

"When later?"

"After the competition, when you were talking to Paladin over near the stage."

"You noticed that?"

"Sure," says Kitty. "And that's when Chester found me again and told me he'd put the collar tips in *his* shirt pocket Thursday night."

"Did he say why?"

"No," says Kitty. "But he didn't expect all the clothes would be gone after their Jacuzzi. Anyway, Chester wanted to come by my shop Friday afternoon to get the collar tips, and I said okay, and he made me promise not to say anything to Paladin."

It's a lovely tale, so far. The only real fact is that Kitty notices everything, especially when I happen to be within range.

I say, "So you found the collar tips in Paladin's laundry when you went back to your shop on Friday afternoon."

Kitty hesitates. "No."

"No?"

"They weren't there."

"How hard did you look?"

"I looked, okay?"

I say, "Maybe they fell out of Chester's shirt pocket. Did you look in the hamper?"

"Yes, I did. I'm not stupid, you know."

"And?"

"There was nothing," he says.

"They might have got caught in some of the other clothes."

"Look," says Kitty, "I couldn't bring my business to a full halt just because Paladin lost his collar tips. I had a pile of work to do for my clients, and most of those dance hall queens will *not* be seen in daylight with their costumes. They do it in total secret. And believe me, if I found those collar tips, I would have called Paladin right away. But I figured he probably had them back at his hotel all along. These divas are always doing things like that. They meet someone new and get all distracted with sex, then they get everyone else into a total panic about something trivial, and then they say, 'Oh, sorry, here they are, right where I left them. Silly, silly me.'"

"But Chester told you he put them in his own shirt pocket. Why would he say that if it wasn't true?"

Kitty doesn't answer.

I say, "Are you having trouble remembering something?"

"Actually," he says, "I did find the collar tips."

"Why did you say you didn't?"

"I don't know. Maybe just to bother you – you and your faux cop act."

Who's calling whom faux?

He says, "The collar tips were in Chester's shirt pocket, exactly like he said. And the pocket was snapped shut, so it was no accident they were in there."

"And then Chester came to your shop and got them." Story finished, everyone lived happily ever after.

"No," says Kitty. "He never showed up and he never called."

"So, what did you do?"

"I called Paladin at the hotel."

"Even though you promised Chester you wouldn't tell him."

"Yes," says Kitty. "By that time I was sick of the whole thing and just wanted those collar tips out of my hands."

"And?"

"There was no answer. He and Chester were probably having a victory fuck to celebrate getting into the finals."

"Does their having sex bother you?"

"Why should it?" says Kitty. "It's *their* honeymoon."

"It's the second time you've brought it up."

"I don't care what Paladin does, or who he does it with.

I get plenty on my own. Look, I told you, I was very busy yesterday and I couldn't keep waiting around for Chester to show up, or keep phoning Paladin about his damn costume jewelry."

"You could have taken them to the hotel yourself."

"I could have," says Kitty, "but I didn't."

"Why not?"

"Because it would be pretty stupid. I mean, how is it going to look if I suddenly show up with the collar tips after Paladin accuses me of stealing them?"

"But you didn't."

"But *he* thinks I did, and then I show up with them in my hand. How does that look?"

"You're right," I say. "Not good. So what did you do?"

Kitty says, "I left them in the shop. I figured, if Chester took them, it's his problem to get them back."

"And did he?"

"Last night at Gunsmoke he came up to me. It was just like that morning. He was desperate to get the collar tips, so I gave him the key to my shop and told him he could go up there and get them himself."

"Why didn't you go with him?"

"I didn't want anyone, especially Paladin, to think we were in this thing together."

"But you were in it together."

"Not really," says Kitty. "It was my bad luck, that's all. And last night I had some good luck. I met Tex."

"His name is Tex?"

Towering Tex.

Kitty nods. "He's from Dallas. He wants to set me up in business down there. I wasn't about to give up a chance like that just to help Chester. You saw how Paladin attacked me yesterday at the hall. I didn't need a repeat performance of that. I wanted to have some fun for a change."

"So Chester went up to your shop to get the collar tips."

"Yes."

"And then?"

"Then you met me near that exit door at Gunsmoke, and then Paladin came by and started threatening me again. That's when

Tex came out of the men's room and we left together."

"Where to?"

"The hotel," says Kitty.

"And what about Chester?"

"The next time I saw him was when I got to my shop this morning, and the police were there. And now I'm here."

"But you called the police from the hotel lobby."

"When?" says Kitty.

"This morning. Your call was traced back to a phone in the hotel lobby, and they got a voice print on you."

"No," says Kitty. "I went straight from Tex's room to my

shop."

"Never mind that for now," I say. "Didn't you wonder what happened when Chester didn't bring back your key last night?"

Kitty stalls. "Once Paladin found me with you and started threatening me again, I didn't care about the key. I just wanted to get out of there, and Tex took me away."

"The cops will get a statement from this Tex guy."

"We have nothing to hide."

"Are you sure you didn't go back upstairs to your shop, just to see what was keeping Chester?"

"No," says Kitty.

"You didn't want to keep Tex waiting."

"That's right."

"Couldn't Tex wait a few minutes for you to go and get your key back? I recall him asking you about your friend."

Kitty's chin trembles. "I told you, I wasn't thinking about the key."

"But your shop, Kitty, and everything in it."

"I didn't care. I just wanted to get out of there."

"I don't believe you," I say. "What if Chester forgot to lock the door? What about all your equipment, and all your fabric, and all those costumes? You weren't concerned about any of that?"

"No," he says.

"I think you did go back, Kitty. I think the thought of all those costumes sitting there with an open door, and all your demanding clients the next day, all that work, all that income —"

"All right!" he says. "All right! I did go back, okay?"

"Okay. Go on."

He sniffles and fights back tears. "The door was open. Chester was in there. He was on the floor, already dead."

"How do you know?"

"I could tell. He wasn't moving. His eyes were open. There was blood all around him. Everything in the room felt like it was all ... stopped. That's why I ran out. I wanted to be safe again, and Tex was waiting downstairs for me."

"Did you touch anything before you left?"

Kitty says, "I took the key and locked the door."

Calm in a crisis, like me.

"Where was it?"

"On the sewing table. I guess Chester put it there. But I don't remember anything else."

I ask, "Why didn't you call the police right away?"

"Because I had a date with Tex."

Sex with Tex, above all else.

Kitty says, "But I was so upset I couldn't do anything, so we just slept together."

"And then you called the police anonymously this morning."

"Yes," says Kitty.

"From a phone booth in the hotel lobby."

"Yes, and they broke in and found Chester's body in my shop."

We sit there quietly a few seconds.

Then Kitty says, "Have the police got Paladin yet?"

"Why?"

"Why do you think?" he says. "He killed Chester. He's insane. You've seen him, and that was just over his collar tips."

Kitty and Fannie Mae, both accusing Paladin.

I say, "When you found Chester last night, were Paladin's collar tips already on his shirt?"

Kitty puts his head in his hands. "I can't answer any more questions."

"Were they or weren't they!" I almost sound like Branco, except an octave higher. Still, it's enough to make Kitty shrink back and answer me.

"Yes, they were there."

"Did you put them there?"

"Why would I do that?"

"To humiliate Paladin."

He says, "Huh?"

"Maybe you wanted to send him a message."

"What message?"

I say, "It was a chance to put Paladin in his place. Like, here's your new boyfriend, and now he's dead, and he's wearing your missing collar tips, and so much for your lucky charms."

Kitty looks at me dubiously. "You think I'd make all that up after finding Chester's body like that?"

"Maybe."

He says, "I'm glad I'm not as sick as you think I am. You're worse than the cops. When you came in here, I thought you wanted to help me, but now I see you want *me* to help *you.* Next thing you'll say that I killed him."

"That's always a possibility."

"If I was going to kill anyone, it wouldn't be Chester."

"Who would it be?"

"That's not what I meant!" he says.

So the delicate kitten has a bit of roar left.

I say, "What about Colt Remington? Would you like to kill him?"

"Who?" says Kitty.

"You two were friendly once."

"When?"

"Kitty, I know you gave his name to the cops, and I was there when they hauled him in. If you hadn't told them –"

"If I gave his name to the cops, then you can't call us friends, can you?"

"He lost a belt buckle recently."

"I don't know anything about it."

"I didn't say you did. I just mentioned it."

"You think just because I had Paladin's collar tips that I have Colt's belt buckle too?"

"The cops are searching your place as we speak."

Kitty trembles. "I guess they'll find it then."

"If you have it."

He says, "I took it the other night when I was at Colt's place."

And that, dear Kitty, is why everything else you've said so

far could also be a lie.

"Why did you take it?"

He shrugs." I don't know."

"Maybe you wanted something of Colt's you could hold near and dear to you? Or else humiliate him with? Maybe my sick theory about the collar tips isn't so far from the truth, eh, Kitty?"

He says, "I've got to get out of here. I've got clients who really need me right now."

I remember when I used to be able to say that – and mean it.

I turn to leave, and Kitty says, "Can you get me out of here?"

"Not up to me," I say, and leave the stuffy little chamber.

* * *

Outside the questioning room a uniformed cop escorts me back to Branco's office. I catch a smirk on the guy's face as sits me down outside the door. I wait there a while for Branco to call me in. Then a plainclothes cop comes by with a big pile of documents and takes it into Branco's office. It's only then that I realize Branco isn't in there, and his office door isn't locked either. The other cop comes out and closes the door behind him. Once the coast is clear, I slip into Branco's sanctum sanctorum.

The pile of documents lies on his desk. I'm about to start leafing through it when something else gets my attention. I hear voices coming from concealed speakers behind an array of large folding panels along one wall. I pull at the edge and the whole thing folds up, accordionlike. Behind the panels is a matrix of television monitors, twelve in all, and each of them shows the interior of an interrogation room similar to the one I've just been in with Kitty. Three of the rooms are occupied and in use, but only one of them gets my full atten-tion – the one in which Branco is questioning Colt Remington.

Trouble is, the sound is too low, and it's garbled by the

voices from the other occupied rooms. I find the master control panel, but it's a hacker's delight – way too many switches, lights, and buttons for someone like me, whose technology level pretty much stops at low-medium-high, like on a hairdryer. I find a volume control on the monitor that's showing Branco's room, and I adjust it until I can hear their voices above the babble from the other speakers.

Colt says to Branco, "I'm trying to cooperate with you, and I'm answering your questions. But you still haven't answered mine, which is, Why did you come and haul me out like that?"

Branco says, "I've explained to you that we wanted to talk to you and we couldn't locate you earlier."

"You didn't have to humiliate me in front of the crowd."

"We had no intention of humiliating anyone."

"That depends on your point of view."

Branco says, "Mr. Remington, we are in the process of questioning everybody who was at the Gunsmoke Saloon last night. That includes you."

"I don't see three hundred guys in here today."

"My crew is identifying and locating every person who was in the saloon last night."

"Good luck," says Colt.

"We'll do it."

"But for now, you singled me out."

"You and a few others," says Branco, "the people who are regulars, the ones who would most likely notice anything out of the ordinary. So, yes, it's true that I wanted to talk to certain people myself."

"Well, now, that touches my heart," says Colt, "to think that I'm some kind of special witness, just for you. Now that we finally understand each other, can I go? I've got a job."

"Speaking of which," says Branco, "what is your relationship to Bistany Evans?"

"She's the boss. I run the music."

"Anything personal between you?"

"Is that any of your business?"

Branco says, "Right now, everything about you is. You used to run a fight club for women."

"So?"

"Why did you give it up?"

"I was forced to."

"By who?"

Oh, Vito!

"My landlord," says Colt.

"Who's that?"

"I'm sure you already know, so why are you asking?"

"It's better if you tell me."

"My landlord is Heather Blossom. Was. Heather made me close down the club because she was afraid of the bad rep."

"Tell me about this club."

"You tell me," says Colt.

Branco reads from a paper in front of him. "The Boston Bobbie Boxers was a group of women who convened ostensibly to learn hand-to-hand combat."

Colt says, "Fancy language."

"Why did you do it?"

"That's a personal question."

"In the sense that I'm asking it of you, personally," says Branco, "then yes, it's a personal question."

"I wonder –" Colt leans forward and looks at Branco's badge. "What's your name? Branco? I wonder, Mr. Branco, would you be so curious if I was teaching men how to fight?"

"That would be completely different," says Branco.

"Why? Don't you teach your female officers how to fight?"

"Yes, but we don't arrange fights between strangers."

Colt says, "But my people weren't strangers. They were club members, they were consenting adults, and they weren't hurting anybody."

"Beating each other up?" says Branco. He's exasperated, shaking his head, the kind of thing he often does with me.

Colt says, "You can preach all you want, Lieutenant. But you don't get it. And the thing you don't get is exactly what makes other people trust me. For one thing, Lieutenant, I'm discreet. For another, I don't care who a person says he is or what he believes. I don't care what anybody says about himself. You can be nobody or you can be the President. You can be a cop or you can be Jesus Christ himself. But when you come to me for help, my only mission is to help you discover and actualize the person you really are. I don't care about the person coming in the door, talking the talk and walking the walk, because that's all an act. But the person who goes out the door has tasted reality. That's the kind of help I can give my clients."

Branco says, "That's some philosophy. How does Bistany Evans feel about it?"

"Bistany?"

"The woman you're working for at the convention."

"I'm just the DJ," says Colt, "freelance, not on the payroll. Bistany doesn't think it's good having someone like me officially connected to the convention. Imagine that? A bunch of homos dressed up like cowgirls, and she's worried about me. She even thought I was gay at first, but now she knows better. Bistany is just another ambitious bitch who wants to be overpowered."

"And you can do that for her."

"I do for her and she does for me."

"And what do you both end up with?"

"Glory, laud, and honor, Lieutenant. Fame and fortune. Isn't that what everyone wants? Even you, I bet, even you wouldn't mind getting your lousy fifteen minutes. Isn't that what what's-his-name said? Fifteen minutes of fame for everyone? But who wants a measly quarter hour? I'm thinking more along the lines of twenty years. That's what I want. Twenty years of fucking glory, laud, and honor."

Colt Remington must be high on something. He's talking like a maniac. Maybe he was high last night when he killed Chester. He took a break, went up to Kitty's place, and stabbed Chester in the back. But why? I'll figure that out later. For now, Colt Remington, you'll get your twenty years and then some. Maybe you think you'll settle in as King Prick at the

Walpole Correctional Facility. Except they'll break *you* in first, the way they do with every new colt that enters the corral. You might begin your stint as Gummy Jaws or Sorry Hole or, if you're really good, just plain old Fuck.

Branco says, "Thank you, Mr. Remington. I appreciate your cooperation. You can go now. Please don't leave town."

Then Branco leaves the interrogation room. Which probably means he's coming back to his office. The office where I am. The office where I am not supposed to be.

I quickly slide the big folding panels closed, then realize I've left the monitor volume on too loud. I get the panels open again, turn down the volume, and then try to slide the panels closed, and, of course, this time they jam! I push and pull and shove, and they won't budge. To hell with it! I turn to flee Branco's office and see his brawny frame filling the doorway.

"What are you doing?"

"Waiting for you," I say.

"How'd you get in here?"

"Door was open."

"Open? Or unlocked?"

"Same difference," I say.

"No," says Branco, "big difference."

He goes to his desk and sits down. There's a dark cloud over his brow. Daddy is displeased. He slides the pile of papers toward himself. "Have you looked at these too?"

I try to smile. "Not yet."

Branco almost smiles back. "Sit down," he says. "How much did you see?"

"Just the last few minutes."

"So you got to see how I do it."

Tantalizing.

He says, "Tell me what you found out from Mr. Chu."

I give him my report, a fact-by-fact account of the session with Kitty. I skip the emotional interludes.

When I'm done, he says, "That's pretty good work. We'll get that Tex fellow in here for a statement, and I'll radio my people at Mr. Chu's shop to bring in that belt buckle."

But the one fact that satisfies Branco most is that Kitty admitted going back and finding Chester's body last night, but then waited until this morning to call the cops.

Branco says, "Amazing how you can get people to talk."

"Thanks to the styling chair."

"Maybe my crew should learn hairdressing?"

"Or just a lighter touch."

Without reply, Branco opens the center drawer of his desk and pulls out a remote control. He pushes a button on it and the panels on the wall slide back smoothly. No wonder they jammed on me. I was probably grinding the gears. Branco pushes another button and a monitor lights up. (It's so easy when you know how.) Then the final button, which provides an instant digital playback of my session with Kitty.

There I am, "on the record", entering the questioning room, and there's Kitty leaping into my arms, pawing me left and right, weeping into my shoulder, gripping me like he's going down for the third time and he's taking me with him.

Branco says, "Is that the light touch you suggest I use?"

"How'd you know about that?"

"There were other eyes watching," he says.

He turns off the video and sits there with a big smirk.

Okay, fine. He gets to grill a he-man like Colt Remington, while I get to console a poison-petalled cherry blossom like Kitty. Is that distinction between me and the cop clear enough?

I say, "I still did good work."

He says reluctantly, "Yes, you did."

"So maybe you can return the favor?"

"Maybe."

"Can you confirm something I heard this morning at The Castle?"

"Depends," he says.

"Fannie Mae Knox told me she got an anonymous phone call telling her Chester Wright was dead. Then she says she called the police to verify it."

Branco says, "She did call us, and we took a report. But

we didn't release any information to her."

"Not even to verify Chester's death?"

"No."

"Why didn't you tell me that at the shop this morning?"

"First of all," says Branco, "I don't have to tell you any-thing. Secondly, we were still trying to verify that alleged anonymous phone call to her."

"And now?"

Branco hesitates, as if calculating how much to tell me. "Okay," he says. "We got a list of all incoming calls to the hotel this morning. We determined where every call was directed – which room, which office, and so on."

"And?"

"A call was directed to Fannie Mae Knox's hotel room at exactly the time she claims it happened."

I say, "Nice to know she watches the clock so closely. Who called her?"

"It originated from a public phone in the hotel lobby." Branco smiles. "The same public phone Wang Chu used for his tip-off to us."

"Well, well," I say. "Which call carne in first?"

"Mr. Chu's."

"So Kitty called you, then he called Fannie Mae."

"Maybe," says Branco. "There's a few minutes between the calls, which means someone else could have made the call to her."

"Hey," I say. "I just thought of something. Did Fannie Mae actually pick up the call made to her room?"

"What do you mean?"

"Did she answer the phone, or did the voice mail kick in?"

"The hotel report didn't say. Why?"

"Maybe she phoned herself from the lobby."

Branco smiles. "I'll check on it," he says. "Meanwhile, I hear you had a little problem last night."

"What kind of problem?"

"A drinking problem."

"Who told you that? Heather Blossom?"

"Among others," says Branco. "Look, Stan, off the record I can use your help, but you're not going to be any use to anyone with a drinking problem."

"Unreliable," I say.

Branco nods. "Sometimes it happens when people have too much time on their hands."

"So I was right."

"About what?"

"Someone drugged me last night to give the impression I'm unreliable."

"Drugged you?" says Branco. "With what?"

I tell him, "Heather claimed it was fermented lemon, something from Italy."

Branco smiles. "*Verbena fresca morta*," he says smoothly.

The sound of it goes right through me.

Vito, baby, talk Italian to me!

He says, "That's not a drug, Stan. My grandfather used to drink it for his digestion. The wormwood will knock you for a loop. You can't get it in this country."

"Heather bootlegs it," I say. "Funny how she didn't mention *that* to you – just that I have a drinking problem."

"Interesting point," says Branco. "Tell you what, Stan, you just keep mixing with these people, nose around, see what else you can find out. But be careful. this isn't a game. It's a murder investigation."

"Have you found Paladin yet?"

"No, why?"

I say, "He seems to be everyone's favorite."

"Meaning?"

"Fannie Mae Knox and Kitty think he killed Chester."

"Which is exactly why I want to find him."

"I'll do it," I say.

Branco grunts. "Just like that?"

"Sure."

He leans forward. "Do you know where he is?"

"No, but how hard can it be?"

He grunts again: Tyro dick thinks he can find someone

my crew can't even locate.

I say, "Funny thing, Lieutenant, all I could manage in your eyes yesterday was gay trinkets. What a difference a day makes."

Branco glowers. "You know, Stan, someday you might try looking at the world over your other shoulder, the one without the big chip on it."

"What chip?"

"The one that's imprinted with the saga of what a sensitive person you are and what a bully I am – how I don't understand you, how nobody understands you, and nobody really cares about you, and on and on, and to me it's all bullshit. I know a lot has come down between us, and you saved my life, but ..."

He pauses, catches his breath.

I say, "You almost sound sorry about that part."

The poor guy really looks exhausted.

He says, "I'm not sorry about anything. I'm just a little tired right now."

"Is everything all right at home?"

He bristles. "Sure, why?"

"Maybe you're not getting enough sleep or something."

"What are you driving at?" he says.

Does Costanza keep you up all night? *is what I'm driving at.*

"Nothing," I say.

There's another pause. Then Branco says, "Sometimes you get so damn wrapped up in yourself, you don't even know when someone cares about you. Look, just forget it, okay? I'm sorry I brought it up."

"No, I want to know, Lieutenant. Tell me. Talk to me."

"I've done enough talking," he says. "If I yap any more, I'll sound like you, and I've got work to do."

He puts his attention to the pile of papers on his desk.

I say, "But I want to talk."

Silence.

"Lieutenant?"

"Go find someone who wants to listen."

I say, "So I guess I'll just keep nosing around then."

"You do that," he says, completely absorbed in the documents on his desk. "Just keep out of trouble."

"Are any of your crew heading back downtown?"

"Hmm?"

"Thought maybe I could get a lift."

"You can call a cab downstairs."

12.

FORGET THE CAB. I take the Orange Line to Back Bay Station, then walk to Newbury Street and Snips Salon. I want to see Nikki, partly for comic relief, partly to reground myself after that session with Branco. All right, I know he cares about me. He has to, right? I saved his life. But to say the words? *Someone cares about you.*

It's mid-afternoon and the salon is busy-busy. Nicole is working, and I stop at her manicure table.

"Having a nice holiday weekend, doll?"

"Benjamin phoned," she says without looking up from her work. "He's very concerned about you."

"I'm fine."

"But he doesn't know that, Stanley. You should call him and put him at ease. It's the least you can do after last night."

Nicole's client looks at me askance.

I reassure her. "It's okay. We're family."

Nicole says to me, "Where would you have ended up if Benjamin hadn't been there? In some emergency room? And then they'd call me as next of kin and I'd have to come running out at some ungodly hour to get you home."

"But you would have come, right?"

"Grumblingly."

"I hope that's not a word from your writing class."

Nicole puts down her cuticle trimmer, a sign that she's

serious. "Stanley," she says, "if you don't phone Benjamin right now, I'm going to prevent all further relations between you, since you obviously don't appreciate his true worth."

She picks up the trimmer and resumes her work.

I say, "I thought you only cared about net worth."

"You can use the phone in the office."

"Like I need your permission, doll?"

I go and call Benjy.

"Penny!" he cries.

Doesn't sound worried to me.

"All better from last night?"

"I'm fine, Benjy."

"That's good. When I left you this morning you weren't in top form."

"Or in bottom form either."

"I'll take you either way, Penny. Hey, I just heard about that cowboy who was killed. It sounds awful, stabbed in the back with sewing shears."

"How'd you hear about it?"

"I have my sources," he says.

Benjy does have an incredible knack for finding out confidential information. Back when he was burning hair, his clients used to accuse him of mind-reading. More recently, the owner of an local independent rag created a job specially for him, as Information Deity. From there, who knows?

Benjy says, "Did you ever meet the victim?"

"Kind of," I say, trying to sound vague.

"What did you think?"

"About what?"

"About him?"

"He seemed like a nice guy," I say. "I'm sorry he's dead."

"Then I'm sorry too, Penny. Will you be working on the murder now?"

"Can't tell," I say.

"But we'll still have the cookout Monday?"

"*We*, Benjy?"

"Excuse me, Penny. *You*. Will you still have *your* cookout?"

"I don't know," I say. "We'll have to play it by ear."

"We?" says Benjy. "Or you?"

"Oh, all right. *We!* Okay?"

The office door opens and Nicole comes in. "I hope I'm interrupting something very private and important."

"I'll only be a minute, doll."

"Take your time, darling."

In unison, Benjy says, "Take your time," but without the darling. That's some relief.

Nicole says, "I'll just sit here and listen."

Benjy says something else.

"Sorry, Benjy, what did you say?"

"If that's Nicole, tell her hi."

"Benjy says hi."

Nicole says, "How is he doing after a dreadful night with you?"

"Sorry, what, Benjy?"

"I said, what are you doing tonight?"

"Probably working on the case."

"Do you need any help?" he says.

Meanwhile, Nicole has taken out a cigarette and is snapping desperately at her empty lighter.

"Could I have a light, darling?"

"Sure, doll, but with what?"

Benjy says, "With anything, Penny. I'll do anything."

Nicole says, "With a match from your pocket."

"What match?" I say.

"I detect the shape of a matchbook in your shirt pocket."

I look, and sure enough, there's a book of matches in there.

"Where did that come from?"

Benjy says, "Penny, what's going on?"

Nicole raises an eyebrow. "Becoming a bit forgetful, darling?"

"Nikki, I honestly don't know how that got there."

"You must have put it there, dear."

"Why would I?"

"Penny?"

Nicole says, "You'd know better than I. Now, would you please light me?"

I fish out the matches. The cover is black with white lettering that says The Cubbyhole.

I light Nicole's cigarette, then examine the matchbook. There's no address, no phone number, nothing inside. Just those two words on the cover.

Benjy says, "Penny, are you there?"

"I'm here, Benjy. I'll call you right back."

"No, I'll hold. I like three-ways, especially on the phone."

Nicole says, "If you can't remember where you got it, then who have you been with today?"

Benjy says, "Are you at a VD clinic?"

"Well?" says Nicole. "Have you seen anyone who might have put it there?"

"Oh, wow!" I say. "Kitty!"

"Kitty?" says Benjy.

"But Branco frisked him."

Benjy says, "What's going on?"

Nicole says, "Who is Kitty?"

Echo from Benjy: "Who's Kitty?"

I tell them, "Kitty is Wang Chu, Boston's pre-eminent costume designer for the local country-western aficionados."

"Oh," says Nicole, "like Nudie was in Los Angeles."

"Nudie?" I say.

Benjy says, "Herman Nudie. The Christian Dior of western wear in the 1940s and 50s."

Is there anything Benjy doesn't know?

I say, "I don't think Kitty is that famous."

And I don't want to think too much on where this matchbook has been. More important is where it's going to take me. But there's no information on it except that curious name. And where do I turn when pondering life's imponderables?

"Benjy?" I say.

"Waiting," comes his singing reply.

"Where is The Cubbyhole?"

"Oh, Penny, yeah, talk dirty to me!"

"I need a phone number for a place called The Cubby-hole."

"Cute name," he says. "What is it? A private club?"

"Looks like it," I say, still fingering the matchbook. "That's all you want? A phone number? That's a cinch."

"When can you find out?"

"Right now, while we talk. Start my little search engine here, click advanced, click Boolean … You know, Penny, with a few lessons, you can do this kind of thing yourself."

"I'd rather have you do it, so I know it's right."

"Sure," says Benjy, then, "Aha! Unlisted and unpublished. No wonder you couldn't find it."

Do I tell him I didn't even try?

"But I have my sources," he says and continues. "Typey-typey-type, dum-dee-dum, doo-dee-doo …"

"Benjy?"

"Mmm?"

"Why the sound effects?"

"Am I doing that again? I don't even hear myself. Okay, here we go."

He gives me the number for The Cubbyhole.

"Thanks, Benjy. I owe you, again."

"Don't mention it, Penny. What are friends for?"

"For more than favors."

"Really?" he says, with that extra-hopeful sound in his voice.

"Bye, Benjy."

"Farewell, Penny."

I hang up.

Nicole says, "He's devoted to you."

"I know."

"I wonder why," she says.

"Because he wants a direct path to you."

"What are you going to do about it? You can't just keep leading him on."

"I'm not leading him on."

"You provoke him, Stanley."

"It's just fun."

"It's more than that."

"Then what should I do?"

"Marry him."

"Nikki, marriage needs more than provocation."

"Not much," says Nicole.

"Okay, I'll admit that Benjy could be an ideal spouse."

"Well then?"

"For someone else."

"Whatever you do, Stanley, don't ever tell him he deserves someone better."

"Why not?"

"Because it's cruel to encourage a person and then make yourself unworthy of him."

"Isn't it better than saying straight out that he doesn't interest you?"

"But he does interest you, doesn't he?"

"Not sexually."

"Are you sure?" says Nicole.

"We haven't done anything."

"Why not?"

"The urge isn't there."

"Maybe you're afraid."

"Of what?"

"Of finding yourself involved with someone who in no way resembles the trophy-man you had before. Of having to admit that you're no longer mourning the one you lost."

I tell her, "I just don't find Benjy sexy."

"Don't you?" she says. "I do. If I were a gay man –"

"But you're not," I say. "Look, Nikki, I like Benjy a lot. Maybe I even love him, in a best-friend kind of way, second to you, of course. But I can't marry him for that, just the way I can't marry you for it."

Nicole shudders. "I see your point."

"Do you?"

"You and Benjamin are at an impasse."

"Another word from your writing course?"

"At least I'm doing something productive with my spare time."

"And I'm not?"

Nicole says, "I'm writing a pilot for a TV sitcom."

"Profound."

"I've set it in a salon just like ours. I'm calling the series Snips."

"Clever."

"You have to admit, Stanley, with the clientele that comes in here –"

"Never mind the ones who work here, doll."

"Present company excluded."

"Present company gets star billing."

"Thank you, darling. The premise of my series is that truth is stranger than fiction."

"Will there be drag queens?"

"Do you think they're necessary?"

"Only if they're straight."

Nicole draws deeply on her cigarette, smiles in pleasure, then exhales. "Why this sudden preoccupation with transvestites?"

"I want to know the identity of a particular Boston monarch."

"That should be easy enough," she says.

"Have you ever interviewed a drag queen?"

"You'll never find out that way. The whole purpose for concealment is so that other people won't know who you are."

"Exactly, doll. So what can I do?"

Nicole says, "Just follow the person home."

"Then what?"

"Look on the doorbell."

"What if there's no name?"

"Stanley, I can't do all of your detective work for you. Isn't it obvious?"

"You mean, if I know where she lives, that's a start, and

just continue from there?"

"I'm surprised you didn't think of it. So rudimentary." Nicole looks at me intently. "Darling, you seem to be trying so hard at this new career that your thinking is becoming faulty. And you're not having much fun either. You know, it's perfectly all right to give up when something isn't working out."

"So you and Branco can call me a quitter."

"Vito again," she says. "Well, never mind that. Just remember, there's nothing noble or glorious in struggling."

"You must really want me back here in the salon."

"You have to admit, Stanley, you were much happier here."

"I think you just want new material for your sitcoms."

"Well, there's that too," she says. "I do want a sexually frustrated thirty-something gay male character, but an interesting one."

"Use Benjy."

"Oh, I plan to, but not for *that*."

She rolls the burning ember off the end of her cigarette, then tamps it lightly until it's extinguished. No messy, broken, smoldering butts in Nicole's ashtray.

"Where are you off to now, darling?"

"I've got to find this place," I say, still fingering the matchbook from Kitty.

"Good luck," she says, and she leaves me alone in the office.

I dial the number Benjy found for The Cubbyhole. A woman answers the phone, which surprises me.

I ask, "Is this The Cubbyhole?"

"Whaddya want?"

"What's your address?"

"Ain't one."

"How do I get there?"

"Up to you."

"But this is The Cubbyhole, right?"

"Whaddya want?"

Return to Go. Try again.

"I have a very important meeting with someone, and I lost the directions."

"What kinda meeting?"

"It's personal," I say.

Silence.

"Business," I say. "Very *personal* business, and I really can't afford to miss it."

That seems to satisfy her, and she gives me directions to the place. It's on Beacon Hill, somewhere within a maze of right turns, left turns, halfway downs, alleys, and dead ends.

Then, I don't know why I do it, but I stupidly ask for a street address again. The woman says nothing and hangs up on me.

Nicole is right: I'm not thinking clearly at all.

13.

I FIND THE CUBBYHOLE on Beacon Hill, in an unmarked alleyway off one of the unmarked streets in the vast tangle of one-ways and dead ends that cover the hill. The entrance is also unmarked, basically a doorway into the basement of the building. Like a twenty-first-century speakeasy, the simple fact is, if you don't know where The Cubbyhole is, you'll never happen upon it. I'm lucky enough to find it with explicit directions.

The door creaks as I open it. Inside, the place is dimly lit and damp. It's basically a converted cellar that reeks of years of spilled booze and smoke. There's no one visible in the place, and all is quiet except for the distant squeak of an ancient ventilating system and the faint sound of recorded jazz from the 1930s. There's a tiny bar against one wall, so I go there and take one of three vacant stools. A few minutes later, a middle-aged woman emerges from behind a beaded curtain.

"Whaddya have?" she says, squinting her pale blue Irish eyes at me. By her voice, I know she's the one who answered the phone earlier.

"Rolling Rock," I say. "In the bottle." This isn't the kind of place to order a martini.

She makes a strange sound, like I said something lewd in a foreign language, then she fishes around in a cold chest behind the bar and pulls out a beer. She snaps off the cap and bangs the long-necked bottle on the counter, where it quickly frosts over. It's been buried in ice, literally, which to my taste is the best temperature for any beer. (You connoisseurs enjoy your tepid brews.)

I pay for the beer, and she disappears behind the beaded curtain. I swing myself around on the barstool and look the place over. Except for the barstools, there's not a chair in sight on the small floor. There are, however, several tiny booths around the perimeter of the place, each one just big enough two people, tete-a-tete. It's the kind of place you'd come to "speak easy" and not be overheard. I wonder how the owner got it zoned. Or maybe it isn't. Maybe it's been this way since Colonial days, which would partly explain the secrecy.

I hear a quiet rustle in the farthest corner of the place, then a creak of wood. One booth back there is situated so that its seats are completely hidden. I get up and stroll over. If it turns out to be a cat-sized Beacon Hill rat, I'll join it for a chaw and a talk.

It isn't a rat, but a black-clad, sleek-haired dancing cowboy named Vaslav Paladin. A killer cowboy. Except that Paladin doesn't look dangerous. He looks scared.

His greeting: "What the fuck are you doing here?"

"Having a beer."

"How did you find me?"

Typical of Paladin, the center of the universe.

"Who says I'm looking for you?"

"This isn't the kind of place where people just drop in."

"Obviously," I say.

"So how did you find it?"

"Someone told me."

"Who?"

"Whom do you think?"

"Christ!" he says, probably offended by my grammar. "Look, I don't give a fuck one way or another."

"Kitty told me."

"Kitty? Right," he says, but he's obviously relieved. "No

fuck either way."

"You know from personal experience?"

"You think I'd get personal with Kitty?"

"He makes your costumes," I say. "That's personal."

Paladin sneers. "And she blows me sometimes. That's personal too, for some people." He waits for my reaction.

I take the seat opposite him, like we have a rendezvous. That's the feeling this place has, that you come here to draw up contracts in the carnal realm.

I say, "Amazing what you can find in someone's laundry."

"What's that supposed to mean?"

"Kitty told me he found your collar tips in your laundry. After all that noise you made about someone stealing them yesterday, it turns out they were in one of your shirt pockets."

"Maybe Kitty was lying."

"Maybe you are. You're both pretty good at it."

"So why did she send you here?"

"Kitty didn't send me, but he did give me this."

I show him the matchbook.

He takes it and smiles. "The little she-cat. Did she find this in my laundry too? When did you see her?"

"This morning, at police headquarters."

"She's with the police?"

"That's right. But why do you keep saying 'she'?"

"It fits, doesn't it? What's she doing in the pigpen? Besides bruising her knees."

"You really don't know?"

Paladin says, "I'm just sitting here minding my own business."

"When's the last time you saw Chester?"

Paladin pulls back.

I say, "Do you know what happened?"

He lowers his head. His whole body seems to shrink a bit. He says, "I heard it on the news."

"What news?"

"I don't know," says Paladin. "I just heard it, okay?"

But Chester's death hasn't been broadcast yet. Benjy

knows, but that's Benjy. So who told Paladin?

I say, "Do you know how Chester was killed?"

Paladin squirms. "He was shot."

"Bad guess."

"Maybe I heard wrong."

"You didn't hear anything."

"Maybe I'm upset," he says, "and I don't remember."

"Why are you hiding here?"

"Who's hiding?"

"You're acting defensive, like you're afraid of something."

He says, "I'm afraid of you boring me to death."

I tell him, "If you know anything about Chester's death, you've got to go to the police."

"What, are you working for them or something?"

"Kind of."

"Kind of?" says Paladin. "What the fuck does 'kind of' mean? Like, if I let you suck my dick you kind of *won't* squeal on me? Fuckin' junior pig!"

The woman appears suddenly from behind the beaded curtain.

"Everything okay out here?"

"It's fine," I say. "Everything's fine."

"Well, keep it down," she says.

"Right," I say. "Down."

The woman retreats behind the curtain.

I say to Paladin, "Just for your information, Chester was stabbed in the back."

Paladin's jaw drops and he sits bolt upright. "Who says?"

"The police."

"But he was on his back."

That gets *me* to sit up.

"So you were there," I say.

Paladin looks around, as though somebody might come out of the woodwork after him. Then he slouches back into the bench. Even in the darkness of The Cubbyhole I can see he looks sad.

"Yeah," he says, "I was there. But I didn't kill him."

"What happened?"

He stares at his folded hands, then says, "Last night at Gunsmoke, Chester disappeared. He does that sometimes, goes off for a while. I don't ask him where he's been. It's none of my business, not yet. We're still getting to know each other." Paladin stops suddenly. "I can't believe he's gone."

"Keep talking."

He grimaces but continues, as if it relieves him to be telling this story, even if it's to me. "Last night Chester didn't come back. I figured, this time it's going to be a little longer. But then he never came back while I was at Gunsmoke. I went to the hotel thinking maybe he went there, but no. So I waited. I tried to sleep, but I couldn't."

"Did you guys argue about anything?"

"No, why?"

"You two looked a little tense last night at Gunsmoke."

"Nothing important," says Paladin. "But when Chester didn't come back to the hotel, I went out looking for him, back to Gunsmoke. It was after three, and the whole place was dark, all except for a light in one of the upstairs windows. I knew that was Kitty's shop, so I went up there. The door was locked. I knocked, I called out, then, I don't know why, but something told me to break in, so that's what I did."

He pauses. His chin trembles. He looks at me crossly, as if I'm trying to make him cry.

"Chester was inside," he says, "on the floor, on his back." Paladin shakes his head. He blubbers a bit as he tries to continue. "There was blood all around him. I knew he was dead."

"Why didn't you call the police?"

"I don't know. *I don't know!*" he wails.

"Did you touch anything? Move anything?"

"No," he says. "I thought about taking the collar tips off him, like some kind of souvenir, but I knew I'd never be able to wear them again. So I just stood there and looked at him. I couldn't even touch him. I know I should've done something, but I couldn't. I just ran. And now I feel like shit."

I ask, "Do you know who might have done that to him?"

Paladin says, "It had to be Kitty. Every time I turned around yesterday, Chester was with her. I don't know what they were up to, but Chester's dead now."

"Kitty thinks you killed him."

Paladin says, "Maybe the little bitch doesn't have it in her after all."

"But even real women kill," I say.

Paladin clenches his jaw and thinks about this. "You know something?" he says. "I forgot all about her."

"Who?"

"The bitch!" he says.

"Which one?"

I can't keep track of them all.

"Bistany," he says with a hiss. "Bistany killed Chester."

"But why?"

He mimics me, whining, "But why?" Then he's back to tough. "Figures she'd stab him in the back, the lying bitch! That's not even her real name. She's from Los Angeles. She used to be an agent out there, for actors, went by the name Ramona Warwitch."

"Bistany Evans?"

"Yes," says Paladin.

"Who told you this?"

"Who do you think?" he says. "Chester! That's where he met Bistany, in L.A."

"Chester knew her?"

"I'm telling you, she was his agent. Except she went by the name Ramona Warwitch back then. Chester wanted to get into the movies – you know, anytime they needed a guy with a bad foot. But nothing ever happened with that. Then there was some problem with money – seven, eight million dollars missing."

"Ramona took it?"

Paladin says, "Probably. But there was definitely a pile of money gone. And there was another woman, Vera something."

"When did all this happen?"

He falters. "I'm not sure," he says. His eyes dart nervously. "All I know is by the time Ramona arrived in Boston, she was Bistany Evans. She lost a lot of weight and dyed her hair, but Chester knew from her eyes that Bistany Evans was really his agent Ramona Warwitch. Dumb bitch didn't even bother to get colored contact lenses."

"So what did Chester do?"

"I'll tell you one thing he didn't do. He didn't blackmail her. She's the one who came to him and tried to make a deal."

"What deal?"

Paladin shakes his head. "I've said enough now."

"You can't stop!"

"No?" he says. "You gonna *make* me talk?"

I say, "Any chance you knew Bistany Evans separately from Chester?"

"What!"

"Did you?"

"You don't quit, do you?" he says. He chews his lip a while, then says, "In a way the whole thing is my fault."

"What whole thing?"

He says, "I used to tend bar at the Four Seasons. About a year ago Bistany Evans walked in, said she was new in town, looking to build a network. I told her I was a dancer and she seemed to like that – maybe a holdover from her agent days – and so she came by Gunsmoke to see me there. That's where she met Heather. Next thing you know, the two of them are planning Mucho Macho Honcho together."

"Just like that?"

"Sometimes things fall into place," he says. "Bistany spent a lot of time at Gunsmoke, planning the convention with Heather and all, and that's how she eventually ran into Chester. It had to happen sooner or later, and it did."

"And so she struck a deal with him."

Paladin says, "That's where I stop."

"Why? Because the deal includes you in some way? You're a fixture at Gunsmoke, after all. And maybe now because of this secret deal with Bistany, Chester is dead."

Paladin tries hard not to cry, but one gasping sob escapes. "If I didn't invite Bistany to Gunsmoke, Chester would still be alive." He clenches his jaw to hold back another sob.

"That's some story, Paladin. Maybe you'll get it right by the time you tell the police."

"You don't believe me?"

"After all the other lies you've thrown at me?"

"This time I'm telling the truth."

"Right," I say. "Tell me, how do you get by now?"

"Get by?"

"What do you do for money?"

He smiles weakly. "I found an uncle with deep pockets."

"How did he feel about Chester?"

For a moment Paladin looks stunned or maybe ashamed of something. "No," he says. "No more."

"I heard you were going to leave Chester after the finals. Was that your doting uncle's idea?"

"Where'd you hear that?"

"Is it true?"

"Who told you?"

"Fannie Mae Knox."

He sniggers. "The pink flamingo. Do you believe all the shit people throw at you?"

Case in point.

"I'll tell you one thing," he says. "When I break up with someone, I do it to his face. I don't kill my ex's, and I certainly don't stab them in the back."

"But you were planning to leave Chester."

"No!" he yells. Then, suddenly, quietly, "In the beginning, yes, that was part of the deal, but I never figured on liking the guy. It all backfired. I wasn't supposed to like him."

Paladin leans toward me, across the tiny table, and breaks down into quiet sobs. I move toward him and hold his heaving torso. It reminds me of Rafik, the strength and the litheness of it. His shuddering body gets me slightly aroused. Christ! This is Chester's lover, and Chester's dead, and now I'm sitting in this dive, getting hard with the guy crying on my shoulder.

The woman comes out from behind the curtain again. "What's going on out here? Hey, none o' that! I got a business to run. Youse two wanna carry on, take it somewheres else."

I reply softly, "It's under control. He just lost a close friend."

She makes a sour face. "Well, I'm sorry," she says, "but keep it quiet. And put some space between youse two." Then she disappears again.

I ask Paladin, "What about the deal?"

He just shakes his head.

"Whom was it with?"

No reply.

"You've got to go to the police."

"And what?" he says. "Get arrested? They always suspect the lover first. Why should I be arrested for something I didn't do?"

"Because it's the only way to stop Bistany."

"You tell them," he says. "I'll take my chances here."

"If I found you, so will she."

He says, "It's a risk I'm willing to take."

"Why won't you go to the police?"

"Because I can't!"

"Are you protecting someone?"

Paladin says, "Maybe someone is protecting me."

"Who?"

No reply.

"Did you call anyone after you found Chester's body last night?"

Paladin is mute. Mute and scared.

I ask him again, "Whom did you call?"

Paladin says, "Look, Tinkerbell, just go away."

"It's for your own good."

"Says who? You and the law?"

I've got to call Branco right away. Call me a snitch, but they've got to arrest Bistany Evans, if only to get her hoofs off the public byways. But first they have to talk to Paladin. I look around the place for a public phone, but there's none. I go to the bar and call the woman out to ask her if I can use her phone. She refuses, big surprise. I don't even bother asking her to call the police for me.

I leave Paladin in The Cubbyhole and go outside. After the confinement in there, the afternoon air clears my head a bit. But I still need a phone. Why didn't I take that cell phone when Benjy offered it? I dash through the maze of streets, down the hill to the commercial area on Charles Street. In the lobby of a snazzy boutique hotel, I find a pay phone and dial Branco's number. He comes on the line, and I tell him breathlessly that I found Paladin. I give him frantic directions to The Cubbyhole.

He says, "You stay with him until we get there!"

"I'm not there!" I say, but Branco has already hung up.

I go back to the Cubbyhole. The door is locked now. I knock and bang, but there's no answer. Can you blame them?

When the police arrive, they nearly batter down the door before the blue-eyed woman opens it. They ask her where Paladin is, and she shrugs and says he left the place right after I did.

The spirit of the speakeasy thrives on Beacon Hill.

Branco turns on me. "What the hell were you doing coming here on your own? You told me you didn't know where Paladin was hiding out."

"I didn't."

"Then how did you end up here?"

"I was following a lead."

"What lead?" he says. "From who?"

Forget the grammar. I hold out the matchbook.

Branco takes it. "What's this?"

"Kitty put it in my shirt when I was at headquarters this morning. I didn't find it until later. You can ask Nicole.

She saw it in my pocket. So I came here and found Paladin."

"Why didn't you call me first?"

"Because I didn't know what I was going to find here. You

want me to call you before I tie my shoes, just in case there's a clue underneath?"

Bad joke. Branco is seething.

I tell him, "Paladin is either running from someone, or he was waiting for someone."

"Running or waiting," says Branco. "Which is it?"

"Well, he seemed relieved that it was Kitty who gave me that matchbook."

"Relieved?" says Branco. "Seemed? Just tell me who!"

"I don't know! Paladin didn't say, but he told me about Bistany Evans, and that's why I think it's her. *She!*"

Branco glowers. "Did Paladin mention any other names? Maybe mine? My wife's? Why don't you pick a name out of a hat?"

"Lieutenant, Bistany Evans is from Los Angeles, which is also where Chester Wright is from. She used to be his agent there. Bistany is also Heather Blossom's chief spokeswoman for the convention – the same convention where Chester and Paladin were about to win a big dancing prize."

Branco shakes his head, like he's trying very hard to keep his temper in check. Why doesn't he understand me?

"Look," I say, "here it is in a nutshell. Bistany Evans and Chester Wright are both from L.A., and they both end up here in Boston at the same convention, and now Chester turns up dead. I don't think it's just a coincidence."

"No? Then how about an accident?" says Branco. "Or maybe you're the accident."

"It's not my fault Paladin got away."

"Then whose fault is it!"

By now the other cops are noticing Branco's shouting.

He takes a deep breath. Then he speaks in very controlled syllables, quietly, so the others can't hear. "I don't care whose fault anything is. This is about you. Your job is to get facts, not collect butterflies. But that's all you're doing, Stan. You're flapping around. And now, because of that, we've lost a crucial suspect."

"I was trying to help you."

"I need reliable help."

That word again, and no fermented lemon now.

I say, "Was I reliable in that fire?"

Branco winces. "Playing your trump out here, in front of my crew?"

"That's not how I meant it."

"All right," he says, "I owe you my life. Now what?"

"You don't owe me a thing. I'm sorry I brought it up."

"But you did."

"I don't like being called unreliable."

"All right!" he says. "Maybe I was wrong to say that."

"Maybe," I say.

He looks at the ground, then he looks up at me. Poor guy. I don't mean to torment him. Honest.

"I don't know how you do it," he says, "but you can get me more riled up more than the people who work for me."

"Maybe it's because I'm not afraid of losing my job."

"Easy for you to say."

"I was like this before I got my money."

"You're goddam right about that," says Branco. "From now on, you take your lead from me. Got that? You're a free agent, but no more improvising in my territory. I just hope I don't end up regretting this whole thing."

"What whole thing?"

"You," he says. "Getting involved with you."

Then he turns away and heads back to his cruiser.

I call out, "Hey, what about that matchbook?"

He doesn't reply. He doesn't even turn around. All he does is wave the hand that's holding the matchbook in the air: Everything's fine now, I've got the evidence, thanks a lot, go away and leave me alone.

14.

ON MY WAY BACK HOME, I stop by Snips Salon. It's well after six o'clock, and the place is finally closing up for the holiday weekend. Nicole is in the back office, having a smoke and a drink – bourbon, rocks. I pour one for myself and join her.

"I think Branco's having a nervous breakdown.

She says, "Instigated by you, no doubt."

"Whose side are you on?"

"How many times did you see Vito today?"

"Three, so far."

"That would do it," says Nicole.

"He yelled at me in front of his crew."

She says, "It shows how much Vito trusts you."

"What does?"

"If he didn't trust you, Stanley, he wouldn't expose his feelings like that, in public."

"Speaking of exposed feelings, Branco's looking more and more like an exhausted sex-slave."

"But that's good, isn't it?" says Nicole. "For him?"

"I can't make heads or tails of it."

"Of what?" says Nicole.

"It's like he's in a cage. He's trying to act tamer, but instead he's even wilder."

Nicole says, "I think you're the one who's wilder, darling, in your imagination. Vito is extremely happy with his wife."

"But he's only doing it to protect her."

"Doing what?"

"Having sex all the time."

"To protect her?" says Nicole.

"So the real world can't see what he did."

Nicole's eyes cross slightly.

I explain. "Branco serves his wife's endless demands because he feels responsible. First, he deflowered her. Then, as if that didn't induce enough guilt, when she was supposed to burgeon with the splendor of young motherhood, instead she became a voracious sex demon."

"Tell me again," says Nicole, "who is having the nervous breakdown?"

"It shows on his face, Nikki. Something isn't right."

"I know what isn't right," she says. "You're still annoyed with him for getting married. After saving his life you hoped things might be different between you two. Well, they are different, Stanley. The man will be indebted to you for as long as he lives, but that does not obligate him to become your lover."

"Nikki! Lover? Branco? With me? It would be the worst thing in the world. Just look at how we don't get along. We'd kill each other. It would never work. You're absolutely wrong."

Nicole says blithely, "It sounds like a love story to me."

"An absurd love story."

"Is there another kind?" she says. "Never mind, dear. Once you find someone –"

"I don't want someone, Nikki. I had someone, and that's enough. I'm not sure I even want another cat."

"As you wish, Stanley. What's on for tonight?"

"Branco wants me to keep nosing around the cowboy klatch."

Nicole smiles. "*Plus ça change ...*"

I ask her, "What about you?"

"I'm working on my sitcom."

"Alone?"

"For the time being," she says.

I finish my drink, we say good night, and I head home.

* * *

By the time I get in, it's almost eight. There's a message from Benjy, so I call him back. That boy has countless phones and phone numbers too, yet he always picks up as though he's reclining at horne, a lad of leisure, when in fact he might be lunching with a State House politician, or plowing through a deadline at work, or having steam room sex.

I tell him what happened at The Cubbyhole.

He says, "So you found the killer?"

"I found who I thought was the killer."

"Don't you mean whom?" he says.

"It's *who*, Benjy. Trust me."

"How do you do it, Penny? Know when to use *who* and *whom?*"

"It's like you and computers," I say. "It's just there."

"So what happened with the killer? Weren't you scared?"

"He got away, and no I wasn't."

"Brave Penny," he says.

"No," I say. "Foolish Penny. Actually, I don't think Paladin killed Chester. But I *am* curious about The Cubbyhole. Could you maybe –"

"Your query is my command," says Benjy, and I hear his fingers already tapping on his computer keys.

I ask, "Where are you, anyway?"

"I'll tell you where I am," he says, "if you tell me what you're wearing."

"This isn't that kind of call."

"Alas, too true," he says. "And where I am is at work."

"On Saturday night of a holiday weekend?"

"At double-time-and-a-half pay."

"Which makes it how much per hour?"

"More than either of us ever got at the styling chair."

"Combined, probably."

"Correct," he says. "Okay, here we go. According to its charter, The Cubbyhole is a private eating and drinking establishment for members only."

"They have a website?"

"No, Penny. I have other resources."

"Like what?"

"If you want to know my secrets ..."

"Never mind. But if The Cubbyhole is for members only, how did I get in today?"

He says, "Maybe they relaxed the rules, or else you gave them a good line."

"Or maybe they thought I was someone else. Paladin was expecting someone when I showed up. Does it say who owns it?"

"A financial entity called – are you ready? – the Dolly Madison Rugala Revocable Limited Partnership Trust."

"Sounds like a Southern Belle with a kink in her lineage."

Benjy says, "Or the wayward wench who spawned Howard Johnson."

"Any names?"

"Not here, Penny. Private trusts don't have to disclose much in the way of public information."

"Meaning the people who own The Cubbyhole are anonymous."

"To us, Penny, yes. It's called privacy."

"Meaning a dead end," I say.

"Meaning a challenge for yours truly," says Benjy. "Anything else for now?"

"How about the dirt on a Hollywood talent agent named Ramona Warwitch?"

"That her real name?"

"You tell me."

Tappy-tap, typey-type, tippy-tappy-happy-type.

"Here we go," he says. "Ramona Warwitch Talent. Oh, looks like she might be defunct."

"Why?"

"The site hasn't been updated for a year. Yeah, everything here is really old."

"Does it say anything at all?"

"She's got, or had, clients throughout Los Angeles, and at

last count, she'd blown every mogul in town."

"You're kidding."

"Says so right here: Best Head In Hollywood."

"Benjy!"

"Easy, Penny. Okay, Ms. Warwitch brags about big-names, but you can never tell with a website. People can say anything they want. Who's going to check?"

"What big names?"

"First one here is some actress named Bistany Evans. Yeah, right, like that's a real name."

"Benjy, that is a real name, kind of. Bistany Evans is the emcee at the Mucho Macho Honcho Convention."

"She sounds like something out of a trashy novel."

"Paladin told me Ramona Warwitch and Bistany Evans are the same person, but you're saying Bistany is one of Ramona's clients."

"Was, Penny. Ramona Warwitch Talent is no more."

"I wonder if there ever was a real Bistany Evans."

Benjy says, "Or Ramona Warwitch, for that matter. Just because there's a website ..."

"One could have invented the other," I say.

"Or vice versa," says Benjy. "Like I said, you can say anything you want on your own website."

"But wouldn't that kind of thing backfire? An agent lying about her clients, she'd be out of business pretty fast."

Benjy says, "Which is exactly where Ramona Warwitch is.

So, anything else on your list? This is a lot more interesting than my deadline."

"Can you search for Gunsmoke Saloon the same way you just did for The Cubbyhole?"

"You mean ownership records, as opposed to marketing stuff."

"Right," I say.

Typing sounds. Then Benjy speaks with a Count Dracula accent: "Veddy interesting."

"Yes?"

"Gunsmoke Saloon is co-owned by – small fanfare, please

– a financial entity we've just encountered, namely the Dolly Madison Rugala Revocable Limited Partnership Trust."

"Some coincidence," I say.

"Is it?" says Benjy. "How about the partner, a Heather Blossom Co?"

"I know Heather Blossom."

Benjy says, "This is Heather Blossom Co. It's a DBA."

"DBA?"

"Doing business as," says Benjy. "It means running a business under an assumed name."

"Why would she do that?"

"To conceal her own name, Penny."

"So who is she really?"

"That," says Benjy, "is exactly what I'm checking on."

"How?"

"I have access to the DBA registry."

"So who is she?"

"Patience, Penny. Patience is a virtue. I ought to know." What would Benjy do with his monumental unrequited love if I ever said yes to him?

"Here we go," he says. "Heather Blossom is the business name for – whoa!"

"What, Benjy?"

"Perkins Cabot Cushing III."

"Talk about a fake name."

"No, Penny. That is not a fake name at all. Just let me get my Boston Register up on the screen."

"Boston Register?"

"It's our version of Debretts Peerage."

"You mean Heather Blossom is ...?"

"Yes, Penny. In real-life Heather Blossom is Boston royalty. She's a Brahmin. That explains the DBA. The Brahmin code of conduct forbids participation in the workaday world."

"Meaning they don't work."

"Not for wages," says Benjy.

"How Brahmin is Miss What's-her-name the third?"

"Brahmin is Brahmin, Penny. Typically, tons of assets,

no cash; countless properties, all crumbling; old furniture worth billions, threadbare carpets. Hey, Pen, this is fun. Why don't you come over later and we can do some more research together?"

"I'm going out, Benjy."

"Where to?"

"Gunsmoke Saloon."

"Again?" he says.

"That's where everyone will be."

"Everyone?"

"Everyone who knew Chester," I say. "And now I know Bistany has a past in Los Angeles, and there's a common financial link between Gunsmoke and The Cubbyhole, so I have some ammunition."

"Ammunition?" says Benjy. "Penny, I'm not so sure you should be doing this. Why don't you tell your cop friend and let him go hunt these people down?"

"Because he just bawled me out for trying to help him."

"All the more reason," he says.

"Benjy, I can't just sit at home while Chester's killer is still out there. Branco's doing whatever he's doing, and so am I. I'm a detective now, and it's not a nine-to-five job."

"Down, Penny, down! You don't have to convince me. But if you're going to Gunsmoke, you need a chaperone, especially after last night."

"But if you're there, Benjy, I'll feel obligated to talk to you, and –"

"Obligated?"

"You know how it is when we go out. We end up talking and cruising and dishing the crowd. But this isn't a social night. I'm going there to work, and if you're with me I'll be distracted. I've got to go alone, Benjy."

"Who's going to carry you out this time?"

"I promise I won't put a thing to my mouth that isn't in a sealed bottle."

"Okay, Penny. Have it your way. I'll just sit at horne, alone and cloistered, researching the true identity of Dolly Madison

Rugala and her entrepreneurial realm, all for you."

"Thanks, Benjy."

We say goodbye.

I'm feeling tired, especially after last night's unidentified chemistry experiment and all the running around today. But as I just told Benjy, being a dick isn't a nine-to-five job. No naps allowed. Instead, I take a shower and change clothes. Too bad I don't own any cowboy duds to conceal my interloping presence at Gunsmoke Saloon. The only prop I have is the bogus cowboy hat Heather stuck on my head last night. I try to straighten out the brim, then decide that the bruised, crushed, "damaged goods" look gives it a rough-and-rumble authenticity.

By ten o'clock, I'm back at the Gunsmoke Saloon.

15.

JUST LIKE LAST NIGHT, the lively thump-thumping of cowboy music is audible from the sidewalk outside Gunsmoke Saloon. On the massive overhead sign, the electric cowboy boots are still dancing away, supercharged and frisky as ever. I can also see lights coming from a second-floor space, probably Kitty's shop, now a crime scene. Chester was killed up there last night, but down here at street level tonight, nothing has changed.

I open the saloon door, and the music comes at me like a tempest. The place is crammed with dancers. Heather Blossom is tending bar, and Fannie Mae Knox sits in her designated corner, surveying all from her velvet throne and within her voluminous mantle of pink. Both of them look briefly my way, then turn away, as if not seeing me.

Separated from the crowd, high above the fray, Colt Remington reigns in his own sanctuary of the DJ booth. He glances toward the door as I enter the place, gives the merest flicker of recognition, then goes about his business of juicing up the crowd. He's wearing a skimpy cutoff top that reveals his hard-won arms and abs, and as he moves about the confines of the booth, the micro-spotlights play on the ripples and planes of his fabulous torso. Meanwhile, the lights on his control panel cast their upward glow, giving his face a stark and sinister look.

I make my way through the mob to the near end of the bar, where there is an unexpected clearing. Along the way I jostle past people who are drinking and jabbering happily, cruising and teasing one another, and generally having a good time, or the appearance of one. When I get to the clear space at the bar, I see why it's there. Rather, I smell why.

Bistany Evans is sitting on a barstool, yammering at Heather and polluting the air, which is already smoggy with numerous cowboy colognes. I scrutinize her, hoping for some sign that will incriminate her. But Bistany conceals any truth about herself under that perpetual broadcast of inanity, hoofbeats, and smell.

Heather sees me and vanishes quickly, or maybe she needs some air. I take a deep breath before entering the lethal zone around Bistany Evans.

"This is some wake," I say.

She turns to me. "Yew again," she says. "Seems like every time I turn around, there yew are."

"No one seems to be mourning Chester Wright."

Bistany chirps back, "Life goes on."

"As long as you're alive."

"That's a good thing," she says. "That's why I'm here tonight – to make a positive, inclusive, and healing show of life."

Show being the operative word.

She goes on. "Yew people in Boston all think the same. Everything is bleak, bleak, bleak – doom and gloom, like there's nothing but winter all the time."

I say, "Someone in Iceland sees the world differently from someone in Bali."

She says, "Yew have control over your own reality."

"But not the weather."

"Your own reality," she says, "is how yew perceive things."

"I perceive winter as wet and cold."

"There yew go," says Bistany. "Yew just proved my point. Yew see winter as bad, someone else sees it as an opportunity to ski. Their reality is cheery, yours is gloomy. And that affects your life."

Her smile is nauseating.

I tell her, "I'll remember that next winter, when I'm skittering around on icy sidewalks."

She says, "It's the same thing with this convention. I wanted to show Heather – Y'know, she is exactly like yew. How can yew people from New England all be exactly the same? I wanted to prove to her that there is more than one way to utilize that young man's death."

"Utilize?"

"Yew've got to use it," says Bistany. "Heather wanted to close down the convention after what happened – out of respect and all. And now she wants to call off the hoe-down tomorrow. But I told her we absolutely, positively *cannot* cancel the hoedown. It's scheduled for Sunday and that's when it has to happen. Otherwise people will end up going home early. Worse, they'll go home feeling *bad*. And yew cannot do that to them."

Never mind Chester Wright going home feeling dead.

"But somebody died," I say.

"That's right," says Bistany with her sickening smile.

"But we're still here."

"What about respect?"

"We can respect him on Monday," she says, "on Memorial Day. In the meantime, we have to use the situation to our advantage. People are feeling uncertain and unsafe, and yew can either send them home that way – oh, that would be nice, wouldn't it? What a nice memory to keep in your heart about the first Mucho Macho Honcho Convention in history, that somebody died and then the whole thing turned into a funeral. Or, yew can turn it all around and use the hoe-down to re-instill a sense of security and joy among the participants. Bring them back into the light and love of community and inclusivity and celebration. Play the music louder and let them dance all the harder. And then, because the human emotional memory always recalls the good times before the bad ones, every person in that crowd will be yours forever because they'll be remembering something good in the midst of something bad. Yew will always represent the feeling of hope within them. And people will always come back to yew if you give them hope."

She almost has a point.

I say, "Is that how people think in Los Angeles?"

"Where?" she says, and I detect a chink in the armor.

"The land of the New Year's Eve picnic."

Bistany looks at me sharply, like a bird that has spotted a bug it ought to eat. *Crunch!*

I say, "You believe that we New Englanders are all exactly the same. Does the same hold true for, say, Hollywood?"

She says, "It can be true for anyone, anywhere. That's what's so wonderful about positive thinking."

"But I'm talking specifically about Los Angeles, your hometown."

"Huh?" she says. "Where'd yew get an idea like that?"

"You could say Chester told me, but not in a mirror."

"Chester? But he's dead." It comes out *day-ed*.

I say, "Why did you close down your agency and flee?"

"Why what?" she says, slightly off-balance.

"Your talent agency, in Hollywood."

"Sweetie, what is it with yew and Hollywood? How would I know about a thing like that?"

"You used to be a Hollywood agent."

"Me?"

"You used to be Ramona Warwitch, Hollywood agent."

Bistany says, "Ramona?"

"Warwitch," I say.

She stares at me with her sick-making smile. "Who's that?"

"The person Chester Wright knew you as in Los Angeles. He was a client of yours out there. There was some money stolen too, eight million or so. When you two met up in Boston you made a deal with him."

"What deal?"

"To keep him quiet. But then you decided to kill him anyway."

"Sweetie," says Bistany, "are yew off your meds or something? Why would I hurt Chester? I needed him. I couldn't succeed without him."

"Was that part of the deal?"

"What deal? Yew keep talking about a deal. Where did yew get this idea? Who have yew been talking to?"

"Whom," I say. "It's *whom* have you been talking to."

The cloven-hoofed she-beast looks at me as though I should undergo psychiatric evaluation. Any more time with this crowd, and who knows?

I tell her, "It was Paladin. He told me all about you." Her leering smile vanishes instantly. "You found him?" The errant yew has vanished again too.

"That's right," I say. "And when he tells it all to the police, so much for you."

Bistany smiles, but this time it's not a fake smile. It's the kind of smile you make as you throw down a winning hand.

"If he goes to the police," she says, "which I doubt he will, since he is their prime suspect."

"Who says?"

Bistany says, "I've been with the police today. We all have. And Paladin can't incriminate me by talking to them."

"But he can arouse their suspicion, cause embarrassment, perhaps a scandal, maybe even close down the convention. Paladin talks, and your little world begins to crumble."

"But they have to find him first," Bistany says with a victory grin. "Meanwhile, I plan to proceed as though nothing's happened, including you and your crazy theories. I'd suggest you do the same."

"Or what? You'll kill me too? Your secrets won't die with Chester."

Bistany says, "I didn't kill him."

"Easy to say."

"I have an alibi," she says. "I was with Colt."

"Colt?"

"That's right. All night."

Another winning hand.

"That's some alibi," I say.

"It satisfied the police."

Branco believed her?

"Now, if *yew* don't mind," she says, "I've got things to do."

She trots off, fumigating her way through the crowd to the far end of the bar. She pauses briefly at Fannie Mae's throne, and they exchange words. Then she continues on, tromping up the metal stairway leading to the DJ's booth. Colt lets her in, and immediately she's got her hands all over him. Maybe the two of them are trying to create their own reality and convince the rest of us too. But with the mood lighting in the booth, it just looks like bad soap-opera sex.

Somewhat recovered from Bistany's noxious vapors, I head toward the regal end of the bar myself. But Fannie Mae sees me coming, and she gets up and disappears down the corridor that leads to the rest rooms. I park myself on the barstool next to her throne and await her return.

Heather Blossom comes to take my drink order.

"Bottled water," I tell her.

"Glad to see you're on the wagon," she says.

"In the bottle, please."

"Sure, darlin'. How else do you think we serve it? In a crystal flute? You want a lime in that?"

"No, nothing. And would you mind bringing it unopened?"

Heather's eyes widen. "Whatever you want," she says.

I manage a smile. "Thanks."

She returns with a bottle. I take out my wallet, but Heather shakes her head. "Keep your money."

"You won't stay in business that way."

"There's more to business than money," she says.

"That's quite an economic theory."

"But speaking of money," she says, "Fannie Mae tells me you have a little. Would you be interested in coming in on the business?"

"Which business?" The one not based on money?

"The convention," says Heather. "If this weekend is any sign, it's really gonna take off. You might want to get in on the ground floor."

I tell her, "Bistany mentioned it this afternoon. Who are the other investors?"

She hesitates. "Right now, it's just me and Fannie Mae."

"Not Bistany?"

"No," says Heather.

"So if the thing goes bust, it's all on you and Fannie Mae."

"Nothing's going bust, darlin'."

"But Bistany has nothing to lose."

"Not financially, but the convention couldn't happen without her. It was her idea, and she's the one who's really in charge."

"Do you know much about her?" I ask. "Like her past?"

"What's to know?" says Heather. "Bistany represents what the public likes. That's why we put her up there where people can see her and hear her."

"*We* meaning you and Fannie Mae."

"You sure ask a lot of questions, darlin'."

"If I'm going to invest money, I want to know what I'm getting into. And I'd want to see the paperwork, and get your real names – yours and Fannie Mae's – before I go any further."

"What real names?"

"You and Fannie Mae. Those are just business names, right?"

"On second thought, darlin', maybe you wouldn't be the right kind of partner for us."

"I'm not a Brahmin, if that's what you mean. And I'd certainly need to know more about the Dolly Madison Rugelach Revocable Limited Partnership Trust."

"The what?" says Heather, slack-jawed.

"Isn't that where half the money for this place comes from? Maybe it's paying for half the convention too."

"I am partners with Fannie Mae, darlin'. I don't know anything about that other – what did you call it?"

I say it all again, then tell her, "You must know about it. How could you not know who your partner is?"

Heather's eyes narrow. "My partner is Fannie Mae. My accountant takes care of the finances. And *I've* got enough to do taking care of people here. Speaking of which, darlin', if you don't mind, I've got other customers to look after."

And away she goes. But she doesn't wait on other customers. Instead, she disappears through a curtained doorway behind the bar.

Meanwhile, Bistany Evans – aka Miss Porno Lite of the DJ Booth – comes clomping down the metal stairway just in time to intercept Fannie Mae, who has just reappeared at the bottom of the stairs. They have another brief tête-à-tête, then Fannie Mae comes to her throne where I have been awaiting her.

"Pumpkin!" she exclaims merrily.

She cocks her head slightly, as though she expects me to genuflect. Instead, I cock my head back, like a 3-D parrot.

I say, "Am I reinstated then?"

"From what?"

"You unknighted me at the convention hall this morning."

"Did I?" she says. "Probably my monthly mood. Pay no attention when I'm like that, Pumpkin." She settles down, then sees that her drink is empty. She looks around. "Where's Heather?"

"I think she went looking for you."

"For me?" says Fannie Mae. "Why?"

"To warn you."

"Of what?"

"Of me. I'm asking too many questions again."

"Such as?"

"Such as what is the Dolly Madison Rugelach Revocable Limited Partnership Trust."

Fannie Mae chortles. "The what?"

I repeat the name.

Fannie Mae looks at me dumbfounded.

I tell her, "Last night Heather told me that you and she were partners here at Gunsmoke. But I found out that a trust is part-owner of the saloon too. So, maybe *you* are that trust."

"Pumpkin, what is the source of your information?"

"The most capable online researcher in Boston."

"Capable," she says, "but is he, or she, reputable?

Pumpkin, I'm sure what Heather meant last night is that I am her partner in an emotional and supportive sense."

"Then what is that trust about?"

"Oh, Pumpkin, I fear you are becoming overwrought. Perhaps you need a vacation."

"I'll take one when all this is settled."

"When all what is settled?" says Fannie Mae.

"Chester's death," I say. "Remember him? Last night he was alive. Tonight he's dead."

"Oh, Pumpkin, yes, it's all just too awful about him, but life does go on. It must."

"Obviously," I say.

"What do you expect people to do? Life is short – too, too short."

"Tick-tock, tick-tock."

"But it's true, Pumpkin. Think of it. If we're lucky, we get a few hundred million breaths. It may sound like a lot, but the number is finite. You do run out eventually. Inevitably. Therefore, you've got to make the most of every one of them. Live every moment to its fullest!"

"Here, here," I reply to Fannie Mae Knox, motivational speaker.

"Oh, Pumpkin, even you with your righteous, empathetic, Chester-loving bones found your way here tonight, didn't you? So why shouldn't everyone else be here as well? Don't you see? If the young can die so tragically and unexpectedly, then we must all live for the moment. That poor, poor boy!"

Over my shoulder I notice a tall man emerging from the corridor that leads to the rest rooms. He's carrying two large garment bags, one over each arm. For a moment, he seems daunted by the crowd in the saloon, but he forges ahead and makes his way through the pressing mobs toward the exit at the other end of the place.

Heather arrives with a fresh drink for Fannie Mae. Fannie

Mae says to her, "And another for our friend."

I remind Heather, "Unopened, please."

She scowls and walks away.

Fannie Mae leans to me, "You see? You think no one cares about poor Chester. But the stress of that boy's death is taking its toll on our Heather, and she's not herself tonight."

"Or else I upset her."

"Did you?" she says. "And what good did it do, Pumpkin?"

Just then, two more men struggle past us and head into the corridor where the other man came out a few moments ago. These guys are also burdened with huge wardrobe bags, the contents of which are hazily visible through the translucent plastic: crinoline petticoats and big puffy dancing skirts.

Fannie Mae casts a glance at the two men, then says to me, "The competition, such as it is."

"For whom?"

"For me, Pumpkin. These boys you see passing to and fro are vying for costume prizes at the hoe-down tomorrow night."

"Never fear. No one can hold a candle to you."

"That's very nice of you, Pumpkin, and tactful too. You can be tactful when you want to be. But the fact is, I'm not in the costume competition. I'm judging it."

"Oh," I say.

"I shall award the prizes."

"As royalty bestows titles."

Fannie Mae frowns slightly. "Tactful yet provocative."

I say, "But why are they here with their costumes?"

Fannie Mae shrugs.

Heather returns with my bottled water, but the cap is off.

I say, "I asked for an unopened bottle."

Heather retorts, "Darlin', I hear hundreds of people telling me things every night, but I've never yet been told how to serve my own customers. And frankly, I'm offended. Truth be known, I don't have to serve you at all. But I always try to make the best of a bad situation."

She leaves us.

"Oh, dear," says Fannie Mae. "Whatever did you say to her?"

"Among other things, I asked her what her real name was."

"I hope you won't make that mistake with anyone else."

"Not yet," I say. "But I do want to ask you something."

"Careful, Pumpkin. Not too personal."

"It's business."

"Oh!" she says and chortles. "I have no head for business."

"But you're very generous with your money."

"When it's for a good cause, yes."

"How do you sign the checks?"

"Hmm?" says Fannie Mae.

"When you contribute money, do you sign the checks Fannie Mae Knox?"

"What an odd question, Pumpkin."

"I'm just curious."

"Curiosity killed the cat."

"It's just a question."

"And the answer, Pumpkin, is that someone else .takes care of those things for me. As I said, business and I are not bedmates."

"Who signs the checks then?"

"Oh, Pumpkin, how should I know? Some nameless person in a financial institution."

"In other words," I say, "your accountant."

"Well, of course my accountant!

"So you don't actually handle your money yourself."

"Not in the way you're talking, no," says Fannie Mae.

"There's simply too much of it for me to keep track of."

Curious, how neither Heather nor Fannie Mae take care of their own money. Is it another mark of true wealth? You don't even touch the stuff that lesser mortals are grubbing for.

Fannie Mae says, "Now why all this concern with my money? Are you going to ask me for some? Is that what all this is about? Because if you are, Pumpkin ..."

"No," I say. "I've got enough of my own."

"That's a relief," she says, then gulps down half her drink.

I ask, "What about Heather's fake name? Is that how she conceals her wantonness?"

Fannie Mae chortles. "Heather? Wanton?"

"Maybe she changed her name so no one will know the kind of business a Boston Brahmin is running. Maybe that trust is her doing as well."

"Pumpkin, that is grotesque!"

Says the drag queen who looks like she came out of a cotton-candy machine.

I say, "She'd have to keep it a secret, owning places like Gunsmoke and The Cubbyhole."

"The what?" says Fannie Mae.

"The Cubbyhole. It's a little speakeasy on Beacon Hill. Maybe you know it."

"I'm sure I have no idea of such things."

"That same trust –"

"Enough!" says Fannie Mae. "All these questions, Pumpkin. You are becoming too tedious."

Just then Colt Remington's voice comes over the PA system.

"Hi, fellas! And gals. I'm taking a break, so I'm turning on the automatic music system. This is the best it can do," he says with a sly laugh, "so you'll all appreciate my live bones when I'm back up here in the booth."

Fannie Mae leans toward me. "Bones not so lively," she says, fluttering her long lashes. Then she waggles a finger between us. "Though I never gossip about other people's intimacies."

Colt's muscular legs appear at the head of the narrow catwalk that leads up to his booth. Like Paladin last night, he jogs his way down lightly, almost without a sound. At the bottom he glances at me sitting in Fannie Mae's throne corner, then turns down the corridor that leads to the rest rooms.

I slide off my stool. "Duty calls."

Fannie Mae says, "Careful, Pumpkin."

I head down the corridor after Colt and call out to him.

He turns, gives me a seething look. The more these people see of me, the more they hate me on sight. Can I blame them? Meanwhile, people pass by us in the corridor, coming and going to the rest rooms. Then another man goes by with a giant garment bag. He passes the rest room and opens a heavy metal door just beyond. He goes in, and it slams behind him like a vault.

"Well?" says Colt.

"Fannie Mae's been saying how short life is, and it got me thinking – maybe it's time to butch myself up. So I thought of you."

"What do you want from me?"

"Help."

He sneers. "I can't make you straight, if that's what you mean."

"Not straight," I say. "Just more like you."

"I'll tell you what then," he says, "get yourself a sex change, and maybe you can pass for a dyke."

"Thanks for the tip. So, how does it feel to be back in the running, now that Chester's dead?"

"The running for what?"

"To be the poster boy for Mucho Macho Honcho's national tour."

"Things change," he says.

"And I always like to know what makes them change. For instance, yesterday you two were at each other's throats, but tonight you're having PG-13 sex in public."

Colt says, "Call it my version of an audition."

"And what about Bistany's problem with your fight club and the bad rep it gave you?"

He says, "She's willing to trust me now. It's people like you we can't trust."

"You trust her?" I say. "She already broke her promise to you when she replaced you with Chester. What's to stop her from doing it again?"

Colt smiles. "There's no one to take my place now."

"There's Paladin," I say. "He'd make a fabulous poster boy."

"That will never happen," says Colt. "I've got something Paladin doesn't."

"What's that?"

"A straight dick," he says, and he flexes his chest and shoulder muscles. I half expect him to beat his tits like Tarzan.

"Is that part of Bistany's campaign, using a straight guy to advertise a gay product?"

Colt says, "Heterophobes like you will never understand."

I say, "Did Bistany take a lot of convincing?"

"Not much," says Colt. "She pretty much plugged me in where Chester got deleted."

"Did you know about the deal she had with Chester?"

"What deal?" he says.

"To keep him quiet about knowing her in Los Angeles." Colt's face freezes.

"Ask her about it," I say, "the next you two are having a horizontal track-meet. Ask Bistany about Ramona Warwitch and the eight million dollars. See if that improves her performance."

Colt says, "You don't know what you're talking about."

"Maybe Bistany convinced you to get rid of Chester for her, and promised you fame and fortune, along with sex on the side to certify your straightness. Must have been irresistible."

"Wrong," says Colt.

"Okay, then," I say, "forget about sex." (Especially forget about sex with Bistany, since it's giving me heterohorrors.) "Maybe you cleared the path for yourself and that national tour."

"You think I killed Chester?"

"Anything is possible with overweening ambition."

"Except I have an alibi," he says. "I was with Bistany."

"All night," I say.

"That's right," says Colt. "During my breaks too."

"And she was with you."

"Right again," says Colt.

"You're telling me that you and Bistany were together at every moment last night."

"Now you get it," he says.

"So maybe you killed Chester together."

Colt says, "We had other things on our mind. Or is that still too much for your little gay brain to comprehend?"

"Not too much, Colt, too incredible. Overnight, you and Bistany have become some kind of triathlon sexmates."

"Someone's got to keep the species going."

"Especially if you've just removed one human along the way."

Colt says, "You really need help, you know that?"

"How does Kitty feel about you and Bistany?"

"I don't give a fuck about Kitty."

"You used to."

Colt clenches his fist. I stick my chin out at him.

"Go ahead," I say. "Smite a defenseless fag. Show me how much you really care."

He plants his feet into the floor and winds up for the hit. My impromptu word play hasn't turn out quite as expected, and now I'm going to need bridgework.

I am saved by Bistany Evans rushing out from a little alcove near the ladies room door.

"Don't do it, Colt!" she shouts. "Do *not* hit him!"

Colt relaxes his stance, but only slightly.

"Where'd you come from?" he says to her.

"I was listening to you two. And we cannot afford any more trouble, so no more fighting, Colt. Okay? Just let him be."

Colt says to me, "You are one sad fuck."

"Ditto!" say Bistany. Then her hands are all over him.

After a small crowd has witnessed their faux foreplay, Colt and Bistany walk away together, hip-to-hip.

Meanwhile, another big-framed cowboy comes into the corridor with a garment bag over each arm. As he approaches the big metal door, I ask him, "What's going on in there?"

He holds up his garment bags. "Costumes, downstairs."

I start to follow him through the door just to check it out, but that's when I hear a lot of rustling behind me – a soft, pinkish disturbance. I look back down the corridor to see Fannie Mae Knox making a big fuss of gathering up her skirts and her pink-beaded reticule as if she's getting ready to leave the place.

First things first, I tell myself. If ever I'm going to discover the true identity of Dame Fannie Mae Knox, I'll have to take Nicole's advice and follow her home sometime. Now's as good a time as any. Fannie Mae clears her usual path through the saloon crowd, and I follow in her wake, a safe distance behind.

Outside Gunsmoke, she gets into a waiting cab. I, alas, have no such luck. There goes Fannie Mae's cab, and here stand I. It stops at a traffic light up ahead. Do I run to catch up? The answer arrives on a golden chariot, literally. At that very moment a motorcycle of monstrous dimensions pulls up to the curb. The behemoth is painted metallic gold with gold-plated accents. The glistening paint reflects the dancing cowboy boots from the electric billboard overhead, making the motorcycle look like a self-propelled casino on the Las Vegas strip. There's even a gold nameplate running along the back fender: Roadmaster. (Is it a Buick? A Buick motorcycle?) Yet for all its size and garishness, the megamachine makes little more than a docile purr.

I approach the cowboy who's sitting high in the saddle, which resembles a tufted leather club chair. He's middle-aged and fine-framed, like some archetypal accountant or bookworm before they all began consuming protein powder. His innate civility seems alien at the helm of such a gigantic and powerful machine.

I say to him, "How'd you like a little adventure tonight?"

His eyes open wide. "That's direct, young man!"

"I'm an investigator, and I want to follow that cab, the one stopped at those lights. Are you game?"

"You're serious!"

The light changes and Fannie Mae's cab starts moving.

"Time is running out," I say urgently.

"Won't they notice us?"

"I rely on your discretion," I say, as if implying something else, something more.

"Then hop aboard!" he says. "I've always wanted to do this."

The guy is an excellent driver and knows instinctively how to keep enough distance between us and Fannie Mae's cab. As for the motorcycle, it's akin to riding on a cloud. The smooth low hum of the engine makes it seem far away. Even its heat is ducted away from us, so that all I feel is the cool night air.

We follow the cab to its destination, which turns out to be atop Beacon Hill, somewhere on the so-called "good" side, behind the State House. When the cab stops, I tell my driver to stop too, leaving enough space between us and Fannie Mae. Up ahead Fannie Mae gets out of the cab and enters her apartment building.

My driver turns his head and says, "Looks like we're here."

"Thanks," I say as I dismount.

"You want me to wait?"

"No, thanks."

"Fun while it lasted," he says, then rides away.

I hurry down the block to the building where Fannie Mae went in. I stand at the entrance and stare at it. I don't know what I expected. I'm here, she's not, and the front door has no directory.

Now what?

The answer comes in a torrent of cawing, screeching cries from one of the top-floor windows, just thrown open. It's Fannie Mae Knox herself, leaning precariously out, her pink wig glowing in the Beacon Hill gaslights.

"Help!" she screams. "Help! Police! Murder!"

16.

HOW DO I GET IN? The intercom system is an enigma machine. There's no directory of building residents, no coded apartment numbers, nothing.

Meanwhile, Fannie Mae is screeching away from an open window high above. Her calls echo like warring ravens within the brick-walled maze of Beacon Hill. I should call the police, but yet again I am without phone. Desperate to get in, I press random buttons on the intercom box, but all I hear is the phone company's squealing message: "Your call cannot be completed as dialed. Please hang up and try again, or dial your operator for assistance."

And there is the answer.

I disconnect the intercom, start over, and this time I press "0". Within seconds a phone company operator comes on the line. I tell him – *order* him – to send the police. "*Now!*" I say. "Send them to ... to ..." I look up at the door. "Send them to number twenty-three ..." Twenty-three what? What street am I on? "Just send the police to Beacon Hill, behind the State House. Tell them to keep their windows open and they'll hear the screaming."

The operator suspects a prank, and he threatens to call the police on me.

I tell him, "Yes! Do that! Send the police to this telephone right now!"

He says, "That's exactly what you're going to get."

Within minutes I hear the siren call of the Boston police. That was fast. So much for needing a mobile phone. But why does a whole battalion of cops arrive to arrest a mere prankster?

Lieutenant Branco leaps from the first cruiser.

I stand there pointing upwards, where Fannie Mae's crowing fills the night air.

Branco says, "What are you doing here?"

"I'm the one who called you."

"Not the call we got," he says. "One of the neighbors –"

"'Twas I, Lieutenant. That phone prankster was me, calling from the intercom." I point to the security box and tell him, "I am calm in a crisis."

Meanwhile, that same security box is being breached by one of the cops. It's so easy when you have a passkey.

Branco scowls at me. "I don't have time for this." He pushes past me and goes in with his crew.

When the path has been cleared, you must take it. So, I slip in behind him and file in with the other cops – a caboose dick. They take the stairs, and they don't seem to mind me following them. Maybe talking to Branco out front grants me some kind of immunity. Still, I stay out of his view.

We get up to the sixth floor and head down the hallway to Fannie Mae's apartment. Once all the cops are in there, I peer through the open door. Directly inside is a large foyer festooned with gilt rococo mirrors – a style befitting Fannie Mae's gilt rococo personality. There's a pervading scent of something floral – bland and sweetish. Maybe it's makeup or some fancy imported cold cream. Given Fannie Mae's lifestyle, there must be buckets of the stuff around.

I slip inside the foyer to see more, careful to stay out of Branco's sight. The living room windows face the street, where Fannie Mae was screaming earlier. There are also two French doors leading to an outdoor balcony on the side. Since the apartment is a few stories higher than everything else around it, there's probably a decent view out there, along with some privacy – not just someone else's brick wall.

At the center of the room is Miss Fannie Mae Knox herself, holding a private audience for Branco and crew while reclining on a recamier, no doubt a copy, just like her. The cops huddle, trying to calm her down, except Branco's not in the huddle. His attention is on the room, the *mise en scène* of the crime, and he's registering every detail.

I sneak a little further inside the foyer. The living room furniture is French provincial, the walls flocked, the lampshades tasseled. It's as though Fannie Mae Knox wants constant reminders to go over the top in her private life as well.

A few cops move slightly and leave an opening, and I see it – or, rather, him – the victim. Vaslav Paladin is lying face up on the floor near the French doors. He's on the hardwood parquetry, where the Aubusson carpet doesn't cover. He's decked out in the same cowboy finery as when I found him at the Cubbyhole this afternoon, except there's also a heavy leather belt pulled tightly around his neck. On one end of the belt is a heavy brass buckle. Looks old, like something from the Civil War.

The cops move in again, blocking my view but opening another space. That's when I hear Branco shout, "How did he get up here?"

From across the room his eyes blaze angrily. Beside him, Fannie Mae looks up from her reclining position. She glares at me, outraged at my intrusion on her command performance.

Branco yells, "Get him out of here!"

Next thing I know, two big cops have me by the arms and are hauling me out of the flat. I scramble to keep up with them, down the long hallway, into the stairwell. I lose my footing completely as they drag me down the stairs.

One of them grumbles, "Use your feet!"

"Okay, guys," I say. "Easy does it. I can go down by myself, honest."

"Sure, you go down," says the other cop.

The first one adds slyly, "We're going down with you. All the way."

Oh, clever wits are they! But I figure, why trip and stumble after them? I pull my legs up and let the cops carry me. But these guys don't want to play. They want to show off their muscles and their repartee.

Their muscles, anyway.

One of them growls, "Get your feet down before we throw you down!"

The other one answers, "We can't rough him up. We got precious cargo here. This is the lieutenant's little buddy, the one that pulled him outta that fire."

Little Buddy? Is that my new persona, my true self?

"Oh, excuse me!" says the other cop, feigning feyness. "I forgot my kidskin gloves."

I tell him, "I prefer gauntlets."

"You shaddup!" comes their unison reply.

At the front door, I am tossed onto the landing, albeit with tough love, and the heavy door is slammed closed behind me. I watch from the street for a few minutes, but I can't see a thing up on the top floor, so finally I give up and walk home.

It's well after 1:00 A.M. when I get in. There's a phone message from Benjy: "Penny, I've been digging in the data mines for you, and I found a small gem. Call me when you get in, if you get in, you little slut."

I phone him back, but his voice mail kicks in, which is odd, but I leave a message: "It's after one. Where are *you?*"

I'm about to call Nicole, but I don't. It's late, and besides, I've got to get tough on my own. So what if Paladin is lying dead in Fannie Mae's apartment? Does that mean I should call Nicole about it? She's probably writing her memoirs anyway, or reading them to her teacher.

I sleep fitfully for a while, then the phone rings.

"Penny!"

"Where have *you* been?"

"At Gunsmoke, looking for you."

"I phoned you."

Benjy says, "I turned my wireless off."

For Benjy, *that's* a sacrifice.

He continues. "The bartender said you left."

"I followed someone home."

"Was he hot and hunky?"

"Yes," I say. "He was also dead."

"Jeez," says Benjy. "And I was hoping you had a good time."

"Here's the good time I had: I was at Gunsmoke taking verbal abuse from everyone I talked to, then I followed Fannie Mae Knox home, trying to find out who she really is, and then she discovered Paladin's body in her living room."

Benjy says, "Who's Fannie Mae Knox?"

"A drag queen."

"You followed a drag queen home?"

"It was the quickest way to find out who she is."

"And now there's another dead cowboy?"

"The boyfriend of the one who was killed last night."

"Coincidence?" says Benjy.

"Not to me," I say.

"Did you get my message?"

"About finding a gem, yes. Some joke."

"Here it is, Penny. The Dolly Madison Rugelach Revocable Limited Partnership Trust was created about twelve years ago by an old Baltimore gal who's still alive and living in Baltimore."

"Not Boston," I say.

"Nope."

"So she's not a Brahmin."

"Penny, she's anti-Brahmin, as in ante-bellum. Baltimo' be da Sout'."

"I can almost hear the banjoes, Benjy. But why would an old Southern gal put her money into Boston business?"

Benjy says, "Maybe she still has mixed allegiance. Maryland was a border state, after all. Or maybe Miss Dolly doesn't know how the money is being used. Technically it isn't hers as long as it's in that trust."

I yawn.

Benjy says, "Am I keeping you up?"

"No," I say with a second, lesser, afteryawn.

"Here's something else," says Benjy. "While I was waiting for you at Gunsmoke, I decided to poke around."

"Poke what?"

He says, "You know that costume maker?"

"Kitty."

"He's got a shop in the basement at Gunsmoke."

"That explains all those guys with costume bags," I say. "But Kitty's shop is upstairs."

"Maybe he has two."

"Maybe."

Benjy says, "I never saw so many big bruisers sashaying around in flouncy dresses. Wasn't it a women's gym down there?"

"It used to be a fight club, but it closed down."

"For women?"

"Yup," I say with another yawn.

"Jeez, Penny, why would women want to do that?"

"Who knows? To be like men, I guess."

Benjy says, "I thought penis-envy was obsolete."

"It's muscle-envy now."

"Maybe someday, humans will be like seahorses," he says.

"Did you know that the females deposit their eggs into the males, who get pregnant and carry the young and actually care for them?"

"No, I didn't."

"Neat, huh?"

"I call it strange, Benjy."

"Like this conversation. Penny, do you think other people are talking about things like this?"

"At two-thirty in the morning? I doubt it."

"Isn't it nice to know that we're unique?"

"We'll talk tomorrow, Benjy. I'm glad you're all right."

"I'm glad you are too, Penny."

So ends another day in the life of a confirmed bachelor dick.

17.

THE NEXT MORNING I'M lying abed, drowsily initiating a round of Happy Wake-Up. It's a playful start to any day, but especially Sunday, the beginning of a new week. What will the new day and the new week hold? Adventure? Surprise? Something that will change my life forever?

Minutes pass, and I head toward the joyful little leap (*la jouissance*, the French call it) that culminates this solo sport. Then the phone rings. Stupidly, I pick it up.

Branco's voice says, "I'm sending a car for you. Be ready."

He hangs up. The clock says eight-fifteen. He's certainly no Sunday morning slugabed, but then, he has a young wife to rev him up. (I wonder what the Italians call it. *Il giuoco?*)

The urge to express myself has withered, and it is I who leap from the bed, and not my joke from me. I perform the fastest ablutions on record, so when the cruiser arrives twenty minutes later, I am spic-and-span ready for my close-up with The Boss Cop.

At the station I am escorted to a secure waiting area and told that Branco has been detained.

So, why the big hurry to get me here?

In that same secure waiting area is Kitty the costumer. He's sitting in a corner chair looking anxious. Whatever is coming down with Branco this morning, Kitty and I seem to be in it together, so I go over to him. Unlike yesterday, when

Kitty pretty much grappled me in the police interview room, this morning he looks up nervously from his chair.

He says, "Go away."

"What's wrong?"

"I don't want to talk to you. You betrayed your tribe."

"What tribe?"

"Queer people," he says.

"Kitty, *I'm* queer, or gay, or whatever we're called."

"But whose side are you on?"

"I'm not on anyone's side. I'm trying to find out what happened. The only people who have reason to mistrust me are the guilty ones. Does that include you?"

"No," he says.

"Then why not cooperate instead of hating me?"

"Because you ruin everything."

"Like what?"

He says, "Before I talked to you yesterday, I had a new boyfriend and a good alibi for Friday night. Then, thanks to you, the cops talked to Tex. And now he left town."

"The police let him go?"

"His family knows some Senator who vouched for him."

"Nice catch for you, then."

"Not anymore," says Kitty. "Tex told me he couldn't afford to be involved with someone who consorted with criminals. And that was it. No more business, no more fun. He's on his way back to his ranch and his mother."

"And you blame me for that?"

"There's more," says Kitty. "Because of what I told you yesterday, the police say I could have killed Chester when I went up to my shop to see what was keeping him Friday night."

"And so now you think I betrayed you, because you told me the truth yesterday."

Kitty thinks a moment. "I guess it's not really your fault. But I trusted you and it didn't work out."

"You didn't do anything wrong," I say, "and you have nothing to lose by talking to me now."

"Maybe not," he says.

I ask him, "Were you ever involved with Paladin?"

"You mean sex?"

"If that's how you were involved."

He says, "I don't get emotional with my clients."

"What about sex without emotion?"

"Depends," says Kitty. "Sometimes when I was fitting him, he'd get a little hard, and I'd blow him."

What price, custom-made costumes?

I ask him, "Why did you give me that matchbook yesterday?"

"I wanted you to find Paladin. If he killed Chester, he'd come after me next."

"Why didn't you tell the police?"

Kitty says, "I don't rat on people."

"But telling me was all right."

"Yes."

"Even though you knew I'd tell the police."

"Not necessarily," he says, sneering at me, the tribal betrayer. "But why do they think I did it?"

"Because Chester was found in your shop, and Paladin was your client. They have to question you."

"Thanks to you."

"No," I say. "I had nothing to do with them bringing you in here. How did you know that Paladin hung out at The Cubbyhole?"

Kitty says, "That's where he met his johns."

"He was a hustler?"

Kitty smirks. "Part-time, very exclusive – like everything else about him."

"Who were his clients?"

"Older queers and younger straights."

"Straights?"

Another smirk.

I ask, "How do you know this?"

"I go there too," he says. "It's easy money, usually."

"You hustle?"

He shrugs. "Why not, if you can?"

"Were Paladin and Colt ever involved?"

"Colt?" he says.

"He's straight. Maybe he got curious and hired Paladin to find out."

Kitty says quickly, "I don't know about that."

"Didn't you just say how well you knew Paladin? All those fittings, all those blow jobs? And you and Colt knew each other too, once upon a time."

Kitty says, "Colt is a jerk and a liar."

Now this is more like it.

Kitty continues. "He says he's straight, but I know better. He's *ho-mo-SEX-ual*." He exaggerates the pronunciation with sissified sibilants.

I ask, "So Colt was one of Paladin's clients?"

"No," says Kitty. "One of mine."

He's pleased at my surprise.

"I was his first guy. He almost fainted the first time I grabbed his crotch. Then he couldn't get enough of me. I think that's what scared him. He probably thought it was going to be a Marine, and instead he lost his cherry to a geisha boy in Boston."

"You were the top?"

"Sometimes," says Kitty. "And sometimes he was all over me. *All* over me." His eyes take on a wistful, faraway look, as he recalls those glorious days when Colt paid for his company.

Wang "Kitty" Chu, costumer and master embroiderer.

"By the way," I say, "geishas are Japanese."

"Whatever," says Kitty with another shrug. Maybe he picked it up from Colt.

"So what happened with you and Colt?"

"He cut me off, completely, just like that."

Odd choice of words.

Kitty says, "I told him it was a mistake, that he should accept what he is and what he likes to do."

"Which is what he preaches to everyone else."

"Except he can't take his own advice," says Kitty. "Like I said, a jerk and a liar. And now he's trying to be straight again, with Bistany Evans. But he'll get tired of her, and he'll try it with some faux-het' guy like himself, and then he'll come back to me."

"So maybe it's a lucky thing that Tex left town."

"Lucky?" says Kitty.

"Leaves you free to go on the national tour with Colt."

"What tour?"

"Now that Chester and Paladin are dead," I say, "Colt can go on tour with Bistany."

"What?" says Kitty. "Why?"

"Bistany probably doesn't care whether her poster boy is a dancer or a caller, as long as he looks good. The point is, are you going along with them?"

Kitty says, "I don't know anything about it."

"It doesn't bother you if Colt goes with Bistany, especially if he's being straight with her?"

Kitty is silent.

"In fact," I say, "it gives Colt a pretty good motive to kill Chester and Paladin."

Kitty says, "So he could go on tour with Bistany?"

"Or maybe *you* killed those guys to clear the way for Colt."

"No way!" says Kitty. "Why would I do anything to send Colt away with Bistany?"

"Because you'd like to punish him," I say, "for dumping you, 'cutting you off' you said, and sticking him with Bistany could be quite a punishment."

Kitty scowls at me.

I say, "Or else, maybe you assumed *you'd* be going with him, once you got him to dump her. Face it, Kitty, you're still totally wrapped up with the guy. Trouble is, he's wrapped up in whatever serves his ambition, which right now means Bistany Evans."

Kitty considers this a moment, then exclaims, "*That's* why he wanted to move my stuff yesterday. He wanted an alibi!"

"Move what stuff where?"

Kitty says, "I needed a place to do the fittings for the hoe-down tonight, and I couldn't go back to my shop, not after what happened there. So I moved my stuff to Gunsmoke, downstairs."

"The police let you take things from the crime scene?"

Kitty says, "Only the costumes and the fabric, .and they checked those over and over. I had other equipment at home, and I moved that to Gunsmoke."

"Must've been a big job to move it all in so quickly."

"Colt arranged it."

"Colt?" I say. "So you've been on friendly terms all along."

Kitty smiles. "In a way."

I say, "And Heather let you move in, just like that?"

"What could she do about it?"

"She could say no."

Kitty says, "Colt already paid the rent in advance for his fight club, but Heather wouldn't refund it, even though she shut him down. So the space was his to use."

"When did the move happen?"

"Yesterday afternoon," he says.

"So you and Colt have an alibi for that time."

Kitty says, "My time is covered. I was with Colt yesterday afternoon, and I saw clients all last night. He's on his own for the time I wasn't with him."

On the one hand, loyal to the death; on the other, betrayal.

Branco and two uniformed cops arrive in the waiting area with Fannie Mae Knox. Branco leads them, with the two cops on either side of the Pink Lady. Branco says to her, "Thank you again for your cooperation."

She nods to him regally, without a word.

As the little group passes Kitty and me, Fannie Mae throws a disdainful glance our way, but says nothing. It's quite a sight, that vision in pink sashaying through the halls of police headquarters. The two cops take Fannie Mae out of the secure area to the elevator, while Branco comes over to Kitty and me.

"Mr. Chu," he says to Kitty, "I'll see you now." To me he

says, "You stay put. You're next." Then he takes Kitty.

Once the coast is clear, Fannie Mae Knox makes a elaborate about-face from the elevator and charges back to the secure area like a stampeding animal – a stampeding pink animal. But she can't get into the secure area. She tries talking through the bulletproof glass, but I can't hear a word. I ask the guard if I can go out, or else can Fannie Mae can come in.

He says, "Better if you go out." And he buzzes the door open for me.

In the hallway Fannie Mae says, "Pumpkin, why did you follow me home last night? You were dazzlingly obvious on that motorcycle."

"I wanted to see where you lived."

"And did you satisfy your curiosity?"

"I certainly got more than I expected, with Paladin dead on your living room floor."

Fannie Mae lifts her nose slightly. "That was the *salon* floor." She lowers her nose a bit and goes on. "Whoever did this had it all planned to the last detail. Someone is out to get me."

"Get you?"

"Yes, me!" says Fannie Mae.

"Then why didn't they kill you instead of Chester and Paladin?"

"Oh, Pumpkin!" she says, and her puffy pink shoulders seem to collapse a bit. "Is that how you feel? You'd rather I was dead?"

"No, I only meant –"

"I didn't say someone wanted to *kill* me. I said they wanted to *get* me. Chester's death has nothing to do with me, Pumpkin. Neither does Paladin's. But by killing him in my apartment, someone is trying to *blame* me. And when I find out who it is, believe me, the word *sorry* will have new meaning."

"What will you do?" I say. "Kill him?"

"Oh, I'll do much worse than that."

Then Fannie Mae Knox storms off like some deranged

and displaced Queen of the Night, paradoxically arrayed in hot pink chiffon on a bright and early Sunday morning.

As if on cue, Branco appears in the secure area, behind the protective glass. He doesn't seem bothered that I'm not in there waiting for him. He sees me and comes out into the hallway.

"I'm holding Mr. Chu for further questioning, and I don't know how long it's going to take, so I'll talk to you now."

"Kitty will keep," I say.

Branco grunts.

In his office he tells me the ME's preliminary report says Vaslav Paladin was unconscious before being strangled with the belt that was cinched around his neck.

"How do they know that?" I ask.

"Massive amount of valerian in his blood."

"The herbal sedative?"

Branco nods.

"Can you actually knock someone out with valerian?"

"Sure," he says, "but you'd have a hard time killing them with it."

"Does it taste anything like lemon?"

"Not at all," says Branco. "Why?"

"I wondered if maybe Paladin got some of what I got on Friday night."

"*Verbena fresca morta?*" he says, snagging me again with his Italian. "No, he got valerian."

I regain my wits. "What about that belt buckle? How did it get on Paladin's body if your crew picked it up at Kitty's shop?"

"They never found it there."

"It's certainly been found now."

Grunt.

"So," I say, "why did you bring me here?"

"To talk," says Branco, "among other things. Why don't you start by telling me your version of last night?"

"Which part?"

"What did you have to drink?"

"Water," I say. "Bottled water."

"Good start," says Branco. "And when did you first see Fannie Mae Knox?"

"Around ten, when I got to Gunsmoke."

"Were you with her all that time?"

"No, but she was pretty much in my sight. She never left Gunsmoke while I was there."

"Okay," he says. "Then what?"

"Then I followed her home."

"Why?"

"Because I want to know who she really is – the man beneath the fluff. Don't you?"

"Obviously," says Branco.

"So who is she?"

"We're working on it."

"What's so hard about finding out?"

"You ever heard of a thing called privacy?"

"Are you having her followed at least?"

"Now we are," he says.

"So I wasn't out of line to follow her home last night." Branco waffles. "You were all right."

"Even though you kicked me out of there."

"We had work to do," he says, "and you were in the way."

"All give, no take."

"That's your job," he says.

"Some job, like Mickey Mouse with all those brooms."

"Close enough," says Branco.

I ask him, "Did you leave one of your crew at The Cubbyhole yesterday afternoon, just in case Paladin –"

"Of course!" he says. "And no, nobody showed up – not Paladin or this other mysterious person you claim he was waiting for." Branco heaves a big sigh. "It's one of the biggest frustrations of this work – you wish you could have just ten seconds with the dead person."

"Lieutenant," I say, "that's a frustration of life. Meanwhile, it sounds like I might have been the last person to see Paladin alive, except for the killer."

Branco grumbles, "Possibly."

"In fact, now that I think of it, without me and my Mickey Mousing yesterday, there's a crucial thread that would never have showed up in your investigation."

"What's that?"

I say, "If I hadn't gone and found Paladin on my own, then you, at this very moment, here in your office, would not know about the connection between Chester Wright and Bistany Evans in Los Angeles."

"I can assure you, Stan, if we had found Paladin, we would have got that out of him, and more."

"But you didn't," I say. "That's my point."

"And my point is that we didn't have time, not after you scared him off."

"But you can't blame me that he turned up dead before you got around to finding him. At least I found him alive."

"All right," says Branco. "So you gave me what you think is a crucial thread. What do you want, a medal?"

"How about a corsage?"

Grunt.

"Fact is," he says, "given what you just told me, I might have to put you in protective custody."

"Why?"

"This 'thread' you just told me – the connection between Bistany Evans and Chester Wright in Los Angeles, and Paladin knowing about it – if the killer knows that you know, it doesn't exactly put you in a good position."

"I didn't think of that."

"Good thing I did then," he says, hinting at a smile. "Now have a listen to this." He swings around in his chair and starts the tape machine on the table behind him. After some preliminary identifying remarks – it's a taped interview of Fannie Mae Knox this morning – Branco skips ahead and then pushes "play" again.

His voice says, "Please tell me what happened when you returned to your apartment last night."

Immediately Fannie Mae bursts into hysterical wails.

"Oh, it was awful! That poor boy! Just lying there on the salon floor. Who would do that? Who would hurt him – and *me* – like that?"

Her voice quavers and fades.

Branco asks her if she is able to go on.

"I think I can," says Fannie Mae, "although I don't suppose this is very appealing, is it, Lieutenant? Someone like me, on the verge of a breakdown?"

I mutter, "What verge?"

Branco shushes me.

On the tape he says, "I make no judgments."

I roll my eyes at him.

He's stone-faced.

Branco asks Fannie Mae again if she can go on.

"For you," she says valiantly, "I will try."

"Thank you. Now, do you have any idea who could have gotten into your place? Do your friends have keys?"

"The fact is," says Fannie Mae, "anyone can enter my flat. I never lock the door."

"Living in the middle of the city?"

"I've never had an uninvited guest until now."

"How long have you lived there?"

"About twelve years," she says.

"And in all that time you've never locked your door?"

"That's right, Lieutenant. I never lock it because, I hope you'll excuse my candor, but the fact is, I often indulge." Her voice takes on coy inflection. "And then I can't find my door key, or the lock, for that matter." She chortles affably.

There's a pause on the tape. I'm sure Branco is giving her the stone face as well.

He says, "Without a key, how do you get in the street door?"

"When I'm in my cups," she says with a demi-chortle,

"there's always someone who'll let me in."

"The building isn't secure then."

"Oh, it is! They know me in the building, and they know my voice, so it's as safe as anywhere else. The truth is, if someone wants to do a bit of bad work, they'll get in no matter how tight you make a place."

Branco says, "What about your balcony door?"

"Now you may think it odd," says Fannie Mae, "but I always keep the balcony doors locked, top and bottom bolts. That is a direct opening to the world outside, so I do offer a bit of resistance there." Again that chortle, friendly, hinting of something else.

Branco says, "Tell me about Bistany Evans."

Fannie Mae pauses before answering. "Bistany is the Executive Presenter of the convention. She is very smart and very capable. She's also very attractive, but that's probably not important to you. Or is it, Lieutenant?"

I gag quietly.

Branco is a cipher.

Fannie Mae goes on. "My dealings with her are strictly business. I invested quite a bit of money in this convention, which I would not have done if I had any doubts about Bistany's abilities."

"Where did you meet her?"

"Here in Boston," says Fannie Mae.

"Did you know she used to be a Hollywood agent?"

I say aloud to Branco, "How did you know that?" Immediately he stops the tape.

"What?" he says.

"Who told you that Bistany Evans used to be a Hollywood agent?"

Branco says, "You did. Yesterday. Remember?"

"Oh, right," I say, "and then you lectured me about being unreliable."

"And you got your thank-you corsage this morning. Look Stan, the arrangement works like this: You give me information and I try to use it. I wanted to throw this Knox dame off guard, and I happened to recall what you told me yesterday, so I put it to her. There was nothing to lose."

"You're welcome, then," I say.

Grunt.

He starts up the tape. His voice says, "... used to be a Hollywood agent?"

Fannie Mae doesn't miss a beat. "I did a thorough background check on her before investing money in the convention. I may seem frivolous, Lieutenant, but I assure you, I don't throw money away. And yes, I knew about Bistany's past. She used a different name – Ramona Warwitch – but other than that, everything seemed in order."

"You didn't mind that Miss Evans changed her name?"

"Who am I to mind something like that, Lieutenant?"

"Did you know that Chester Wright was also from Los Angeles?"

"Goodness!" says Fannie Mae. "Do you think there's a link?"

"You tell me."

"There must be," she says. "Otherwise why bring it up?"

"What do you think that link might be?"

"If she was an agent, perhaps Chester was a client. After all, he was an entertainer of sorts. But if that's true ... Oh, no!" says Fannie Mae. "This is very bad. If Bistany ... Oh, the convention will be a shambles."

There's a pause.

Branco says, "Miss Knox?"

"Lieutenant, what if Bistany Evans killed both those boys?"

"Why do you think that?"

"Perhaps Chester knew something illicit, something horrible about her in Los Angeles that never showed up in my enquiries. My information was all gathered legitimately, but who knows what *isn't* in the records? And perhaps Chester arrived here in Boston and began to blackmail her about it – her illegitimate past."

"Do you have any idea what it was?"

"No, but it must have been something awful if she killed him for it. Paladin too." She gasps. "I've just thought of something even more dreadful. What if Bistany thinks I know this awful secret as well?"

"You're getting a bit carried away, Miss Knox. This is all speculation on your part."

"Lieutenant, I don't intend to tell you how to do your job. I can only tell you what I know and what I observe, and then what I conclude from those things. But now, if I may be so frank, I am concerned for my very life. If Bistany Evans killed those boys for knowing whatever it is they did, she will most certainly come after me."

"But you claim not to know what they knew."

"I claim the truth!" says Fannie Mae. "But Bistany Evans doesn't know that!"

"Now, Ma'am," says Branco.

"Oh!" shrieks Fannie Mae. "*Ma'am?* Now you've wounded me, Lieutenant, to the quick. Ma'am, indeed!"

There's a long pause on the tape, and I can almost see Fannie Mae rearing back and looking down her nose at Branco.

Finally, Branco speaks. "My apologies, Miss Knox. I've never interviewed a person quite like you."

She says, "And I've never been questioned by the police before. I suppose we're both a bit nervous, eh?"

More silence on the tape.

Branco says, "Can we continue now?"

"Yes, of course."

"How well did you know Chester Wright?"

"I don't recall that I ever spoke to him."

"Never?"

"Well," she says, "perhaps in passing."

"What did you talk about?"

"I don't recall," she says again. "I don't even recall talking to him. I'm simply trying to be agreeable."

"That's not important," says Branco. "Truthful answers are."

"As you please," says Fannie Mae.

"What about Paladin?"

"What about him?"

"Did you know him?"

"As well as any other dancer who comes into the saloon on a regular basis."

"No special interest?"

"What are you implying, Lieutenant?"

"No implication, Miss Knox. I'm just asking if you had any special interest in Paladin."

"Nothing beyond my usual interest in an attractive young male."

There's another pause on the tape. I look at Branco. He avoids my eyes.

Fannie Mae says, "I know they were a couple, if that helps."

"How did you know that?"

"It was common knowledge. You see, that's why I came to those conclusions just now, Lieutenant. Carried away, I believe is what you said of me. The fact is, if Chester knew some dark, horrid secret about Bistany in Los Angeles, and then they met up by chance here in Boston, she'd have to kill him to protect her secret. And if Chester had told Paladin the secret, she'd have to kill him too."

Branco says to me, "Now watch how she turns."

On the tape he says to Fannie Mae, "Would you please tell me your legal name?"

"Oh, Lieutenant," she says coquettishly, "a gentleman never asks, and a lady never tells."

"Which applies to neither one of us," Branco says flatly. "Since this is a double-murder case, I need your full legal name."

"I refuse to supply it."

He says, "Because of the nature of this investigation, I may have to resort to extreme measures."

"Meaning?" says Fannie Mae.

"Meaning a court order for the full disclosure of your personal life."

"If you obtain that order, Lieutenant, I'll have the District Attorney in here so fast you'll wish you'd asked me to go buggy-riding instead."

"Do you know the D.A. personally?"

"We are longtime family friends."

Branco says, "In your other life."

"That is as it may be. There is no call for rudeness."

"You certainly know your rights."

Fannie Mae says, "It is every citizen's duty. I am cooperating with you, Lieutenant, and that is the extent of what you can expect of me – unless you formally charge me, in which case, I'd have my private attorney present within the half-hour."

"Would he be in costume too?"

There's a pause on the tape. I glance at Branco. His question sounds like something I'd say. Is my presence eroding his technique that much? He may be in worse danger than I am.

Fannie Mae says, "There was no need for that remark."

Branco says, "My error."

"Are you charging me, Lieutenant?"

"No."

"Then this entire line of questioning is moot. Here I am, trying to cooperate – and trying to keep it as light and entertaining as possible, which is the best anyone can hope for in this sorry world – and in return you have become hostile."

Branco says, "It won't happen again."

Her reply is icy. "True, since this interview is finished."

There's a rustle of pink chiffon on the tape.

Branco says, "The lab is still examining your flat for evidence."

"No matter," she says. "I've taken a room at the Park Plaza for the duration of the convention."

"Then why did you go home last night?"

She says, "I longed for my own surroundings. Haven't you ever felt that way, Lieutenant? Or are you devoid of such feelings?"

Branco's phone rings. He stops the tape to take the call. He listens, then says, "I'm on my way," and hangs up. He says to me, "What do you think of the interview?"

"What do I think?"

"I'm asking you," he says.

"It sounds like a performance."

Branco says, "Do you believe any of it?"

"What do you care what I think?"

"I'm trying to understand your logic."

"My gay logic, you mean?"

"Frankly," says Branco, "yes. I'm trying to learn something from you, how you think, how you perceive things."

Why am I bothered by his words?

He says, "That's why I brought you in here this morning. I wanted you to have some time with Mr. Chu in the secure area, and I wanted you to hear some of Miss Knox's interview."

"No wonder that cop was so cooperative."

"He was instructed to help wherever possible."

"And you arranged it all just to get my take on things."

"That's right," says Branco.

"As a gay man."

Branco twists his mouth. "Informally, off the record, yes."

"I don't like it," I say.

He says, "I don't blame you. In a way, Stan, I'm exploiting you, and I apologize. But I wouldn't do it if I didn't think it would help."

"It matters that much to you?"

"Yes," he says. "It matters if we're ever going to work together."

Work together? Well, then, yes, Vito, yes! All is understood, accepted, and forgiven. I'll gladly be your gay advisor and informer – your Little Buddy.

Yes, I know. Sad. But you don't know Branco.

He says, "Anything important from Mr. Chu?"

"Only that he and Colt Remington used to be a couple."

"You mean that big guy and –"

"The butterfly," I say. "Yes."

The Little Buddy is already dispensing factlets.

Branco makes a quiet whistle. "They named each other as suspects, which is why I've got them both in here now."

"All's fair in love," I say. "When will you arrest Bistany Evans?"

Branco says, "They just brought her in. That's what that phone call was."

There's a knock on the door, and Branco's sergeant enters.

He tells her, "I'm on my way."

She hands him a sheaf of papers. "Those reports you wanted." She smiles at me, probably another accomplice in Branco's audition of the Little Buddy this morning.

Branco puts the papers on his desk and flips through them.

I discern a partial address on the top sheet and recognize Fannie Mae's apartment building.

The sergeant says, "There are still four units to do."

I see a yellow Post-It with four numbers on it, each one a digit and a letter. They look like apartment numbers.

She says, "We're short-handed, and we'll try to finish later. Maybe."

Branco grunts. At her! So I'm not the only recipient of them.

I commit the four numbers to memory just as he removes the papers from his desk.

The sergeant leaves, and Branco stands up.

"Time to go," he says, and we leave his office.

Outside headquarters I jot down the four apartment numbers I memorized. Yes, I'm going to take reports from those apartments. I'm a free agent, after all. Haven't I been reminded of that a thousand times in the past forty-eight hours? So I'll free-agent my way into those apartments and show Branco I can do more than just provide an alternative, Little Buddy's perspective on his world.

18.

ARMED WITH THE FOUR apartment numbers, I arrive on Beacon Hill, at the other end of the world from police headquarters. In the bright, post-noonday light, Fannie Mae's apartment building sits grandly, a massive brick structure that occupies most of the block. The cornerstone says 1927, which in Boston means yesterday. Tall windows all around give light to cavernous interiors. The place seems to represent the height of spacious city living at the height of those roaring, extravagant times, everything realized with proper Bostonian discretion, of course.

I decide to start with the lowest number and work my way up, maybe finish my self-assignment with a nice view of Boston from high atop Beacon Hill. But first I have to get into the building, and I don't have the assistance of last night's police brigade.

My first apartment is 1-A, but the intercom has only a number keypad, no letters. So, maybe you press a number for a letter, according to its alphabetic position? A is 1, B is 2, and so on? Hell, what can I lose? I press "1" twice and wait. A phone starts ringing, then a woman answers.

"Hello?" Her small voice is tremulous.

I tell her I need to get into the building to take reports on the incident last night.

"Can't hear you!" she says.

"Please let me in," I say.

"What?"

Then the door buzzes open, and I am inside.

I find apartment 1-A easily. Despite the solid, heavy construction of the building, the sound of a loud television gabbles its way through the door. I knock, but no one answers. Twice more, then I resort to banging, but still without results. I know she's in there – she just buzzed me in.

The resident across the hall opens her door slightly, sticks her head out – another granny gal – warbles quietly. "She's hard of hearing. You have to press the door button." Then she retreats.

Door button? Where? Then I see a small mother-of-pearl disc built discreetly into the door frame. I press it a few times and wait. The television behind the door goes silent. A few moments later, the door itself opens. The woman is small and frail, slightly bent, but with lively eyes. She smiles brightly and says, "Good afternoon."

I introduce myself and tell her I'm there about the trouble last night, and would she mind answering a few questions?

She says, "You'll have to speak up, dear."

I repeat my little spiel more loudly.

"Oh," she says. "Did you just ring the doorbell?"

"Yes," I say.

"Then you'd better come in."

I follow her inside.

A large reclining chair sits directly before a colossal television. The silver-screen images of Robert Mitchum and Jane Greer move silently across the screen. A tray table holds a pot of tea, a plate of various shortbreads, a bone china cup and saucer, and a pint of top-shelf gin.

"Would you like some tea, officer?"

"No, thanks, Ma'am."

"I won't report you."

I'm tempted, but I refuse again, then tell her I'm not with the police.

"Eh?" she says.

Never mind. I take her name, then begin the questions.

"Were you home last night?"

She says, "I'm home every night. I never used to be. You wouldn't believe it to see me now, but I was quite a pert young thing in my day. Out on the tiles every night."

"I'm sure you were. But the police were here last night, and apparently you weren't in when they rang your doorbell."

"I was here," she says. "I'm always here. But if it was late, I was probably in bed. When I take my hearing aids out, I'm deaf as a post. And my doorbell is a light that blinks, but not in the bedroom. Are you sure you don't want some tea?"

"No, thank you, Ma'am. Tell me, before you took out your hearing aids yesterday, did you hear anything unusual? Or see anything out of the ordinary?"

"I saw it all on the news," she says, "this morning. That was a surprise. Nothing much happens in this building. It's like a mausoleum. And then all of a sudden, someone gets killed here."

All of a sudden is right, especially. for the victim.

I try another tack. "Do you know the person in the apartment where it happened?"

"They're not a mixing crowd here."

I tell her, "She wears a lot of pink."

"Oh, her!" says the woman, and she laughs. "Yes, I know her. She's colorful, that one." She leans close to me, and I can smell the gin, really high-class stuff. She lowers her voice and says, "I think she's really a man." Then she winks and laughs again.

I ask, "Are you friendly with her?"

"I'm friendly with everyone, young man, and why not? You spend the same amount of effort. Why not start out friendly? Sure, you meet some duds, but you never know when you're going to meet someone interesting."

"How friendly are you with the woman in pink?"

"How friendly?" she says.

"Do you know who she really is?"

The charming little tippler thinks a moment. "I just call

her the lady in pink."

"So when you say you're friendly, you mean casually. You don't really know her well."

She makes a wrenlike shrug. "I'm friendly, that's all."

"Have you ever buzzed her in, the lady in pink?"

"Buzzed?" she says.

"Has she ever rung your doorbell to be let in?"

"No," she says. "Nobody rings my doorbell these days, except the mailman. He forgets his key sometimes. That's who I thought you were. When I was a girl there were lines of young men ringing my doorbell. He's a nice young man too."

"Who?"

"The mailman," she says. "Now, if you're not going to join me, officer, I'm going to have my tea without you."

"I'll have to take a rain check, Ma'am."

"Come back anytime. I'm always here, and I always have a fresh pot of tea."

"Thanks," I say, and head out the door.

Dragnet was never like this. I might just take her up on the offer, once the case is closed and I'm off-duty.

The second apartment on my list is one floor up. The person who answers the door is a young woman – very young. In fact, she looks like she's trying to be thirteen. Maybe she is.

I introduce myself and ask her if her parents are home.

She says, "How should I know?"

Defiant from the start.

I tell her I'm helping with the investigation, and I need to talk to her parents.

"They live in Dover," she says, like it's too much trouble to say the words.

Dover is an ultra-posh town west of Boston, beyond the suburbs.

"*I* live here," she says.

Apparently Mommy and Daddy spared no expense to get their peevish progeny out of their respective hairstyles. And speaking of hair, someone is really burning the shafts on this girl's head.

I get her name, then ask her, "Were you home last night?"

"No."

"Do you know what happened here?"

"I saw it on the news," she says. "It was way cool to see my building on TV."

"Cool?"

"Like, someone was really dead," she says, "like *here.* It's always like, somewhere *else* people get killed and then they get on TV. But finally it happened here. It was like, *wow!*"

Like, yikes.

I ask, "Do you ever buzz people into the building without knowing who they are?"

She glowers at me. "Do you think I'm stupid?"

"Is that a no?"

"Yes, that is a no." Then, just to make it clear, she repeats it like the petulant brat that she is, all in one word: "No-I-do-not-buzz-people-into-the-building-without-knowing-who-they-are. *Okay?* Now, I'm going out and I have to get ready."

Fair enough, fair maiden. But before I leave, I tell her, "You ought to ease up on the chemicals, or you'll permanently damage your follicles."

"Don't preach to me!" she rails. "I do what I want with my body!"

"It's not your body, Miss Thing, it's your hair."

"What's wrong with my hair?"

"It's like *dying*, doll. Like really, like on TV."

"Do you know how much I paid for this?"

"Too much," I say.

"The guy who did it –"

"Don't name names!" I screech. "Professional ethics forbid gossip about fellow estheticians."

She is stunned by my outburst. Well, maybe a little real-world fright is good for someone whose only emotional truth comes from television.

I say to her, "But you can mention the salon, if you want."

Tentatively she says, "It's on Newbury Street, near the Ritz."

I gulp. "Not Snips?"

She tries to smile, but it's an alien gesture. "Do you know Ramon? Isn't he a hotty? I just love him!"

Too hot for his own good and the good of others. Armed with the criminal's identity, I'll report this calamity to Nicole. How dare Ramon let her walk out of Snips looking like that? And where was Nicole when the heinous crime was committed?

I continue my rounds to anonymous subject number three, who lives two flights up, on the fifth floor. But he or she is still not home. Wherever the lucky, holiday-celebrating bastard is – out of town or just off the premises – the report will have to wait.

So then, finally, my last visitation. Onward to the top floor and apartment 6-D.

From the setup on the other floors, I know how the apartment numbers run, and 6-D will be at the same end of the building as Fannie Mae Knox's apartment. There are only four apartments up here – talk about square footage! – and the doorways are slightly staggered, meaning the top floor residents don't have a direct, face-on view of each other's comings and goings.

As I walk down the hall I notice a shallow table at the far end, near the door to 6-D. There's a huge vase of fresh-cut flowers on top, and they fill the hallway with a sweet, bland, familiar fragrance. Last night I didn't notice the flowers or the gorgeous piece of furniture they're sitting on. There were other distractions after all: a caterwauling drag queen, a small army of cops, and a dead dance divo.

The furniture and the flowers give a sense of refinement, as though that end of the building is reserved for people of the highest taste and breeding – a bit of irony, considering Fannie Mae Knox's flamboyant persona and Paladin's dead body within her overdecorated premises last night.

As I pass by Fannie Mae's digs, I see the bright yellow police tape running across the partially open doorway, and just within, a cop standing guard. I slip by quietly on my way to apartment 6-D at the end of the hall.

I press the discreetly recessed door button.

I wait.

I press it again.

Again I wait.

I'm about to press the button a third time when I hear the door being unlocked. It's pulled open slightly, and a man's voice says weakly, "Who is it?"

"Stan Kraychik."

The door opens a bit more, and I recognize the person standing there and leaning against the door jamb with his crown of silvery white hair. It's F. Lloyd Newbegin, the man I met at the Boston Vade Mecum Society on Friday afternoon. He's holding a small icepack against his left cheek, and he's wearing a fine silk robe over fine silk pajamas. In the dim hallway light he looks drawn and tired. He squints at me, as if trying to figure out why I look familiar.

"We've met before," I say.

"Excuse me?" he says softly.

"At the Vade Mecum Society."

"Sorry," he says. "Can't say as I recall."

"The belt buckle."

"You've lost me, young man." He starts to close the door.

"The Civil War belt buckle," I say. "I came to see you on Friday afternoon. You were just leaving for the weekend."

"Ah, yes," he says. "Of course. You'll have to excuse me. I'm not feeling well." He shifts the icepack slightly.

"Toothache?" I say.

"No, just a bump. Refrigerator door at my friend's place. I was getting ice cubes and didn't expect it to close on my face."

He manages a smile, and his teeth are very nice – white and straight and even and – I suddenly realize they aren't the same teeth Mr. Newbegin had on Friday afternoon. But how do you ask a Boston aristocrat where he got new choppers on a holiday weekend?

I say, "You're lucky your teeth weren't damaged."

He looks at me askance.

So much for delicacy.

"I'm sorry to disturb you," I say, "but it's important, about the trouble next door."

"I've been away," he says. "But I had to return sooner than planned. Caught some kind of bug or something. Got in just a little while ago. I laid down for a nap when ..." He waves his hand feebly. "There are some men out on my balcony making a ruckus, measuring, looking, whatever they're doing. Honestly, there is no consideration."

"I'm sorry you're not well."

He says, "The whole purpose for buying into a building like this is to ensure your privacy. In this day and age, that's the very least you should get for your money – some peace and quiet. But does it help? Not when half the Boston police are parading around on your balcony, and to hell with tranquility."

Tranquility. A potpourri of tranquility. That's what the hallway flowers smell like. The Boston Vade Mecum Society.

"I'm sorry," I say again, "but this is important. Has anyone from the police spoken to you yet?"

"They've done plenty to disturb me, that's for sure."

I say, "If you can manage it, I'd like to ask you a few questions. It won't take long."

"Are you with the police?"

"I'm taking reports," I say.

Vague enough?

He closes his eyes and heaves a sigh. "Very well."

I expect him to invite me inside, but he doesn't.

I ask, "Will you be all right talking here?"

Again he waves his free hand. "Just get on with it."

"You haven't been here all weekend. Is that correct?"

"Yes, that's right. I was out of town visiting friends."

"Where?"

"In Rockport," he says.

Rockport is a coastal town north of Boston. It started as a granite quarry in Colonial times, then evolved to an artist colony, and is now an endless real estate auction.

Mr. Newbegin continues. "We went out for dinner last night. Apparently I ate something that didn't agree with me, and so I returned home today. I don't like being a sick guest."

"How did you travel?"

"By car."

"So you were well enough to drive."

"Yes," he says, "but really, I must –"

"Just another minute, please. What time was it?"

"Was what?"

"When you got back here?"

"Just a little while ago," he says. "You can ask those officers next door if you need corroboration."

"And where did you have dinner last night?"

"At the White Crow," he says.

"Nice view," I say.

His eyes flash brightly for a second. "You know it?"

I nod. "The wine list is impressive."

He chuckles softly, no *har-har* today. "Young man, you don't know what you're talking about. Rockport is a dry town."

"Including restaurants?"

"As of last night it was."

He's passed my little test. I, the quasi-alcoholic with North Shore connections, know all too well that Rockport is BYOB at all times. Apparently Mr. Newbegin knows it as well.

I say, "Do you know about the trouble next door?"

"No," he says, "but I guessed something was wrong, with the police banging about like that. What happened?"

"Someone was killed."

He stands up straight. "Here? In the next apartment?"

"That's right."

"When?"

"Last night."

"Oh," he says. "Well, I'm very sorry for that unfortunate creature. When I'm feeling better, I'll have to do something."

"Do something?"

"Send flowers, make a contribution, something."

"Why would you do that?"

"Because it's what's done, young man. Have you no sense of propriety? It's just that, right now, I'm not even well enough to think about it, let alone do anything."

"Mr. Newbegin, it isn't your neighbor who was killed."

"No? Then …?" He shudders. "Did that sorry creature kill someone? That would be too awful, to have a neighbor who is a killer. Do the police have her now?"

"No, but she is under investigation, along with others."

"You mean she's walking the streets?"

"Innocent until proven guilty."

"Hard to believe she'd kill anyone," he says. "Poor thing. It's such a tragedy when people turn out like that. Still, I say live and let live. Should she be pilloried for who she is?"

I ask, "Do you happen to know who she is?"

"Who?"

"Your neighbor."

"I have no idea," he says. "Wears a lot of pink, that's all I know. Frankly, we aren't the mixing kind of people in this building, for which I am eternally thankful. There's nothing worse than having some neighbor at your door, unannounced and wanting something. Here we respect privacy and maintain a sinecure of quiet."

Mr. Newbegin relishes the word.

I'll try it on Nicole later.

He goes on. "This is a sanctuary from the constant pushing on the street, the crowd mentality, etcetera." He moves the icepack from his cheek to his temple, and I see a slight bruise on his jaw. "I'm afraid I have one of my migraines coming on," he says. "The mere thought of those pressing mobs is enough to throw my nervous system into a fit."

I say, "Maybe the flowers are bringing on your headache."

"No, no," says Newbegin. "My headaches come right after receiving a great shock. To think my neighbor is a killer!"

"Who puts them there?"

"Puts what?" he says.

"The flowers."

He snaps at me. "Why are you asking so many questions?"

"Sorry, it has to be done."

He quickly retreats into docility. "No, I'm sorry, young man. I'm not well, you see. As for the flowers, I choose them."

"They remind me of the ones at the Vade Mecum Society."

"You're clever to notice," he says. "They are from the same florist. Now, if you don't mind ..." He wilts again into the doorframe. "It really is a bad time. You must excuse me."

"Just one more thing, please. You're being very helpful. Have you ever buzzed your next-door neighbor in?"

He hesitates before answering. "Will it incriminate me?"

"I'm just gathering information," I say.

"But I won't have to appear in court or anything?"

"You might have to make a formal statement."

He considers this, then says, "The truth is, I let her in quite often. I think she drinks, and the poor thing needs all the help she can get. That kind of charity costs nothing."

"Do you buzz other people in as well?"

"No," he says. "And now, I really must lie down."

He recedes into his apartment and pulls the door closed.

Dick work done, I turn to leave. But first I stick my face in the flower arrangement just outside F. Lloyd Newbegin's door and inhale. There's something about that sweet scent that niggles me. It's here and it's at the Vade Mecum Society. I'm standing there, sniffing flowers like Ferdinand the Fairy Bull when a cop comes out of Fannie Mae's apartment, nearby. He sees me and smirks. Maybe he recognizes me from last night, or headquarters, or somewhere. I straighten up, smile at him, and wave. He comes over to me.

I tell him, "I was here last night."

The cop eyes me warily. "Thought you looked familiar."

"I know Lieutenant Branco. Just doing a bit of clean-up duty here."

"That so?" he says. "For the lieutenant?"

"Kind of," I say. Just two syllables, but my voice wobbles like those two old gals on the first floor. I plant my feet into the floor and ask him, "Do you know when that guy got in?"

Not quite butch, but not a tremulous, withering soprano either. I point toward Mr. Newbegin's doorway.

The cop stares at me, then says, "About half an hour ago."

"Thanks," I say, attempting a grunt that will never happen. Then I head down the hall and out of the building.

19.

I GET HOME AROUND four-thirty. I do some deep breathing to relax myself before phoning Branco to report my delinquent activities on Beacon Hill. But – relief! – he's not available, and my nerve-wracking confession can wait.

I call someone more simpatico.

Benjy answers on the first ring.

I say, "Are you still raking in holiday pay?"

"Penny! Where are you? What are you wearing?"

"Rev up your fingers, Benjy. I need your help."

"I'll be right over."

"I need the unexpurgated truth on Miss Fannie Mae Knox."

"Her again? Penny, what is this fixation with drag queens?"

"It's not a fixation. It's one particular drag queen."

"That's worse," says Benjy.

"But this one is secretive, and it bothers me."

"Intrigues you is more like it. In the old days, you'd shampoo them and break down their defenses."

"I'd shampoo their wigs, Benjy. And their defenses are unbreachable."

"Tough as titanium."

"And just as expensive," I say. "But those days are gone. I don't do hair anymore, and neither do you."

"But we still have each other," he says.

"Right. So, now, what about Fannie Mae Knox?"

Benjy sighs. "Maybe she has a website."

He does his typing-talk routine. Is this how new languages are born?

"Okay, Penny, my stellar search talents turn up nothing relevant on a Fannie Mae Knox. And yes, before you ask, I have tried all reasonable alternate spellings. The only thing is a pile of links on low-cost mortgages for first-time home-buyers."

"That's not her, unless she owns the company."

He says, "It's a government agency."

"Maybe that's the joke, Benjy. She fashions herself a combination real estate mogul and Fort Knox."

"Do you have her address?"

"I do now, since I went back there today."

"To her place?" he says.

"You can't get everything from a computer."

"You almost can, Penny."

Benjy types the address information I give him.

He says, "It looks as though the property in question is actually owned by a person named Fannie Mae Knox."

"But that's her drag name. What's her real name?"

"Hang on," he says. "Let me dig a little deeper here."

More typing, more sound effects. Moments pass.

"Server is slow today," he says. Then, "Nope, that's how the property is registered, Penny. Fannie Mae Knox."

"It can't be."

"Penny, it's a fact. I can't change it."

"But she's a drag queen."

"So? They're entitled to own property."

"But it's a fake name."

"Fake yes," says Benjy, "but it might still be legal. Movie stars do it. Why not drag queens?"

"But someone, somewhere must have a record of who she was before she was Fannie Mae Knox."

"It's called the CIA, Penny. And no, I don't have access."

"Who does?"

"Your cop friend, probably."

"So he can find out."

"If he wants to," says Benjy.

"Can you check the DBA registry?"

"Ah," he says. "My Penny is such a quick study. We only touched on DBA's yesterday."

"Doing business as, you said. Yesterday it was Heather Blossom. So who's doing the business as Fannie Mae Knox?"

"I'll do it with you, Penny. Anytime."

"Focus, Benjy. Focus on the task at hand."

Benjy types and asks me, "Why aren't you game, Penny?"

"This investigation is my game."

"But when it's over?"

"I can't think that far ahead."

"You're no fun."

"Probably not. Just tell me if Fannie Mae Knox is a DBA."

"Okay, Penny! Jeez, who starched your knickers? I have a T-1 line, but sometimes the other servers are slow."

"I feel as though time is running out."

"It is, Penny. For all of us. Okay, here we go. Well, looks like Fannie Mae Knox is not a DBA per se, but I've got one more database, and that one lets me search in retrograde inversion."

"Retrograde inversion?"

"Kinky, huh?" says Benjy. "It means is going backwards, upside-down."

"And that's going to yield a useful answer?"

"Oh, ye of little faith ..." Benjy makes soft cooing sounds as he types commands and his computer does his bidding. Then, finally, he says, "Well, well."

"Well, well, what?"

"Penny, does this sound familiar? The Dolly Madison Rugala Revocable Limited Partnership Trust."

"That's the company that owns The Cubbyhole and half of the Gunsmoke Saloon."

"Almost bingo, Penny! It's not quite a company, but yes,

you retained your lesson well from yesterday."

"You taught me, Benjy."

"When are you going to teach me a few things, Penny?"

"I doubt I can. Focus, Benjy."

"Right. So! The Dolly Madison Rugelach Revocable Limited Partnership Trust owns The Cubbyhole and part of Gunsmoke, okay?"

"So far, so good."

"Now, get this. It also owns a business entity called Fannie Mae Knox."

"How can a business own a person?"

"The same way Snips Salon owns you."

"Bad joke, Benjy."

"Sorry. But remember, Penny, it's a trust, not a business. And you're also confusing Fannie Mae Knox the drag queen with Fannie Mae Knox the business entity."

"So, unconfuse me."

"You have Mercedes Benz the car company, right?"

"Yeah ..."

"That's the business entity. Now, over in the next town lives a guy named Stanley Benz who has a daughter named Mercedes, okay? She's the person."

"It's a stretch, Benjy, but I follow you."

"You follow me in a stretch 'Benz? Very cute, Penny."

"Benjy ..."

"Okay, the point is, they're just names. The business entity and the person could be, coincidentally, absolutely and intimately connected, as in being the *same thing*, but they might also be totally and absolutely unrelated, as in not being the same thing in any way, shape, or form whatsoever."

"So," I say, "Fannie Mae Knox the person lives in an apartment that just so happens to be owned by Fannie Mae Knox the business entity, which in turn is owned by the Dolly Madison Rugala Limited Partnership Trust."

"Revocable," says Benjy. "Yes."

"I still don't get it, but never mind."

"More important," he says, "is that we know there's a real

Dolly Madison Rugala living in Baltimore."

"So maybe it's time to *cherchez la femme*."

"Maybe," says Benjy.

"Except I can't go to Baltimore. Maybe we can phone her."

"We?" says Benjy.

"Me, then."

"Penny, if you were a Baltimore dowager, would you trust a phone call from a private dick in Boston?"

"No."

"So maybe your cop friend can phone her."

"I doubt Branco will follow up on this," I say. "It's what he calls my crystal-ball gazing."

"I bet his are like titanium – rare, precious, tough."

"Titanium is also lightweight, Benjy."

"Then I take it all back."

I say, "Those flowers are still bothering me too."

"Balls to flowers, that's my Penny."

"There are flowers in the hallway near Fannie Mae's apartment."

Benjy sighs. "Back to the drag queen?"

"And they smell familiar."

"Familiar like what?"

"Like makeup or something. I remember from the ballet, when I was in the dressing rooms, the smell of cold cream the dancers used to remove their makeup."

"See why I love you, Penny? There you are in a ballet company dressing room, and what gets your attention? The cold cream. So maybe it's not the flowers you're smelling. Maybe it's your drag queen's makeup. You know how much they use."

"She's not my drag queen."

"Our drag queen, then," says Benjy. "Is she *our* drag queen?"

I say, "But she's not the one with the flowers. It's her neighbor, the guy who works at the Boston Vade Mecum Society."

"Maybe he bought them for her."

"But he has the exact same flowers in his office."

Benjy says, "Then maybe *she* bought them for *him*. Maybe they're secret lovers or something."

"No, he told me he orders all the flowers."

But speaking of secret lovers ...

"Benjy, I might have to cancel the cookout tomorrow."

"Why? Is the drag queen having a private party or something?"

"No," I say. "It's Branco. I doubt he'll be there. The way this investigation is going, I might not even be there."

"Penny, life goes on, even with a murder investigation."

"So it might be just you and Nicole."

"And your cop's wife," says Benjy. "She'll be there."

"We'll have to play it by ear."

"And do what?" says Benjy. "Pull out frozen entrees and throw them in the microwave?"

"Benjy, it's a cookout, not a *cordon bleu* showcase."

"Cooking on the barbee isn't limited to fast food."

"The what?"

"The barbee, short for barbeque."

"Short where, Benjy?"

"In better cooking circles."

"Such as?"

"Penny, I attended the Culinary Institute when I lived in San Francisco."

"Is that when you were also a champion two-stepper?"

"That's right," says Benjy. "I met my dance partner in cooking class."

"The straight guy from Oregon who dances with men."

"That's California for you."

"First a dance trophy, now a chef's toque. Why don't I know these things about you?"

Benjy says, "Because you don't give me a chance."

"A chance for what?"

"To show you how much I can do for you."

"Benjy, let's just keep it simple, so there's no big letdown if it doesn't happen."

"Sure, Penny. I can wait."

"I mean the cookout, Benjy."

"That too," he says. "Do you still want that wireless phone? I can bring it tomorrow and give you a lesson."

"I guess it's inevitable."

"You'll never be the same."

"That's exactly what I 'm afraid of."

We say goodbye.

I have one more call to make before getting ready for the big hoe-down tonight. I phone Nicole and report on Ramon's criminal acts on that young woman from Beacon Hill.

Nicole is utterly blasé. "He's going to make the necessary adjustments, Stanley, at no charge to her."

"He'll extort a tip."

"Everyone makes mistakes, darling, including you."

"Nikki, I never let anyone walk out of Snips looking like that."

"Ramon was especially tired that day."

"Ramon is especially tired, period."

"Now you see why I need you back in the shop, to keep on top of things, so a crisis like that doesn't happen again."

"Doll, the only way I'd come back now is on the condition that Ramon is out."

"Don't be cruel, Stanley. He brings in a lot of business."

"But he can't do hair."

"There's more to life than exemplary hair care."

"With that attitude, doll, you'll lose your reputation."

"It's our reputation, Stanley, once I get you to sign the papers."

"I'll have to be a silent partner, Nikki."

"That's genetically impossible."

"Then I'll exercise *droit du seigneur*."

"Darling, I believe that's a feudal custom where a land-owner had sex with a vassal bride before her husband did. And I never suspected you were inclined toward Ramon that way."

"Repelled, Nikki. *Repelled.* But to continue your feudal

exposition, if that young bride turned out not to be a virgin, she could be drummed off the land forever."

"You're making that part up."

"And since Ramon is anything but virginal, I say good riddance!"

"Stanley, this may be our first business disagreement."

"Hardly, doll. By the way, I might have to cancel the cookout tomorrow."

"But it's less than twenty-four hours away. Your guests are counting on it."

"Here's the guest list, Nikki. You, me, Branco and wife, and Benjy. Who in that tiny group is going to be heartbroken if I cancel the event?"

"Benjamin, for one."

"Benjy is the only one."

"Costanza too, probably. She doesn't seem to get out much."

"Have you talked to her?"

"She calls me occasionally," says Nicole. "Poor girl never expected that Vito's work would keep him away from home so much."

"What, she wants servicing during daytime hours too?"

"Stanley ..."

"Once that baby arrives, she'll be busy enough."

"That's a chauvinist attitude."

"Vocabulary alert!"

Nicole says, "I predict once that baby is born, Vito will spend much more time at horne, and you'll eat your words."

"But right now," I say, "Branco is in charge of a double homicide investigation, so he probably won't be at the cookout. And if he's not there, what's the point of having it?"

"Ah," says Nicole. "So that's how things stand."

"What things?"

"The things in your version of the world, Stanley."

"What do you mean?"

"Never mind, dear. What are you doing tonight? It's Sunday, which means *two* videos, right? Alone as usual?"

"Not this week, doll. I'm still on the case too, as a free agent, so I'm going to the Mucho Macho Honcho Hoe-down."

"Will Benjamin be there?"

"It's work, doll, not play."

"Too bad," she says. "Still, it sounds better than staying at home alone."

"In my sinecure of quiet," I say, plying F. Lloyd Newbegin's word on her.

Nicole makes a little gasp.

"What's the matter, doll?"

"Stanley, that's a malapropism."

"I knew you'd be impressed."

She stifles a laugh. "You might want to look up the word." Then she hangs up.

Phone calls completed, I throw together dinner: a chicken breast braised in butter and olive oil, spiked with lemon and capers, and a spinach souffle on the side (frozen and nuked – sorry, Benjy).

While I shower and change for another night of dick work, I think about all the people who are spending the holiday weekend doing "normal" things like partying, drinking, cooking out, being with friends, getting a head start on their tans, and otherwise debauching themselves. Then I think of Chester and Paladin, who are both nowhere and doing nothing, as far as anyone on terra firma can say for sure. And then I stop thinking.

Dressed and ready, I'm on my way, outside and just pulling the door closed when I hear the phone ringing. The answering machine picks up. It's Branco. I rush back in and pick up.

"Hi, Lieutenant."

"Out of breath again?"

I'm always out of breath when you call, Vito.

I say, "I was just leaving for the hoe-down."

"I hear you paid a call on Beacon Hill today."

"Uh ..."

"What did you do," he says, "memorize the apartment

numbers from that paper on my desk?"

"A free agent takes whatever he can find."

"You told one of the lab guys I sent you up there."

"Not quite," I say.

"Close enough."

I admit it. "Close enough."

"Why did you do it?"

"You mean go up there?"

"Use my name!" he says.

"Because," I say, stalling, "because I wanted to check on something, a very simple fact, and that cop knew the answer, so I dropped your name to help me get it. It was in the line of work, if that matters."

"Don't do it again," he says. "Now, did you find anything I ought to know about right away?"

I skip the boring bits and go straight to the fact that F. Lloyd Newbegin is Fannie Mae Knox's next-door neighbor.

Branco says, "What about it?"

"Two things. Number one, his teeth."

"His teeth?" says Branco.

"His teeth were new."

"So?"

"Where does someone get new teeth on a holiday weekend?"

Branco says, "Maybe he already had them."

"Odd thing number two – the flowers in the hallway."

"Christ!" says Branco.

"Newbegin has flowers in his office that smell exactly the same."

The phone is silent.

"Lieutenant? Hello?"

Eventually Branco comes back on. "Sorry, Stan. I've got a lot of things going on here."

"Here's something else," I say. "Have you run across any reference to a Dolly Madison Rugala in Baltimore?"

"No, why?"

"She's an old heiress who created a trust that owns Fannie Mae Knox's apartment, along with half of the Gunsmoke Saloon, and all of The Cubbyhole."

"You've been busy," says the cop.

I've been a good Little Buddy.

I say, "My contact has."

He says, "You tell your contact to call me immediately."

"Roger!"

"Is that his name?"

"No, his name is Benjy."

"Who's Roger?"

"Roger," I say, "as in, 'got it' or 'will do.'"

There's another pause on the line.

"Lieutenant?"

"Sorry, Stan. It's crazy here."

"What happened with Bistany Evans?"

He says, "It didn't take much for her to retract her alibi with Colt Remington. Everything went up in smoke, and I barely put the screws to her."

Maybe the hope of another kind of screw unhinged her.

I say, "So you arrested her? Guilty as charged."

"Don't cheer yet, Stan."

"What finally convicted her?"

"Stan, you're jumping the gun."

"Was it that business in Los Angeles?"

Branco says, "That turns out to be absolutely true. Bistany Evans told me the whole story about being Ramona War-witch, and it all checks out, totally legitimate."

"What about the stolen money?"

"We're still working on that," he says.

"Did she deny it?"

Branco says, "I can't discuss it."

"Why not?"

Silence on the phone.

"Lieutenant?"

He says, "I can't ask Bistany Evans anything because I've just released her."

"You what?"

"Just now," he says. "I had to let her go."

"But she's guilty."

"No, Stan, you said that."

"You could have held her."

"Look," he says. His voice is hard. "She made one call to Los Angeles, got her lawyer on the line, and the first word out of his mouth to me was 'harassment'. No hello, no name, no nothing. Just 'harassment'."

"And you backed down?"

"I had to! I'll stand my ground when I know I'm right. I'll risk my job on it. But I don't have the evidence. And I certainly don't owe you an explanation."

"So you let Bistany Evans go."

"I had to!" he says again.

"Then I guess I'll see her at the hoe-down."

"I don't want you to go there, Stan."

"Why not?"

"Just ... don't go."

"Something coming down?"

Branco says, "I can't discuss it."

"Will you have undercover people there?"

"I said I can't discuss it!"

"You don't have to tell me who they are."

"Damn right!" says Branco.

"I thought we were working together."

"You stay home tonight," he says. "I'll call you later."

"Later when?"

But he's already hung up.

Stay home?

Right.

20.

IT'S AFTER SEVEN WHEN I arrive at The Castle. The hoe-down is scheduled from six to ten, maybe to ensure enough time afterwards for budding romances to continue their surge toward full bloom. And if the hoe-down proves romantically barren, there's still time to hit the bars and clubs, where, even on a holiday weekend – especially on a holiday weekend – you'll probably find a willing bed-buddy. Face it: You *must* get laid over Memorial Day weekend. Otherwise, your summer will be sex-barren. It's as reliable as the ground hog seeing his shadow in February.

Or not.

Unlike my previous visits to The Castle, when the sidewalk thumped with the beat of music, tonight there is no discernible sound coming from the big hall. Nothing. *Nada. Nihil.*

In the foyer, there is no pink anyone selling tickets or checking passes. The last chance for love is apparently a free-for-all. But I see a crowd milling about inside the great hall. As soon as I go in, a brief, ear-splitting sound blasts from the PA system:

BY YOUR MAN!

Then it goes silent.

Impatient murmurs and mutterings throughout the crowd: "C'mon!"

"Let's go!"

"Just fix it!"

"Buy a new one!"

YOUR MAN!

I recognize the strangulated snippet as Patsy Cline.

STAND B–! STAND B–! ST-ST-ST-ST-ST!

Exasperated moaning from the crowd.

And poor Patsy's got a digital stutter.

I see Heather Blossom and Fannie Mae Knox standing together near the stage, so I go over there.

"Evening, ladies. What's the problem here?"

"Problem?" comes their unison reply.

GO WALKIN'! WALKIN'!

Ever-increasing irritation within the crowd.

"That problem," I say. "The music, or lack of it."

Fannie Mae explains. "With Bistany, er, indisposed, we put Colt in charge of the hoe-down as master of ceremonies. But then we needed someone to run the music, so he's teaching Kitty how to work the sound system."

"Doesn't seem to be happening," I say.

WALKIN'! WHEN I! WALKIN'! WA-WA-WA-WA-WA-WA!

Heather stands there beaming, as if things couldn't be better. "More important," she says, "now that everything is settled, we can plan for the future and get things back the way they were, before we all got swept away by Bistany Evans and her fancy ideas. From now on it will be just the Gunsmoke Saloon in Boston, which is exactly how it ought to be in a town like this."

Boston, where culture progresses in retrograde inversion.

Fannie Mae says, "Fortunately I had the foresight not to put any funds directly into Bistany's hands. Who knows where the money might have ended up?"

I say, "Maybe back in Los Angeles."

Heather and Fannie Mae both swallow nervously.

CRAZY!

Heather says brightly, "What's sad is how Bistany seemed so nice. I never thought of her as a killer. It's just awful. I'm sure glad the police finally got her."

"But they don't," I say. "Not anymore. They released her."

"Released her?" say Heather and Fannie Mae simultaneously.

"On what grounds?" says Fannie Mae.

"Lack of evidence."

Suddenly Heather looks very worried. "You mean, she's free?"

"And running wild," I say.

CRAZY!

Heather says, "Maybe we should do something about the music."

I say, "I still can't make sense of that trust."

"Then perhaps you should leave it," says Fannie Mae.

"But there are so many links to it – Gunsmoke Saloon, The Cubbyhole, your apartment ..."

Fannie Mae's and Heather's jaws drop in tandem.

Fannie Mae says, "Someone has been very busy behind the scenes. Have you told the police about your little discovery, Pumpkin?"

"They don't seem to care."

She smiles. "At least someone has some sense."

"But I figure, since you two are linked by that trust, then who knows? Maybe you're secretly married or something."

CRAZY FOR FEELIN'!

"Married?" says Fannie Mae, and she attempts one of her chortles.

Heather says, "It's not for want of trying."

Fannie Mae raises her pink-gloved hand to halt any further comment from Heather. Then to me she says, "It is an indication of your own uncouth and limited scope, Pumpkin, that you cannot imagine two people sharing a trusting and mutually beneficial friendship without sex coming into it."

"Who mentioned sex?" I say. "I was thinking about the financial advantage. You just said 'mutually beneficial'. Maybe you two set up the trust to protect the shared wealth between you. You're in business together, after all. So maybe marriage is an additional way to protect the assets.

Fannie Mae says, "We are partners in business, yes. But that doesn't require the bond of matrimony."

"Just a thought," I say.

"Perhaps you think too much, Pumpkin."

But Heather is standing there, looking wounded. Maybe she *feels* too much.

The crowd suddenly applauds as Colt and Kitty descend from the DJ booth together. They trot up onstage, and despite Colt's hard horsy flanks and Kitty's delicate pussy paws, their footsteps are in absolute synchronization.

Colt grabs the mike and says, "Sorry about that, folks. We're in kind of a crisis situation here, and I was trying to show Kitty how to run the sound system."

Kitty leans close to the microphone. "I can do more than sew."

The crowd responds with hoots and hollers and catcalls.

Colt grins. "But I decided to put it on the presets. And before I fire it up, Kitty and I would like to say something."

Frustrated grumbling from the audience.

"It'll only take a minute," says Colt, "and then we'll all get back to dancing and kicking up some serious shit. The fact is, after what happened to Chester Wright and Paladin, and now with Bistany Evans being arrested –"

A huge incredulous roar rises from the audience.

"That's right," says Colt. "Bistany killed those boys. And because of that, Kitty and I have decided to call a truce and to make a pledge to each other in public."

"We've seen the light," says Kitty, "and it is love."

Love? Light? From sexual antonyms?

Someone yells, "I thought you were straight, Colt."

Kitty says, "We have an understanding. Colt can be straight whenever he needs to be, and it's all right with me. Just as long as I'm the only guy." Kitty leans close to Colt. "Honey."

Honey?

Fannie Mae mutters, "I think I may spit up."

Colt says, "Life is easy once you accept who you are."

Kitty says, "Right after the convention we're heading down to Orlando."

Heather says, "Aw, a June wedding."

Fannie Mae rolls her eyes.

Colt says, "When you come right down to it, we're the kind of people who need to live in a theme park –"

Kitty finishes the sentence. "– where we can help meet the entertainment needs of others."

Colt says, "Now, there's just one more thing I want to say to you all. After all this bad business, I realize all the things I've been doing to other people – messing with their heads and their bodies – it was all to prove how strong I was, how much power I had over them. But I don't want to develop that side of myself or anyone else. So as of this moment, there will be absolutely no more fighting or head-shrinking for me ever again. From now on it's the simple life."

Simple life? Or simple mind? In one brief holiday weekend, a savage macho beast is tamed by a willowy wily costumer. That country music sure is right-powerful stuff.

Colt says, "I think I'm just about the happiest man alive today."

Kitty says, "Me too."

"And so," says Colt, "to celebrate the courage it took for me and Kitty to come to our personal place of happiness and joy, we are asking you, the audience, to give us permission to award ourselves the prize for The Most Together Couple."

Stunned silence from the crowd.

Next to me, Fannie Mae mutters, "How dare they!" Her words, though quiet, echo through the momentary stillness of the hall. Then she says to Heather, "That was not part of the agreement."

Heather says, "Do you want me to go up and –"

"No," says Fannie Mae. "Leave it. Just leave it!"

Onstage, Colt and Kitty await the verdict of the audience.

One person yells out, "Do whatever you want, but let's dance!"

The crowd cheers at that.

But now there's a new disturbance near the entrance. An all-too-familiar voice is demanding to know, "What is going on here?"

It's Bistany Evans, and she looks like a vengeful queen come to regain her throne from the unworthy usurpers. I leave Fannie Mae and Heather and move quickly to head her off at the pass. On the way I see that the Loco Moto Mavericks are also in the hall. Maybe there'll be some real entertainment in this place after all.

I get to Bistany and stand in her way.

"Yew!" she says. "Move it!"

"How many more people are you going to kill to keep your dark and dirty little secret?"

"What secret?"

"Whatever Chester knew about you. That's why you killed him, because of what he knew about you in Los Angeles."

Bistany screeches, "That is not why I killed him! I mean, I did not kill him!"

"And then you had to kill Paladin because Chester told him all about you."

"I did not kill anyone!" says Bistany. "Look yew, I told the police everything, and they let me go. So what is your problem?"

"My problem is that you're getting away with murder."

"What exactly do yew think I'm so afraid people are going to find out about me?"

"I don't know," I say, "but it was enough to make you –"

"That's exactly right!" says Bistany. "Yew don't know, and that is why I am so sick and tired of yew. So have a listen to what I'm going to say and maybe yew'll learn something."

She pushes through the crowd toward the stage. As she makes her way, people recognize her and applaud her arrival. By the time she's up on the stage, the entire audience is cheering her return.

And I thought she was the enemy.

She grabs the microphone from Colt and addresses the

audience. "Hi, yawl! Are yew glad I'm back?"

The cheers are deafening. It's like a game show where the host humiliates the players *and* the audience.

She says, "Now, I promise we're going to have some fun tonight, fellas. But first I want to share with yew and bring healing and closure to some awful lies being spread about me. Yes, I did know Chester Wright in Los Angeles. Yes, I was his agent out there. And yes, I did close my agency down without any warning to any of my clients, and I left them all high and dry. I have carried the heavy guilt of what I did with me for the past year. But the circumstances could not be helped. And this is the god's-honest truth: I never took a cent from anyone that I didn't rightly deserve. I made the best of a bad situation, and now I put myself before yew all and ask your forgiveness. Even though yew may not know me personally, I'm asking yew to look in your heart – it will cost yew absolutely nothing but a kindly thought – and try to find a way to forgive me for all the bad things I did in Los Angeles, and for which I am now truly repentant."

A low murmuring throughout the crowd.

"Oh, thank yew!" she says. "I knew I could count on yew! And just so yawl know the *whole* truth, I'm telling you the real reason the Boston police suspected me. It was all thanks to the negativity of one single person. That's how bad negative thinking is. One bad thought can make an entire police force think a person is guilty. So, do yawl want to know who the Most Negative Person in Boston is?"

Here she dramatically points an accusing finger at – whom else? – me.

"*Yew!*" she says. "Yew've made my life a living hell since Friday, and this is all your fault!"

My fault? What did *I* do? Try to get her arrested, tried, and convicted of two murders. That's all. And she still hasn't denied killing Chester or Paladin, or told us any dark and dirty secret either. Just that she was an agent who bolted with funds.

No matter, the crowd is howling in accord. They're probably going to tar and feather me now. But before they have a chance, Bistany turns on Colt and Kitty, who are still onstage and looking stunned by her impromptu expiation and cleansing ceremony.

She says to them, "I don't know what yew two are up to, but I have a hoe-down to run. Colt, yew get your butt back up in that DJ booth. Now!"

But Colt replies, "I'm through taking orders from you. You can run the music yourself."

He and Kitty link arms and head off the stage. Kitty looks back over his shoulder and bares his teeth at Bistany.

"*Bitch!*" he says.

Bistany screams back, "You're the bitch, you little bitch!" The audience cheers.

Kitty lets go of Colt, turns, runs back, springs into the air, and throws himself onto Bistany.

But she flips him off with a Judo throw.

He does not land softly.

She says to the audience, "Colt taught me how to do that." They cheer.

Colt poses for a face-off with her, and she taunts him.

The audience begins a rhythmic applause that grows into mob chanting: "*Go! Go! Go! Go!*"

But Colt reconsiders the attack, and instead he backs off. He's seen the light, after all. So, he goes and gathers Kitty up off the floor, and they leave the stage together, stooped and vanquished.

The audience hoots and boos their departure.

It's not a game show. It's a sports arena.

"*Now!*" says Bistany, "does anyone out there know how to DJ?"

One guy yells, "Me!"

Bistany says, "*Yew* are hired! Get your butt up in that booth and make some music for the rest of us."

Meanwhile, Fannie Mae Knox is making her way toward the exit door. I get there just before she does, and I stand in her way.

"I met your neighbor today," I say.

"My neighbor?"

"The gent who buys the flowers for the table outside his apartment door, across the hall from you."

Fannie Mae says, "Mr. Newbegin *selects* the flowers, Pumpkin. They are purchased cooperatively by all the top-floor residents. And that is not a table they're on. It is a Hepplewhite console. Now, please let me pass."

CRAZY!

I say, "Poor Mr. Newbegin. He wasn't feeling very well."

"That's too bad," says Fannie Mae. "But I'm sure it didn't deter you, did it, Pumpkin?" She forces a bland smile at me. Nice teeth. She hasn't replaced *hers* this weekend.

She makes another move to leave, and I block it.

"Let me pass, Pumpkin."

"You can't leave until you've judged the costume competition."

"That's later," she says, "if we're lucky. With this debacle, who knows? Now, let me pass!"

"But you'll miss the showdown."

"What showdown?" she says.

"That proves Bistany is the killer."

Fannie Mae says, "Nobody can prove anything against anyone, Pumpkin. In fact, now that everything is out in the open about Bistany, *whom* will you pursue?"

"Not everything is out in the open yet."

"No?"

"You got pretty upset when Colt and Kitty were going to award themselves that prize for Most Together Couple."

She says, "They didn't succeed."

"But if they had?"

"I would not have allowed it."

"You have the final say."

"The first and final say," she says.

"The purse-strings."

"Since you prefer bluntness, Pumpkin, yes."

"Is that how it was for the dance contest too? Was it

rigged for Paladin and Chester to win?"

She says, "That prize was to be a reward, an encouragement for his talent."

"Paladin's."

"Yes."

"Yet you told the police you hardly knew him."

"One can admire from a distance, Pumpkin."

"Maybe you yearned to be closer."

"Oh, Pumpkin," she says, "are you going to become tedious again?"

"If you really felt strongly for Paladin, it must have been difficult not to express it somehow."

"But I did express it," she says, "with that prize for him."

"Did you help Paladin in other ways?"

"How?"

"Gifts," I say. "Those collar tips. Paladin told me they were a gift, but he wouldn't identify the giver. Did he really not know? Or was he being discreet?"

Fannie Mae's eyes narrow and she stands firm.

I say, "And what about Chester?"

She flinches. "I could tolerate whatever was necessary for Paladin's success."

"Tolerate?"

"The infatuation would pass."

"Paladin's? Or Chester's?"

"Both," she says.

"And if it didn't?"

"We'll never know now, will we?" she says. "So sad."

I say, "It must have been painful to watch them dancing together, Paladin holding Chester instead of you. Are you the person Paladin was waiting for at The Cubbyhole yesterday?"

"The where?" she says.

"It would explain how you knew about Bistany and Chester in Los Angeles – if Paladin told you."

Fannie Mae says, "That's enough, Pumpkin! Next you'll be saying that Chester told me."

"Did he?"

"Why do you keep harping on such a small thing?" she says.

"What difference does it make now? Everyone knows about it."

"But they didn't know about it yesterday afternoon, when Paladin told me."

"There's no proof of that," says Fannie Mae. "Anyone could have known. I suspect all this insistence on one or two little details is really about you, Pumpkin. You, you, you. You're desperate to interpret things to fit your own ends. Perhaps you' re trying to prove something to that lieutenant. Hmm? Have I touched a nerve? Are you the lieutenant's little mascot, perhaps? Does he throw tidbits your way, and do you scramble after them like a good little dog? You see, I can be provocative too, Pumpkin. And irritating. But what is the point of it all? Why do you want to irritate me? Next you'll be accusing me of killing Paladin – and Chester too, probably. You'll find some way of saying that I put those collar tips on his body, and that Civil War buckle on Paladin's. But you can't do that, can you, Pumpkin, because it isn't so. I don't care how much you distort the facts. The truth is, you have steered yourself off-course, and you're quite lost."

I say, "How did you know it was a Civil War belt buckle?"

"Hmm?"

"The belt buckle on Paladin's body. How did you know it was a Civil War artifact?"

Fannie Mae shrugs. "It looked old enough."

"But it's not been stated anywhere that it was a Civil War belt buckle."

"There you go again," she says, "trying to make something out of nothing. A mere slip of the tongue, and you're ready to hang me."

"A telling slip," I say. "And yet one more thing that lets me see through the pink haze that surrounds you – your pink camouflage."

"Be careful, Pumpkin. You think you're on the verge of uncovering something important, don't you? Well, what if you have? What if the very thing you're thinking right now is true? What good will it do you, or those boys? They're gone now."

"But you aren't gone, either one of you."

"You can't prove a thing," she says.

"The teeth, the costumes, that chortle – everything about you is an act."

"That doesn't mean it isn't true. If you think I'm such a good actor, Pumpkin, have a look at this."

Fannie Mae bends slightly away from me and takes something from her billowing pink skirts. Before it registers, she whirls around me and gets me in a neck lock. As I gasp for air, she flashes a large knife before my eyes.

"Was there anything about *this* in the police reports?" she says. "What? Nothing to say, Pumpkin? Lost your voice? Don't you recognize it? You're so lucky with chance discoveries and recognitions."

There's definitely a man choking me now.

The people nearby clear away from us. They watch us apprehensively, and that's all they do: watch.

"This," says Fannie Mae, "this is an authentic Civil War bayonet spear. The Vade Mecum Society might find it missing from their collection, except that I happen to know the curator of that collection personally." She chortles. "You don't like that sound, do you, Pumpkin? Too theatrical for you? But I do know that curator. I know him far more personally than I ever knew Paladin. And what are you going to do about it?"

Calm in a crisis, that's the only masculine trait I can boast. As I gasp for air, I don't panic. Instead, I hear the lyrics to "Miss Otis Regrets", who pulled a gun from under her velvet gown and then shot her lover down. Madame. Except that this Miss Otis has an antique knife to my throat and she smells of floral cold cream. Or maybe a funeral parlor.

Fannie Mae says, "You're like a persistent and nasty little dog – yapping, yapping, always yapping. You don't know what you're doing, and you don't care. You set your sharp little teeth in and hang on till the death. Anyone with any sense would let go, but not you – you and your utter disregard for the things some of us must do to get along in this sorry world. I try to live my time in a lovely dream, but you doggy people are always hounding me, reminding me that we are on the earth, and our feet are in dirt, and there are no dreams, only pursuer and prey."

More people are gathering around us. They know something is wrong, that something very bad might happen, and they might actually witness it all, frame by frame. Like on TV.

Fannie Mae notices them. "What are you all looking at?"

Bistany's voice comes over the PA system. "Fannie Mae, is he bothering yew?"

"Not anymore!"

I'm quickly becoming an anaerobic animal, but I can still see. Colt and Kitty are huddled together in a nearby alcove. The intrepid new DJ starts playing "Back in My Baby's Arms".

Heather is also standing nearby, watching along with the others, waiting to see what happens next. She gazes adoringly at Fannie Mae, as if I'm the one creating havoc, and Fannie Mae, Heather's own true love wouldn't hurt a flea.

Well, I may be a yappy little dog, but I don't have fleas. Just incipient asphyxiation. And why isn't anyone trying to help me? Is this my punishment for blaming Bistany Evans?

Bistany's voice comes over the PA system. "Fannie Mae, is there some problem over there? I can't see from up here. Do yew want someone to give you a hand? Should I call the police or something? Yew give me the word and I'll do it. Fannie Mae? Can anyone tell me what's happening? Why are yawl just standing there? What is going on?"

Suddenly the PA systems buzzes loudly, then crackles, then squeaks and squawks and howls with feedback, and finally goes out with a loud *POWP!* Bistany's voice and the music are silenced.

At least I'll die without her being the last thing I hear.

Just then the watching crowd begins to rustle. A turbulence moves through it, the same way water churns and bubbles when the tide turns. Moments later, people clear the way for three members of the Loco Moto Mavericks, who glide their glistening wheelchairs directly up to Fannie Mae and me.

The lead guy says, "Maybe you ought to let him go now, lady."

Fannie Mae says, "You think he should live and I should die?"

"Nobody has to die."

"Oh but we all die," she says. "It's what life comes down to – the struggle through time until the final defeat. Why not have some say in the matter?"

The knife digs in a bit. Not bad for an old blade.

The Loco Matos move in, but Fannie Mae stops them.

"It will be on your consciences," she says.

"All right, all right," says the leader, and they back off.

My one hope, vanished, just like that.

Meanwhile, the crowd continues to watch. What else can they do? Pray? Grateful are we that we be not in the clutches of the bloodthirsty transvestite beast, but that we may continue to dwell in our own vouchsafety.

From game show, to sports arena, to church.

Calm in a crisis.

And definitely not nice.

That's me. *I.*

Then who appears without fanfare?

Branco.

Branco and the cavalry. Rather, a bunch of other cops.

At that same moment, the three Loco Moto Mavericks get up out of their wheelchairs – undercover cops! – and press the crowd back to make room for the Branco and his crew.

Then the inexplicable happens: Fannie Mae releases me.

Just like that. It feels as though she melted behind me, and suddenly I can breathe again. I almost fall to the floor but stay on my legs and scramble to Branco's side.

The cops move toward her, and she halts them with her pink-gloved hand.

"One moment, please," she says. She looks at Branco. "You

were considerate to me, Lieutenant, in spite of who I am. Please, may I address the audience? I feel I owe it to them."

Branco doesn't reply, doesn't nod. He doesn't do anything. Maybe he's too incredulous that something like this can really be happening in Boston. Besides, Fannie Mae is still wielding that knife, so at least one person stands to get hurt.

Another moment passes. Nothing happens. Nobody moves. Then Fannie Mae reaches up and pulls off her wig.

It's F. Lloyd Newbegin underneath, but you knew that.

In a flash – Eureka! – I realize that all those flowers he keeps around him are to obscure the persistent and lingering scent of Fannie Mae's makeup and cold cream. Some guys hide their truth behind a wife, F. Lloyd Newbegin hides his behind flowers.

His voice is suddenly stentorian, like some famed orator from Civil War days. "It was the collar tips," he says to the great assembly. The words echo through the high open space of the hall. "If I had known," he says, "I would never bought them for him, for Paladin." Newbegin shakes his head pitifully. "I created Gunsmoke for him too. He needed a place to develop his dancing, and I needed an investment opportunity. Heather wanted to realize her secret dream too, so it worked for all of us." He says to Heather, "But it was really our secret."

Through her tears, Heather nods lovingly at him.

"After that," says Newbegin, "Bistany and the convention materialized, and I sensed that Paladin would finally achieve the fame he deserved, and he would thank me. Who would guess that Bistany – yes, you, Bistany – would catalyze all that ensued."

Bistany yells from the stage, but she can barely be heard without her microphone. Something about "Yew son-of-a-bitch!"

F. Lloyd Newbegin continues. "Bistany with her *inclusivity* campaign." He chuckles. "Such nonsense. But because of her scheming with fate, my Paladin became coupled with Chester. And who was Chester? A boy with a limp. My Paladin was a god. A god to whom I had made fitting sacrifices, to whom I had paid homage, for whom I had done everything. And because of all I had done, the god looked briefly upon me with favor. But Chester meant far more to him than anything I could do or give him."

The cops start to move in again, but F. Lloyd holds up the bayonet spear, and the officers halt.

"I regret that I killed Chester," he says. "I didn't intend to. I always watched him when we were in proximity. Friday night when he left Gunsmoke, I followed him up to Kitty's shop. I intended to reason with him, to pay him to leave Paladin, anything! But he wouldn't yield. Called me sad, old, hopeless. Then he repeated things, intimacies I'd shared with Paladin. He laughed. He and Paladin had laughed together about me. And where was I? Left with the party persona I had invented to hold onto my dreams."

He shakes his head.

"Sad, very sad," he says. "The scissors were there, and I used them. With Chester gone, Paladin would finally experience a sense of loss, that utter emptiness of knowing no matter how hard you work and hope and pray, that you are not going to get what you want. But no such defeat for Paladin. He called me in the middle of the night after he found Chester's body. He wanted me to help him find Chester's killer! Even dead, the boy controlled my Paladin. So, yes, I planned his death – got him unconscious with valerian – easily concealed in those fruity drinks he liked so much – then I strangled him. As much as Paladin had hurt me, I didn't want him to suffer. He did kick once – a spasm, but I don't think it was pain – and he broke my denture, the one I wear as a normal man."

F. Lloyd smiles toward me.

"When you came by my place today, I had my fancy-dress teeth in. Clever you for noticing, especially since Paladin never once suspected that I, F. Lloyd Newbegin was Fannie Mae Knox. He never bothered to observe the most elemental truth about me – about anyone – that we are far more complex than the visible person we present to the world."

F. Lloyd keeps his eyes on me.

"From the very outset I knew that if anyone was going to expose me, it would be the likes of you. Even my slip of the tongue – *Civil War belt buckle*." He chuckles again. "It was no slip. It was time to be caught, and I wanted to be caught by you because you are so moral and noble and sure of yourself. You think you *know* what you believe in, but what do you know? I don't even know who I am, else how could I kill two young men in love?"

Branco says, "That's enough now. Drop the knife."

F. Lloyd Newbegin holds up a finger. "My final word. A warning to all you young bucks who see men like me as nothing more than desperate, paunchy cash-cows. Love is dangerous. You must suppress the urge. Never yield. For here you see the sorry consequence of surrendering to love. Love kills."

F. Lloyd presents himself to Branco. "You can take me now."

Branco says, "Drop the knife."

Someone in the audience yells, "Pathetic old queen!"

F. Lloyd whirls toward the voice. "Would you have my head? You all forgave Bistany when she confessed. And you all cheered briefly for Colt and Kitty. Why not me? Because I'm old? Because I killed someone? Two people? If I were young and handsome, would you forgive me? If I were a tough young brute, would you find my actions *exciting*?"

The heckler says, "Get him out of here! Let's dance!"

Branco nods to one of his crew to go and shut the yapper up.

F. Lloyd says, "How would you have me do it? Should I put this dagger to my own throat, like this?" He puts the knife to his throat and holds the pose dramatically. "And then should I plunge it in, like this?"

The cops run to stop him, but it's too late. Blood is spurting everywhere. He knew exactly where to put the big blade before shoving it in.

Heather runs from the crowd and throws herself onto F. Lloyd's body. "Oh, Floyd, Floyd! Why didn't you wait? No one would have known. I told you I forgive you. I forgive everything you ever did." She looks up at me accusingly. The front of her gingham dress is drenched with blood. "This is all your fault!"

Everything is my fault, doll.

Onstage, Bistany Evans is dumbfounded, finally.

Kitty and Colt tremble in each other's arms.

* * *

After the body of F. Lloyd Newbegin, alias Fannie Mae Knox, has been removed to the morgue, I ask Branco, "What brought you here?"

He explains. "I'd already arranged an undercover team to be here to watch Bistany Evans. But when you told me about Fannie Mae Knox's next-door neighbor, I radioed my crew to go and question him. Funny thing – he'd gone out."

"Despite his dire illness."

"Meanwhile," says Branco, "we'd tailed Fannie Mae from headquarters back to the Park Plaza, where she remained in her room. Or so we thought."

"Don't tell me," I say. "Adjoining rooms."

A nod from Branco. "She goes in one door, half-an-hour later, Newbegin comes out the other door. Time passes. He returns to his room, half-an-hour later, she comes out her door."

"Talk about a quick-change artist."

Branco says, "And you happened to catch him at home."

"As a free agent," I say.

Grunt, goes Branco. Then he says, "The adjoining residences brought it all together. Newbegin probably used the balcony to enter and leave Fannie Mae's place when necessary."

"But Fannie Mae probably never used the balcony."

"A wise decision," says Branco, "dressed like that."

So concludes the first and probably last International

Mucho Macho Honcho Convention in history. I mean, how can you top an event like this, even outside of Boston?

I get home and phone Nicole, but she's not there. I leave a message: "Tomorrow is definitely on and the Vito Brancos will definitely be attending."

I call Benjy, and he's not home either. I tell his voice mail: "We're on for tomorrow. I've decided on burgers and beer, Branco-style. See you at four, if not before."

Neither of them calls me back, so I take myself to bed and wonder if I have the requisite psychological strength to continue being Branco's Little Buddy. Friday morning I had balked at hunting down missing trinkets. But would this be any better, spending day and night tracking down people who kill for what they consider very reasonable reasons?

21.

THE NEXT DAY, MONDAY, is the actual holiday, and it's pouring rain. Thunder, lightning, the whole show. But New England luck is holding: no snow.

I don't go out to shop for food. Why bother, when a cookout is hopeless? In fact, I don't go out for anything except a quick run to the liquor store. I've decided to take everyone out to dinner, and I make a reservation at Bobby's Beef 'n Brew, a steak house on Shawmut Avenue, just a block away. Nothing fancy, just good food and a full bar. It will be fun to surprise my friends, to have cocktails at my place then toddle off to a restaurant.

Meanwhile, with the rain and wind outside, my high-tech HVAC is getting a good workout. *My* workout? I make a pot of coffee and hunker down with some videos. I also try calling Nicole and Benjy again, but all I get is their respective voice mails. Maybe they're out shopping together for Benjy's trousseau.

Nicole arrives at four, alone, under an umbrella the size of Rhode Island. She's dressed to the tits in an expanded copy of one of her vintage Paris originals: a black-on-white polka dot party dress.

"Going somewhere summery, doll?"

"Just a holiday cookout," she says.

"Where's Benjy?"

"He'll be coming later."

"When later?"

"Does it matter?"

"Yes, doll. Plans have changed. I have a little surprise for everyone."

"Really, darling? Tell me about it while you get me a drink."

"If I tell you, it won't be a surprise."

"Then just get me the drink," she says. "One of your nerve-numbing Cosmopolitans would be nice."

"Not beer?"

Nicole shudders as she lights up a cigarette. Within seconds my state-of-the-art air filtration system kicks in to keep everything morning-meadow fresh – but no flowers! I mix Nicole's drink, adding enough for myself.

"By the way," she says, "I see you've dressed up too. Is that part of the surprise?"

Before I answer, the doorbell rings. It's Branco and his young wife, Costanza. They're slightly wet from the rain. Branco is mouth-wateringly casual in gray slacks and a burgundy crewneck that complements his olive skin and steel-gray eyes. Costanza wears a dress of pink pique knit. Pink? How can she with impunity wear pink? Doesn't the color bother Branco, remind him of a certain pink-chiffon self-sacrifice last night? Even I have a moment of sadness for Fannie Mae and her alter ego.

But in the words of Bistany Evans, life goes on.

Branco hands me a chilled bottle of Pinot Grigio, which brings me right back to now. Costanza hands me a box of Italian cookies. "Home-made," she says. "For coffee, later." The bottom of the box is warm.

Costanza asks for a glass of wine. "It's good for the baby."

Brava, girl!

While I open it, Branco pulls a bottle of local ale from my fridge. Then he asks for a glass.

A glass?

Nothing about this cookout, starting with the weather

and continuing on to the wardrobes and the beverages, is turning out as expected.

Drinks in hand, Nicole and Costanza take a tour of my house's framework. And some girl-talk, probably.

I ask Branco, "Can we discuss the case?"

"Depends," he says.

"I still don't know what Bistany's deep dark secret was."

He tells me, "In addition to being an agent, she ran an escort service under the name Vera."

"Vera," I say. "Paladin mentioned the name, but it was a friend of Bistany."

"No," says Branco. "Vera was Bistany. Once she started talking yesterday afternoon, there was no stopping her."

"A catharsis-seeker."

Branco grunts – even here, even off-duty.

"So, that's it?" I say. "Bistany's big secret is that she was a hooker?"

"Not a hooker, Stan. An escort service."

"The subtlety eludes me. What about the missing money?"

"One of Vera's new customers arrived for his first date with a briefcase full of cash. When Vera saw the money, she also saw a brighter future for herself. So, while he was asleep she took the money and ran."

"You mean she stole it."

"All depends on how you interpret the facts."

"Another subtlety," I say.

Branco says, "Her client was found dead the next day. Vera assumed she'd be accused of it. Then she read that the guy was running from the L.A. mob, and she figured they'd come after her."

"So she left town."

"Exactly," says Branco. "But she didn't have to. Turns out the L.A. police found the mobster who killed her client."

"But she didn't know that."

"Not until yesterday," he says. "We found out in our investigation and informed her of it as well."

"And the money?"

"She's going to return it."

"She still has it?"

Branco says, "She invested it."

"Not in Mucho Macho Honcho?"

"No," he says. "Overseas account."

"And now she's returning it?"

He explains. "The bank it was embezzled from is very happy to get the principal back. And, since Bistany didn't steal it from them, they're not going to prosecute."

"Just like that?"

"They're working out a deal," he says.

"And she goes free."

"She's still worried about the mob."

"Looks like there'll be another persona and business scam in her future. But where does Chester come into it?"

Branco says, "Chester worked for her."

"But she was his agent."

"Right, and she got him work." Branco grins, eyebrows raised.

"You mean ..." I say with a gulp, "... Chester was an escort?"

Branco nods. "A specialty item. Some people have a penchant for imperfection."

"Wow," I say quietly.

My Chester, my dream of boyhood bliss, was a male escort. And Paladin was a hustler. And together they'd found a moment of happiness. Kind of puts my nonexistent love life in perspective.

Branco says, "By the time Bistany arrived in Boston she had completely changed her appearance – lost weight, dyed her hair, changed her speech style – but Chester knew who she was right off."

"And she was afraid he'd turn her in."

"Which is why she cut that deal with him."

"The deal!" I say. "What was that deal?"

"The deal was that special dance prize," says Branco.

"Most Together Couple."

"Right," he says. "Bistany promised Chester a national tour if he'd keep quiet about her. He agreed, since he was ready to go legit as a square-dance caller. Then Bistany sold Fannie Mae on the idea as well, who saw the prize as a chance for her own protege, Paladin."

"Fannie Mae said the prize was her idea."

"No," says Branco. "In fact, we've got another person in custody who swears it all started with Bistany."

"Heather Blossom?"

"That's right," he says. "She was Newbegin's confidante."

"Does she know how he killed Paladin?"

"Yes," says Branco. "Newbegin was going to meet Paladin at The Cubbyhole, but once you flushed him out of there, he went to Newbegin's place and waited for him there. Newbegin showed up fresh from his costume change at the Park Plaza, took him inside, got him unconscious ..."

I say, "All this from Heather Blossom?"

Branco nods. "She knows everything Newbegin did, both as himself and as Fannie Mae Knox."

"Making her an accessory after the fact."

"For two counts of murder," says Branco. "I swear she's eager to serve time. She's carried a torch for Newbegin since she met him last year."

I say, "At an exhibit of cowboy art by Mr. Bryce Timothy at the Boston Vade Mecum Society."

Branco says, "How'd you know that?"

"I didn't. It just came together now."

"And that," he says, "is the sign of a good dick."

While I try to regain consciousness, Nicole and Costanza return. I know they've heard pretty much everything we've said, since my place is wall-less.

As if to prove my point, Nicole says, "I still don't believe any person could conceal his identity the way that man did."

I tell her, "F. Lloyd Newbegin had a very bland face, doll. That fair complexion and those vague features are the best ones for a total disguise, because the face doesn't exert a personality of its own."

"Like yours, you mean?" says Nicole.

I stick out my tongue.

"Still," she says, "to claim your own lover never recognized you is preposterous!"

"That word, doll, is reminiscent of Sherlock Holmes, who was always donning costumes and duping Dr. Watson and Mrs. Hudson, both of whom knew him intimately."

"Stanley, those are just characters in books."

"Sometimes you have to suspend disbelief in real life too."

Nicole asks Branco, "How did that man manage to procure the collar tips and the belt buckle before killing the two boys?"

Procure?

Branco says, "Both items were in Wang Chu's costume shop. Newbegin put the collar tips on Chester's body, and he took the belt buckle with him."

I say, "He probably recognized it from my mentioning it earlier that day." I ask Branco, "What about the other money, the Dolly Madison Rugala Revocable Limited Partnership Trust?"

"Soon to be revoked," says Branco. "We phoned the woman in Baltimore, and she's notified her lawyers. The money will now go directly to the Vade Mecum Society, no longer filtered through her late nephew and his dubious investments."

"So Dolly was Newbegin's aunt?"

Branco nods. "He changed his name once he got her to put a pile of money into that trust. He also separated the first two letters of his first name. Floyd Rugala became F. Lloyd Newbegin. The new name marked his new beginning as an entrepreneur."

"Where'd you hear all this?" I ask.

"From Heather Blossom," says Branco. "She's been spilling her guts at headquarters. She and Newbegin were business partners, remember."

"Though she wanted more."

Branco says, "It's always sad when a person chases after

someone and there's no hope of getting what they want."

A pregnant pause, as the four of us look at one another.

The doorbell rings. I open the door. Benjy dashes in from the pouring rain.

"Stand clear!" he says.

Six handsome male models parade into my house, a full brigade of cater-waiters who immediately commandeer the kitchen with noisy chatter about the weather and the house and the holiday and Oh!

Benjy goes to the door and calls out, "Okay, guys, your turn!"

Two beefy movers carry in a large round dining table and set it up. A second trip and there are five chairs around it. Within minutes two of the caterers have transformed it into a formal dining setup, complete with white linen, china, silver, crystal, candles – the works.

Benjy says quietly to me, "Surprise, Penny."

Nicole looks on, bemused.

I introduce Benjy to Branco and Costanza.

Benjy's reaction to meeting the cop in person for the first time is a simple, stunned, "Oh."

I tell Branco, "Benjy is my contact, in case you want to talk shop."

Costanza says, "And he is such a cute boy!"

"Isn't he?" says Nicole.

I tell Benjy, "I was going to take us all out for dinner, but this is even better. How did you manage it, last-minute, on a rained-out holiday weekend?"

Benjy says, "I have my sources."

"I'll pay you back, I insist."

"In services only," he says. Then he pulls me aside and lowers his voice. "Besides, I wanted to impress your cop and his wife. She's not showing as much as I expected, Penny. You made her sound like the *Hindenburg*."

"I guessed wrong."

Costanza appears and drags Benjy off. "Let me get you some wine, you cute thing."

As she leads him away I hear him say, "Vodka Stinger."

Nicole comes up to me. "Such excellent taste in that young man. And so generous."

"He's trying to get me to propose."

"So?" says Nicole.

"Nikki, can you see me married to a phone queen?"

Branco is suddenly behind me. "Then you'd be snagged too."

Outside there is a flash of lightning and a crack of thunder. Costanza screams. Benjy laughs. I look at Nicole and Branco. No one says a word.

Elsewhere people are off by the ocean, weeping that their holiday weekend is being ruined by rain. Others are getting down and dirty with their holiday honey.

Me? I'm exactly where I want to be.

GRANT MICHAELS

Grant Michaels, the pen name of Michael Mesrobian (1947–2009), wrote six mystery novels centering on Stan Kraychik, a gay hairdresser turned amateur detective. "I wanted to do something that would really entertain readers. What could be more outlandish than a gay hairdresser who solves crimes?" said Mesrobian concerning the 1981 debut of *A Body to Dye For*.

Boston was home for the author. He studied at Boston University then settled in San Francisco. Returning to Boston in his mid-30s, he began writing novels, landing a deal with St Martin's Press' Stonewall Inn imprint. His friends loved him for his incredible sense of fun, wit and giggles. He had a great love of music, good food, gin martinis and sometimes great scotch. An independent spirit, his conversation was filled with truth, beauty, an artistic bent touching on dance, piano, drama, writing, art, ballet, and opera.

He made an ideal travel companion, as one friend relates, who shared a 3-week tour of France and Spain taking in the beautiful European male eye candy. Another friend recalled taking ballet classes with him where he invented the "rescue pas de deux". This involved showing up next to his friend at a difficult moment, providing someone to grab on to for support. The ballet teacher was not amused, particularly by the giggling.

All six novels were shortlisted as Lambda Literary Award finalists in the Gay Men's Mystery category.

About ReQueered Tales

In the heady days of the late 1960s, when young people in many western countries were in the streets protesting for a new, more inclusive world, some of us were in libraries, coffee shops, communes, retreats, bedrooms and dens plotting something even more startling: literature – highbrow and pulp – for an explicitly gay audience. Specifically, we were craving to see our gay lives – in the closet, in the open, in bars, in dire straits and in love – reflected in mystery stories, sci-fi and mainstream fiction. Hercule Poirot, that engaging effete Belgian creation of Agatha Christie might have been gay ... Sherlock Holmes, to all intents and purposes, was one woman shy of gay ... but where were the genuine gay sleuths, where the reader need not read between the lines?

Beginning with Victor J Banis's "Man from C.A.M.P." pulps in the mid-60s – riotous romps spoofing the craze for James Bond spies – readers were suddenly being offered George Baxt's Pharoah Love, a black gay New York City detective, and a real turning point in Joseph Hansen's gay California insurance investigator, Dave Brandstetter, whose world weary Raymond Chandleresque adventures sold strongly and have never been out of print.

Over the next three decades, gay storytelling grew strongly in niche and mainstream publishing ventures. Even with the huge public crisis – as AIDS descended on the gay community beginning in the early 1980s – gay fiction flourished. Stonewall Inn, Alyson Publications, and others nurtured authors and readers ... until mainstream success seemed to come to a halt. While Lambda Literary Foundation had started to recognize work in annual awards about 1990, mainstream publishers began to have cold feet. And then, with the rise of e-books in the new millennium which enabled a new self-publishing industry ... there was both an avalanche of new talent coming to market and burying of print authors who did not cross the divide.

The result?

Perhaps forty years of gay fiction – and notably gay and lesbian mystery, detective and suspense fiction – has been teetering on the brink of obscurity. Orphaned works, orphaned authors, many living and some having passed away – with no one to make the case for their creations to be returned to print (and e-print!). General fiction and non-fiction works embracing gay lives, widely celebrated upon original release, also languished as mainstream publishers shifted their focus.

Until now. That is the mission of ReQueered Tales: to keep in circulation this treasure trove of fantastic fiction. In an era of ebooks, everything of value ought to be accessible. For a new generation of readers, these mystery tales, and works of general fiction, are full of insights into the gay world of the 1960s, '70s, '80s and '90s. For those of us who lived through the period, they are a delightful reminder of our youth and reflect some of our own struggles in growing up gay in those heady times.

We are honored, here at ReQueered Tales, to be custodians shepherding back into circulation some of the best gay and lesbian fiction writing and hope to bring many volumes to the public, in modestly priced, accessible editions, worldwide, over the coming years.

So please join us on this adventure of discovery and rediscovery of the rich talents of writers of recent years as the PIs, cops and amateur sleuths battle forces of evil with fierceness, humor and sometimes a pinch of love.

The ReQueered Tales Team

Justene Adamec • Alexander Inglis • Matt Lubbers-Moore

Mysteries from ReQueered Tales

A Body to Dye For
Grant Michaels

A Stan Kraychik Mystery, Book 1 – Stan "Vannos" Kraychik isn't your everyday Boston hairdresser. Manager of Snips Salon, which is owned by best bud (and occasional nemesis) Nicole, Stan thought this day was an ordinary one. A delivery van backed into the salon's rear driveway and accidentally spilled gallons of conditioner, leaving Stan and hunky Roger) embracing in a gooey mess trying to staunch the flow, with little success as they slid and slipped with Nicole watching on with rolling eyes. Later Roger is found murdered.

Stan's client, Calvin Redding, who owns the apartment where Roger's body was found, can't explain why the body is dressed in little more than bowties. Enter Lieutenant Branco, dark, muscular, Italian, (straight) of Boston PD Homicide who immediately suspects everyone, especially Stan. In an attempt to clear his name, Stan travels to California, takes up mountain climbing, eavesdropping, spying, schmoozing, and a little bit of schtupping, all in an attempt to find the truth.

Grant Michaels' zany series of adventures starring Stan Kraychik garnered multiple Lambda Literary Awards including a 1991 nomination for Best Gay Men's Mystery. For this new edition, Carl Mesrobian reminisces about his brother Grant in an exclusive foreword, and Neil S. Plakcy provides an introduction of appreciation.

Love You To Death
Grant Michaels

A Stan Kraychik Mystery, Book 2 – Valentine's Day is fast approaching and everyone has a sweetheart, except Stan Kraychik, Boston's sassiest hairdresser. Ever hopeful of meeting Mr. Right, Stan attends a gala reception that culminates in a death by poisoning, and romantic problems take a back seat to murder. Then Boston police arrest Stan's friend Laurett Cole, who leaves her four-year-old son in Stan's care. In his quest to free Laurett from suspicion and himself from his ill-mannered ward, Stan finds himself exploring the secrets of a revered Boston institution, the Gladys Gardner Chocolate Company. There, along with the sweet edibles, he finds an assortment of not-so-delectable murder.

A Lambda Literary Awards Finalist in 1993, this new edition includes a foreword by Frank W. Butterfield

And don't miss ...

Dead on Your Feet: Stan's new boyfriend, choreographer Rafik, is accused of murder

Mask for a Diva: Stan nabs a gig as wig master to a summer opera festival but the final curtain for one star comes down early

Time to Check Out: Stan takes a holiday to Key West but a dead bodies turns up anyway

Dead as a Doornail: In the midst of renovating his new Boston brownstone, Stan becomes the (unintended?) murder target

Let's Get Criminal
Lev Raphael

A Nick Hoffman / Academic Mystery, Book 1 – Nick Hoffman has everything he has ever wanted: a good teaching job, a nice house, and a solid relationship with his lover, Stefan Borowski, a brilliant novelist at the State University of Michigan. But when Perry Cross shows up, Nick's peace of mind is shattered. Not only does he have to share his office with the nefarious Perry, who managed to weasel his way into a tenured position without the right qualifications, he also discovers that Perry played a destructive role in Stefan's past. When Perry turns up dead, Nick wonders if Stefan might be involved, while the campus police force is wondering the same about Nick.

"*Let's Get Criminal* is a delightful romp in the wonderfully petty and backbiting world of academia. Well-drawn characters make up a delicious list of suspects and victims." — Faye Kellerman

"Reading *Let's Get Criminal* is like sitting down for a good gossip with an old friend. Its instant intimacy and warmth provides clever and sheer fun." — Marissa Piesman

Originally published in 1996, the first book in the Nick Hoffman Academic Mystery series is now back in print. This edition contains a new foreword by the author.

The Edith Wharton Murders
Lev Raphael

A Nick Hoffman / Academic Mystery, Book 2 – Nick Hoffman, desperate to get tenure, has been saddled with a thankless task: coordinating a conference on Edith Wharton that will demonstrate how his department and his university supports women's issues. There's been widespread criticism that SUM is really the State University of Men. Problem is, he's forced to invite two warring Wharton societies, and the conflict between rival scholars escalates from mudslinging to murder. Nick's job and whole career are on the line unless he can help solve the case and salvage the conference.

"Is vulgar literary taste sufficient motive for murder? Actually, killing is too kind for the vindictive scholars in Lev Raphael's maliciously funny campus mystery *The Edith Wharton Murders*." — Marilyn Stasio, *The New York Times Book Review*

"A savagely funny satire of academic pretensions and posturings. Definitely on my list of the year's best!" — Dean James

"Among the pleasures of this mystery is its detailing of the day-to-day domesticity between Nick and Stefan – and of that essential mystery that lies at the core of even our closest relationships." — Katherine V. Forrest

Originally published in 1998, this edition contains a foreword by Gregory Ashe (*Hazard and Somerset* series) as well as a new introduction by the author.

And don't miss ...

The Death of a Constant Lover: The son of a professor is murdered on a campus bridge and Nick's presence puts him in the middle of trouble

Little Miss Evil: When cryptic messages in Nick's mailbox escalate into another corpse on campus, the reluctant sleuth is back on the case

GRANT MICHAELS

In the Game
Nikki Baker

A Virginia Kelly Mystery, Book 1 – When businesswoman Virginia Kelly meets her old college chum Bev Johnson for drinks late one night, Bev confides that her lover, Kelsey, is seeing another woman. Ginny had picked up that gossip months ago, but she is shocked when the next morning's papers report that Kelsey was found murdered behind the very bar where Ginny and Bev had met. Worried that her friend could be implicated, Ginny decides to track down Kelsey's killer and contacts a lawyer, Susan Coogan. Susan takes an immediate, intense liking to Ginny, complicating Ginny's relationship with her live-in lover. Meanwhile Ginny's inquiries heat up when she learns the Feds suspected Kelsey of embezzling from her employer.

“The auspicious debut of a black writer who brings us a sharp, funny and on-the-mark murder mystery.”
— *Northwest Gay & Lesbian Reader*

“An entertaining assortment of female characters makes Baker's debut promising” — *Publisher's Weekly*

“It has adventure, romance, and some of the best internal dialogue anywhere.” — Megan Casey

Nikki Baker is the first African-American author in the lesbian mystery genre and her protagonist, Virginia Kelly is the first African-American lesbian detective in the genre. Interwoven into the narrative are observations on the intersectionality of being a woman, an African-American, and a lesbian in a “man's” world of finance and life in general.

First published to acclaim in 1991, this new edition features a foreword by the author.

And don't miss ...

The Lavender House Murder: Ginny and Noami in Provincetown

Long Goodbyes: A Christmas return home ends in murder

The Always Anonymous Beast
Lauren Wright Douglas

A Caitlin Reece Mystery, Book 1 – Val Frazier, Victoria's star TV anchorwoman, is Caitlin's newest client. She is the victim of a viciously homophobic blackmailer who has discovered her relationship with Tonia Konig. Tonia is a lesbian-feminist professor, an outspoken, passionately committed proponent of nonviolence. She is enraged by her own helplessness, she is outraged by Caitlin's challenge to her most fundamental beliefs, and by Caitlin herself, whom she considers "a thug".

As Caitlin stalks the blackmailer and his accomplices through the byways of the city of Victoria, she uncovers ever darker layers of danger surrounding Tonia. And she struggles against a new and altogether unwanted complication: she is increasingly attracted to the woman who despises her.

> "A very accomplished first novel, which is distinguishable by an elegant flair for description and an obvious love of the language." — Karen Axness, *Feminist Bookstore News*

> "Douglas' book is snappily written, peppered with wit and literary allusions, and filled with original characters."
> — Sherri Paris, *The Women's Review of Books*

Douglas's debut novel in 1987 began a six part series for Caitlin Reece. This new edition includes an introduction by the author and a foreword by legendary Katherine V. Forrest.

And don't miss ...

Ninth Life: Caitlin is hired by a woman code-named Shrew, to pick up a package. Caitlin is sickened to the depths of her being by the contents of the package: a blind and maimed cat, and photographs of animal experimentation. And now Shrew is dead. As a member of the militant animal rights organization Ninth Life, she had infiltrated Living World, a cosmetics company. The other members of Ninth Life suspect she was betrayed by someone within their own ranks and murdered because of what she learned.

Sunday's Child
Edward O. Phillips

A Geoffry Chadwick Misadventure, Book 1 – Lawyer Geoffry Chadwick is 50, Canadian, single, gay and, after a brief struggle with a hustler who tries to shake him down, a murderer. Herein lies the device for this macabre, funny, first novel. Although Geoffry must dispose of the body – which he does by dropping off sections of it around town at night – the trauma of the murder affords him the opportunity to reminisce and ruminate: on the recent termination of his affair with a history teacher; on the not-so-recent deaths of his wife and daughter; on the alcoholism of his mother; on growing old; on being gay. The visit of a nephew and the New Year's festivities only serve to intensify his thoughts. Although Chadwick is abrasively disdainful early on, he is fascinating when he loosens up. Phillips keeps the reader hopping with throwaway quotations from Donne and scatological references and puns.

First published in 1981, and a Books in Canada First Novel nominee, this new edition contains a foreword by Alexander Inglis.

And don't miss ...

Buried on Sunday: "One of the problems with weekends in the country" says Geoffry Chadwick's genial host in *Buried on Sunday,* "is that people feel free to drop in unannounced." And sometimes that includes criminals on the lam: forget the hors d'oeuvres, everyone is now hostage. Winner of the coveted Arthur Ellis Best Novel Award from the Crime Writers of Canada.

Sunday Best: Geoffry gets roped into planning a wedding for his niece Jennifer, but the groom has closet issues and a sexy latino chauffeur has a mixed agenda. Then there is widowed Montreal socialite Lois, mother to the groom, who casts her net for Geoffry ...

Working on Sunday: Geoffry Chadwick has a stalker. But between avoiding Christmas parties, gift shopping, moving his mother into a senior living facility, handling his recently widowed sister, and dealing with the loss of his long-term boyfriend Patrick, Geoffry Chadwick does not have time for a stalker.

Death Trick
Richard Stevenson

A Don Strachey Mystery, Book 1 – Don Strachey isn't exactly the most sought-after private eye in Albany, New York. In fact, this gay P.I. has gotten to the point of having to write checks to pay his tab at the cheapest lunch counter in town. And he isn't sure that the latest one, for the grand total of two dollars and ninety-three cents, is going to clear.

Surprisingly he's hired to locate Billy Blount, the gay heir to one of Saratoga Springs' upper-crust families. On top of that, Billy, a young and outspoken gay activist, is wanted for the grizzly murder of the man he slept with on his last night in Albany – a man he'd never met before that night.

"Sassy and sexy ... Don Strachey is a private dick who really earns his title." — *Armistead Maupin*

"This murder mystery, recounted with sassiness and wit, is full of true-to-life details about contemporary gay existence. Stevenson uses the yarn to poke fun at straitlaced parents, homophobic cops and greedy gay bar owners ... This is a great lazy-day read – and politically correct, yet!" — *The Advocate*

Written just before the onslaught of AIDS, *Death Trick* is a time capsule of gay life as it existed in smaller towns in America. A foreword for the 2022 edition by Michael Nava (Henry Rios series) is included.

And don't miss ...

On The Other Hand, Death: When the giant Millpond Company finds its plans for a mega-shopping mall stymied by the refusal of an elderly lesbian couple to sell their home, the ladies are subjected to ugly vandalism and frightening death threats. The powerful director of Millpond in turn hires Don Strachey, Albany's only gay detective, to protect the ladies, find the culprits, and clear the corporate name. Strachey accepts with misgivings that deepen rapidly as kidnapping, extortion, and murder darken the lives of Albany's gay community.

Simple Justice
John Morgan Wilson

A Benjamin Justice Mystery, Book 1 – It's 1994, an election year when violent crime is rampant, voters want action, and politicians smell blood. When a Latino teenager confesses to the murder of a pretty-boy cokehead outside a gay bar in L.A., the cops consider the case closed. But Benjamin Justice, a disgraced former reporter for the Los Angeles Times, sees something in the jailed boy others don't. His former editor, Harry Brofsky, now toiling at the rival Los Angeles Sun, surprises Justice from his alcoholic seclusion to help neophyte reporter Alexandra Templeton dig deeper into the story. But why would a seemingly decent kid confess to a brutal gang initiation killing if he wasn't guilty? And how can Benjamin Justice possibly be trusted, given his central role in the Pulitzer scandal that destroyed his career?

Snaking his way through shadowy neighborhoods and dubious suspects, he's increasingly haunted by memories of his lover Jacques, whose death from AIDS six years earlier precipitated his fall from grace. As he unravels emotionally, Templeton attempts to solve the riddle of his dark past and ward off another meltdown as they race against a critical deadline to uncover and publish the truth.

"Wilson keeps the emotional as well as forensic suspense up through the very last sentence. The final scene is not only a satisfying explanation of the crime, but a riveting study of the erotic cruelty of justice." — *The Harvard Gay and Lesbian Review*

Awarded an Edgar by Mystery Writers of America for Best First Novel on initial release, this 25th Anniversary edition has been revised by the author. A foreword for the 2020 edition by Christopher Rice (*Bone Music*) is included.

Murder and Mayhem
Matt Lubbers-Moore

An Annotated Bibliography of Gay and Queer Males in Mystery, 1909-2018.

Librarian and scholar Matt Lubbers-Moore collects and examines every mystery novel to include a gay or queer male in the English language starting with Arthur Conan Doyle's "The Man with the Watches". Authors, titles, dates published, publishers, book series, short blurbs, and a description of how involved the gay or queer male character is with the mystery are included for a full bibliographic background.

Murder and Mayhem will prove invaluable for mystery collectors, researchers, libraries, general readers, aficionados, bookstores, and devotees of LGBTQ studies. The bibliography is laid out in alphabetical order by author including the blurb and author notes, whether a hard boiled private eye, an amateur cozy, a suspenseful romance, or a police procedural. All subgenres within the mystery field are included: fantasy, science fiction, espionage, political intrigue, crime dramas, courtroom thrillers, and more with a definition guide of the subgenres for a better understanding of the genre as a whole.

A ReQueered Tales Original Publication.

The Male Homosexual in Literature: A Bibliography *and* The Male Homosexual in Literature: Supplement (2020)
Ian Young

Ian Young's bibliography has served as a basic guide to English-language works of fiction, drama, poetry and autobiography concerned with male homosexuality or having male homosexual characters. Entries include titles published through 1980. Works are identified by author, title, place of publication, publisher, and date. For easy reference, entries are numbered and a title index is provided. Five highly acclaimed essays on gay literature by Ian Young, Graham Jackson and Dr. Rictor Norton, including essay on gay publishing, round out the listings. A title index of gay anthologies completes the work.

The present *Supplement* includes titles overlooked in the *Bibliography* Second Edition, plus works written before the 1981 cut-off date but published later, including works published for the first time in book form.

ॐ

**If you enjoyed this book,
please help spread the word
by posting a short,
constructive review at
your favorite social media site
or book retailer.**

**We thank you, greatly,
for your support.**

And don't be shy! Contact us!

*For more information about current and future releases,
please contact us:*

E-mail: *requeeredtales@gmail.com*
Facebook (Like us!): www.facebook.com/ReQueeredTales
Twitter: @ReQueered
Instagram: www.instagram.com/requeered
Web: www.ReQueeredTales.com
Blog: www.ReQueeredTales.com/blog
Mailing list (Subscribe for latest news): https://bit.ly/RQTJoin